HAPPIEST DAYS
THE ALTERNATIVE
SCHOOL LOGBOOK 1986–1987

JACK SHEFFIELD

LARGE
PRINT

First published in Great Britain 2017
by
Bantam Press
an imprint of Transworld Publishers

First Isis Edition
published 2018
by arrangement with
Transworld Publishers
Penguin Random House

A catalogue record for this book is available
from the British Library.

ISBN 978–1–78541–569–2 (hb)
ISBN 978–1–78541–575–3 (pb)

Published by
F. A. Thorpe (Publishing)
Anstey, Leicestershire

Set by Words & Graphics Ltd.
Anstey, Leicestershire
Printed and bound in Great Britain by
T. J. International Ltd., Padstow, Cornwall

For my wife, Elisabeth

Contents

Acknowledgements

I have been fortunate to have had the support over many years of a wonderful editor, the superb Linda Evans (now retired), and I am now under the guidance of my new editors at Penguin Random House, the dynamic duo of Bella Bosworth and Aimée Longos. Sincere thanks for bringing this novel to publication supported by the excellent team at Transworld, including Larry Finlay, Bill Scott-Kerr, Jo Williamson, Sarah Harwood, Vivien Thompson, Brenda Updegraff and fellow "Old Roundhegian" Martin Myers.

Special thanks as always go to my hard-working literary agent and long-time friend, Philip Patterson of Marjacq Scripts, for his encouragement, good humour and the regular updates on the state of England cricket.

I am also grateful to all those who assisted in the research for this novel — in particular: Adrian Barnes, managing director of Justtech Ltd and church organist, Medstead, Hampshire; Stella Cunningham, former evacuee and retired wages clerk, Storrington, West Sussex; Tony Greenan, Yorkshire's finest headteacher (now retired), Huddersfield, Yorkshire; Ian Haffenden, ex-Royal Pioneer Corps and custodian of Sainsbury's, Alton, Hampshire; David Haigh, programme management consultant and fishing enthusiast, Medstead, Hampshire; Ginny Hayward, family record keeper and supporter of the Watercress Line, Medstead, Hampshire;

Ian Jurd, retired builder, churchwarden and Southampton FC supporter, Medstead, Hampshire; John Kirby, ex-policeman, expert calligrapher and Sunderland supporter, County Durham; Freda Lawes, long-standing member of the Mid-Hants Railway Preservation Society, Ropley, Hampshire; Roy Linley, lead architect, strategy and technology, Unilever Global IT Innovation, and Leeds United supporter, Port Sunlight, Wirral; Helen Maddison, primary-school teacher and literary critic, Harrogate, Yorkshire; Jacqui Rogers, clinical imaging support worker, allotment holder and tap dancer, Malton, Yorkshire; and all the terrific staff at Waterstones, Alton, including the irreplaceable Simon (now retired), the excellent Sam, Scottish travel expert Fiona, plus Bridget and Ysemay; also, Celia and the Cambridgeshire Collection team in the magnificent state-of-the-art Cambridge Central Library.

Finally, sincere thanks to my wife, Elisabeth, without whose help the *Teacher* series of novels would never have been written.

Prologue

Life.

One journey . . . many pathways. Choosing the right one can be difficult.

So it was in the summer of 1986.

I knew the next conversation would determine my future career. Over the years my happiest days had been at Ragley School and I prayed they would continue. I took a deep breath, gripped the telephone a little tighter and listened to her words. They were calm and precise.

Miss Barrington-Huntley, the chair of the Education Committee at County Hall in Northallerton, paused and I heard a shuffling of papers. "Mr Sheffield," she said, "further to your interview today, I should like to offer you the post of headteacher of Ragley and Morton Church of England Primary School."

The relief was palpable.

I said simply, "I accept."

It was then that Miss Barrington-Huntley moved seamlessly into a more familiar mode. "Congratulations, Jack, and I'm sorry you had a long wait for the decision . . . but you will appreciate we had a very strong shortlist and there was much to discuss."

"I fully understand."

"You will receive all the formal paperwork in the post during the coming week and do call me if you have any concerns. In the meantime, enjoy your well-earned summer holiday."

I replaced the receiver and my wife, Beth, smiled up at me while our three-year-old son, John William, continued playing happily with his Lego.

"Well done, Jack," she said. "I know how important it was to you."

That evening, as the sun set over the distant Hambleton hills, we sat on our garden bench and celebrated with a glass of Merlot while breathing in the soft scent of the yellow "Peace" roses. Beth rested her head on my shoulder and I caressed her honey-blonde hair. Our lives had moved on. It was the beginning of a new journey and the unknown was just around the corner.

That was six weeks ago and now the school summer holiday was almost over. A new academic year stretched out before me. For the past nine years I had been Ragley's headteacher, but the closure of Morton School in the next village meant the two schools were to be amalgamated next January at the start of the spring term. It had required an interview for the post of headteacher of the newly formed school and I had been given the opportunity to continue in my post.

On Sunday, 31 August I was sitting at my desk in the school office sifting through the mail from County Hall and the academic year 1986/87 was a few days away. An amber light slanted through the tall Victorian windows while motes of dust hovered like tiny fireflies in the shafts of autumn sunshine.

Meanwhile, on the office wall, the clock with its faded Roman numerals ticked on. In spite of the usual apprehension, I had always found the dawn of a new school year to be an exciting time, but little did I know that a battle was about to commence.

However, on that distant day all seemed calm as my tenth year as a village school headmaster in North Yorkshire was about to begin. Up the Morton Road the church clock chimed midday. I took a deep breath as I unlocked the bottom drawer of my desk, removed the large, leather-bound school logbook and opened it to the next clean page. Then I filled my fountain pen with black Quink ink, wrote the date and stared at the empty page.

The record of another school year was about to begin. Nine years ago, the retiring headmaster, John Pruett, had told me how to fill in the official school logbook. "Just keep it simple," he said. "Whatever you do, don't say what really happens, because no one will believe you!"

So the real stories were written in my "Alternative School Logbook". And this is it!

CHAPTER
ONE

Smile of the Tiger

School reopened today for the new academic year with 101 children on roll. A workman from County Hall was on site preparing the ground for the arrival of the temporary classroom later this month. Letters were posted to the four teachers shortlisted for interview on 17 September.

Extract from the Ragley School Logbook:
Wednesday, 3 September 1986

It was a morning of bright sunshine on Wednesday, 3 September, the first day of the school year, and all seemed well in my world.

As headmaster of Ragley village school in North Yorkshire, I felt a sense of keen anticipation as a new term stretched out before me . . . but, of course, on that fine autumn morning I had no idea what lay in store. Problems, like dark thunder clouds, were on the distant horizon and they were coming my way.

At our home in Kirkby Steepleton in the hallway of Bilbo Cottage my wife, Beth, was saying goodbye to our son, John William, when our childminder, Mrs Roberts, arrived. She had driven from her home in Hartingdale

1

where Beth had once been the local village school headteacher. Since then, Beth had secured promotion to a larger Group 4 headship at King's Manor Primary School in York. Like me, Beth was keen to have an early start and she lifted three-year-old John and gave him a hug.

"Now be good for Mrs Roberts," she said.

"Yes, Mummy," said John.

She kissed his cheek, stroked his fair hair and passed him to me. I knew it was always a wrench for her to say goodbye, but that was the pattern of our lives.

Beth's new headship had proved a success. After glancing through the contents of her black executive briefcase, she checked her appearance in the hall mirror. Her smart two-piece business suit emphasized her slim figure and she tucked her hair behind her ears before hurrying out to her car. Beth had finally said farewell to her ageing Volkswagen Beetle in exchange for a more upmarket, five-door, blue 1981 VW Golf CD diesel. According to Beth, it was a bargain at under £3,000 and matched the status of her new job. Even so, I missed the familiar Beetle.

Regardless of Beth's regular attempts at persuasion, I knew I could never part with my Morris Minor Traveller. It was like an old friend and I gave the yellow-and-chrome AA badge on the radiator grille a quick polish with my cuff for good luck. Then it was my turn to leave for my three-mile journey on the back road to Ragley village.

It was always a joy to travel through North Yorkshire in early autumn and as I drove past Twenty Acre Field the last of the harvest was waiting to be gathered in. Beyond the hedgerow the cornfield swirled in the light breeze like a restless ocean — rather like my thoughts — and I wondered what the new school year would bring.

Then it happened . . . the unexpected!

As I drove slowly up Ragley High Street I spotted a distinctive, mud-smeared Land Rover coming towards me. It was my familiar adversary, Stan Coe, local pig farmer and serial bully. Our paths had crossed many times in the past and there was no love lost between us. To my surprise, he leaned out of his window, waved and smiled. I simply stared in astonishment. He had definitely *smiled*. Puzzled, I wondered if he had turned over a new leaf . . . I should have known better.

Still shaking my head in disbelief, I turned in through the school gate and drove up the cobbled drive. I parked my car, picked up my old leather satchel and walked to the school entrance, where Ruby, the caretaker, was leaning on her broom.

"G'morning, Mr Sheffield," she greeted me. "A lovely day." In her triple-X, bright orange overall and with her rosy cheeks, she cut a cheerful figure.

"Hello, Ruby," I said, "and thanks for all your work during the holiday."

"Allus a pleasure, Mr Sheffield," she replied with a smile.

Ruby had been thrilled when she passed her driving test at the first attempt during the summer holiday. It was thanks to the regular lessons and considerable patience of her friend George Dainty, who had become

3

her constant companion. Now she pushed a few strands of wavy chestnut hair from her eyes and nodded across the playground. "We've gorra early bird, Mr Sheffield."

A solitary workman was busy on the far side of the school grounds. A new temporary classroom was due to arrive later in the month to cater for our growing numbers and preparations were already under way. Ruby leaned towards me with a conspiratorial whisper. "That's Billy 'Ardcastle from Easington what does jobs f'County 'All. 'E were 'ere at t'crack o' dawn. Good worker, is Billy."

Reassured, I walked over to speak to him. He appeared deep in thought as he stared at the strip of spare ground.

"Good morning, Mr Hardcastle," I said. He was standing next to a pile of bricks and a wheelbarrow full of recently mixed mortar. "I'm Jack Sheffield, the headteacher."

"Mornin', Mr Sheffield," he said with a friendly smile, "pleased t'meet you." He was over six feet tall with shoulders like an American football player and the build of a Sherman tank.

"You look deep in thought," I observed.

He nodded in acknowledgement. "Ah allus give a job two coats o' lookin' over afore ah start."

"Two coats of looking over?"

He grinned and stroked his stubbly chin. "Yes, ah try t'imagine what it'll look like when it's all done an' dusted, so t'speak."

"And what do you think?" I asked.

4

He rubbed the back of his weather-beaten neck with the thick fingers of his right hand. "Well, 'ow ah see it is if we build t'base a yard o' two further back than it is on t'plan, y'could 'ave a nice bit o' garden in front of y'new classroom. It'd catch t'sun summat perfec' an' t'kiddies would probably like that."

I was impressed. It was a sensitive thought for such an apparently rugged individual. *Don't judge a person on first impressions* crossed my mind. "Then let's do that," I said, "and I appreciate your consideration."

He picked up his trowel and speared the perfect mortar mix. "Well, ah'd best crack on."

"Thanks for the prompt start," I said, "and I'll make sure the children don't interfere with your work."

"Let 'em look, Mr Sheffield," he replied with a grin. "Ah'm used to an audience." With that he began to build a first tower of bricks on which the base of the new classroom would be placed and I walked into school.

In our shared office the school secretary, Vera Forbes-Kitchener, was already hard at work. Vera, a tall, elegant sixty-four-year-old, looked immaculate in her Marks & Spencer two-piece, charcoal-grey business suit. "Good morning, Mr Sheffield," she said.

A lady in a shabby raincoat that stank of cigarettes was sitting in the visitor's chair and her two children were standing beside her, their faces smeared in chocolate.

"This is Mrs Longbottom," explained Vera.

"You've gorra lovely school, Mr Sheffield," remarked Mrs Longbottom, who had just arrived in the village after moving from Leeds.

"Thank you for saying so," I said, "and welcome to Ragley." I felt reassured as I sat down at my desk in the far corner by the window.

"Yes, we're very proud of our village school," said Vera with an enigmatic smile. She opened the new admissions register, unscrewed the top of her fountain pen and looked across to my desk on the other side of the office. "Mrs Longbottom's daughter, Sigourney, is about to commence full-time education in *your* class, Mr Sheffield, and her son, Tyler, will be in Class 3." The two children stopped chewing their Curly Wurly bars and gave me a curious look.

They both had their mother's craggy features and all three sported distinctive spiky brown hair that resembled a chimney-sweep's brush. The girl was a tall ten-year-old in a baggy grey bat-wing sweatshirt, blue jeans with holes in the knees and white pixie boots. Her eight-year-old brother, Tyler, was wearing a Leeds United football shirt with the name RITCHIE on the back, grubby blue shorts and a pair of battered sandals. They both looked as though they had been dragged through a hedge backwards.

"So have you any questions, Mrs Longbottom?" asked Vera.

Mrs Longbottom looked across at me, hesitated and then turned back to Vera. "There is summat," she said.

"Yes?" enquired Vera.

"Well, ah were jus' wond'rin'," continued Mrs Longbottom, staring thoughtfully out of the window.

I glanced up from my desk. "Go on," I encouraged her. "We're here to help."

She looked firmly at her two children. "Sigourney," she said, "go outside to t'playground an' wait there with y'brother."

Sigourney chewed her Curly Wurly thoughtfully. "Don't wanna," she replied defiantly.

Mrs Longbottom smiled apologetically at Vera. "She's gorra temper, 'as our Sigourney. She likes 'er own way."

Finally, with a reluctant shrug of her shoulders, Sigourney nodded to her brother and they both wandered off. Mrs Longbottom got up and closed the door firmly, and I wondered what was coming next. It was clearly something of import.

She stared at the closed door for a moment, sat down again and spoke in a husky whisper. "Ah were jus' thinkin' about, y'know . . . sex."

"Sex!" echoed Vera, her cheeks flushing rapidly.

"Yes," said Mrs Longbottom, " 'cause as you'll 'ave noticed, our Sigourney's growin' up fast."

"Yes, I suppose she is," agreed Vera cautiously.

I decided to speak up. "Well, if it helps, our local staff nurse comes in to show a film to the school leavers about growing up," I explained, "and parents are invited."

"Ah well . . . that's good to 'ear," said Mrs Longbottom. She sighed, stood up and turned to leave, then paused as if she had remembered something else. "Y'see, ah were really thinkin' 'bout my eldest, Chantelle."

7

"Chantelle?" repeated Vera, wondering how parents came up with these names.

"Yes," said Mrs Longbottom. "Y'see, back on Gipton Estate in Leeds our Chantelle went to a real *forward-thinkin'* school."

"Really?" Vera sounded unimpressed by the implication.

"What do you mean by 'forward-thinking', Mrs Longbottom?" I asked.

"Well, she 'ad a brilliant up-t'-date teacher called Miss Clemence an' she taught 'em 'bout growin' up an' suchlike."

"Did she?"

"Yes, an' mams an' dads were invited in . . . an' ah'll tell y'summat f'nothin', Mr Sheffield . . ."

"Yes?"

"No one could put a condom on a cucumber faster than Miss Clemence."

There was a moment's silence while Vera lost the power of speech.

"Oh . . . really?" I murmured.

Mrs Longbottom opened the office door. "Anyway, mus' fly," she said. "Ah've got t'get to t'Co-op in York." With that, she hurried off with the confident step of a satisfied customer.

"Oh dear," sighed Vera.

"What is it?" I asked.

"I was thinking about Shirley in the kitchen," she said quietly.

"Shirley?" I wondered why our school cook had entered the conversation.

"Yes," said Vera thoughtfully, "it's salad for lunch and when I spoke to her earlier she was . . . well . . . chopping *cucumbers*."

I winced and glanced up at the office clock. It was 8.15a.m. and a new school year had begun.

I walked out to the entrance hall where Anne Grainger, the deputy headteacher, was clutching large sheets of sugar paper and a box of safety scissors. "Morning, Jack," said Anne, a slim, attractive fifty-something, with a slightly strained smile. "Here we go again."

Anne taught our youngest children in the reception class and her commitment and loyalty towards Ragley School were always evident. Her classroom was a riot of colour and activity, and the children in her care always enjoyed a stimulating start to their school career.

"Morning, Anne," I replied. "Another year . . . let's hope for a good one."

Anne stared thoughtfully out of the window where Billy Hardcastle was making good progress. "It will certainly be challenging when all the Morton children arrive," she said. "Most of them are reception children and young infants."

Our neighbouring village school was due to close at Christmas. According to our education authority it was for "economic reasons" and Morton's twenty-eight children on roll would be transferring to us in January.

"I'm sure we will be well prepared," I said, "and we can redistribute the children when the new teacher arrives."

Anne raised her eyebrows and hurried off to her classroom. She was too experienced to count her chickens. It also occurred to me that, from her guarded demeanour, there was something else on her mind.

Our other two Ragley teachers were in the school hall preparing for school assembly.

"Morning, Jack," said Sally. "Pat and I thought we would extend the recorder group to the younger ones this year."

"Good idea," I said.

Sally Pringle taught the eight- and nine-year-olds in Class 3. A ginger-haired, freckle-faced forty-five-year-old with an unconventional dress sense, Sally was our art and music specialist. She was tuning her guitar prior to leading the choir in a rendition of "Kumbaya". In her purple cords, a baggy mint-green blouse and a vivid mustard waistcoat, she looked relaxed in her work.

Next to Sally stood a tall twenty-nine-year-old with a long blonde ponytail. Pat Brookside was our newest member of staff and taught the six- and seven-year-olds in Class 2. A county-standard netball player, she lived in Easington with her partner, David Beckinsdale, a handsome thirty-one-year-old and a recently qualified general practitioner who stood six feet three inches tall in his stocking feet.

"Hello, Jack," she said. "I wondered if we could have a word at the end of school? I've got a few more ideas for after-school activities. Also, David mentioned this morning he would be happy to call in to do an assembly on First Aid — in conjunction with the school nurse, of course."

"Excellent," I said, "and please thank David."

I glanced up at the hall clock. "I think I'll wander down to the school gate to welcome the new starters."

The old oak entrance door creaked on its Victorian hinges as I walked outside. The stone steps under the archway of Yorkshire stone had been worn away by the patter of feet of generations of children. I stepped out into the sunshine, where boys and girls with sunburned faces were running around the tarmac playground, which was surrounded by a waist-high wall with high, iron railings topped with decorative fleurs-de-lis. Two ten-year-old girls in my class, Rosie Appleby and Jemima Poole, were winding a long skipping rope while Hayley Spraggon skipped effortlessly. They were chanting:

> Rosy apple, lemon, pear,
> Bunch of roses she shall wear,
> Gold and silver by her side,
> I know who will be her bride.

I walked down the cobbled drive towards the school gate and leaned my gangling, six-foot-one-inch frame against one of the twin stone pillars that flanked the wrought-iron gate. Excited children were rushing by. Eight-year-old Patience Crapper arrived with her friend Becky Shawcross. "Becky's got 'iccups, Mr Sheffield," announced Patience with a grin.

"Oh dear, Becky," I commiserated. "Go in and see Mrs Grainger and she'll give you a drink of water and that will make your hiccups go away."

Becky considered this for a moment.

"No thank you, Mr Sheffield," she said with a mischievous smile. "I like it when my teeth cough."

I watched them run happily on to the playground to join in the skipping game and reflected on their life.

During the summer holiday they had played games in the certain belief they would live for ever. To be an eight-year-old during those long August days was to be *immortal* . . . in the certain knowledge that friendship never dies and *true* friends will always be by your side. It was good to be young and run wild in the fields and woods and explore the local streams and ponds.

As I watched the children it occurred to me that friendship was really quite simple when it began. Only later did it become complicated.

Now many of the new starters were arriving with their parents and the playground was filling up. I looked back at the busy scene in front of the school that over the years had become my second home. It was a Victorian building of weathered red brick with a steeply sloping, grey slate roof and high arched windows. For the time being, the bell in the incongruous bell tower was silent, waiting for the moment to announce the beginning of another school year.

Opposite the school lay the village green, dominated by the white-fronted public house, The Royal Oak. It stood in the centre of a row of cottages with bay windows, pan-tiled roofs and tall chimneys. I looked

12

down the High Street bordered with grassy mounds where the village shops were preparing for another day. Prudence Golightly's General Stores & Newsagent had been open since half past seven to catch the custom of the villagers who worked in York and she was doing a roaring trade.

Next door, outside the butcher's shop, Old Tommy Piercy was instructing his grandson, Young Tommy, to rearrange the pigs' trotters in the shop window. Then came the village Pharmacy, where Peggy Scrimshaw was once again berating her husband, Eugene, for wearing his Captain Kirk *Star Trek* uniform under his white coat. Outside his Hardware Emporium, Timothy Pratt was making final adjustments to the alignment of his new range of *Dynasty* garden gnomes on a trestle table. Meanwhile, Dorothy Robinson, assistant in Nora's Coffee Shop and wife of Little Malcolm the local refuse collector, was standing in the doorway and listening to Chris de Burgh's recent number one, "Lady In Red", playing on the juke-box. It was clear Dorothy had something on her mind as she hummed along and stared thoughtfully up the High Street.

Next door, Diane Wigglesworth was taking down a photograph of Toyah Willcox from the window of her Hair Salon and replacing it with one of Kate Bush, while Amelia Postlethwaite, the postmistress, was yawning while unlocking the door of the Post Office. She was smiling following a night of unrestrained passion with her new husband, Ted Postlethwaite, our local postman.

The shopkeepers of Ragley village, like me, appeared content in our gentle backwater of North Yorkshire on this fine autumn morning. However, in the wider world, life tended to be a little more dramatic.

For this was 1986. It was the year that Bill Gates became one of the world's youngest billionaires when his Microsoft company was listed on the New York Stock Exchange; unemployment in the UK had risen to 3.25 million; IBM announced its first laptop computer; and the *Sun* newspaper alleged Freddie Starr had eaten a live hamster. Gary Lineker was briefly Britain's most expensive footballer when he was transferred from Everton to Barcelona for £2.75 million; and the first Merseyside FA Cup Final ended in a 3–1 win for Liverpool. Britain's oldest twins, May and Marjorie Chavasse, had celebrated their 100th birthday, and Prince Andrew had married Sarah Ferguson. On the near horizon, Alex Ferguson was shortly to be appointed as manager of Manchester United and the London Stock Exchange was preparing itself for the deregulation of financial markets that would become known as the "Big Bang". Also the government had launched its "safe-sex" campaign following concerns regarding AIDS.

We also said a final farewell to James Cagney, the Duchess of Windsor, Henry Moore, Cary Grant and Harold Macmillan, but in Ragley village the talk was not of cabbages and kings but rather the price of a loaf of bread in the General Stores.

At nine o'clock I walked back into school and rang the bell while the children assembled in their classrooms. There were a few tears in Anne's reception class, but they were shed mainly by mothers saying goodbye to their children as their loved ones commenced full-time education.

In my classroom there was great excitement as monitor jobs were allocated. They carried considerable status and Tom Burgess looked as though he had won the football pools when he was appointed official bell-ringer. Claire Buttershaw and Michelle Gawthorpe were asked to look after the library books on account of the fact that they *always* had clean hands. Likewise, the neat and tidy Rosie Appleby took on the role of hymn-book monitor. Stuart Ormroyd and Jemima Poole, two outstanding mathematicians and both on the highest blue box of workcards in our School Mathematics Project, were put in charge of the school tuck shop. Rufus Snodgrass became dinner-money monitor; the tallest pupil, Barry Stonehouse, nodded knowingly when asked to be chalkboard cleaner; and Sigourney Longbottom, to my surprise, volunteered to be the paintbrush monitor, a particularly messy job. Finally, the lightning-quick Hayley Spraggon became the monitor for delivering messages from one teacher to another.

Within minutes, after each child had received a collection of manila-covered exercise books, a reading record card, a wooden ruler, a Berol pen, a pencil with a rubber on the end, a tin of Lakeland crayons and a *First Oxford Dictionary*, we began our first lesson: namely, a piece of writing about our holidays. Predictable, maybe, but I knew from experience it worked, particularly with those children who had almost forgotten how to write during the long holiday.

Our local vicar and chair of governors, Joseph Evans, the younger brother of our secretary, Vera, called in during morning assembly. After welcoming all the new children he led us in our school prayer:

Dear Lord,
This is our school, let peace dwell here,
Let the room be full of contentment, let love abide
   here,
Love of one another, love of life itself,
And love of God.
Amen.

At 10.30a.m. Tom Burgess undid the rope from the cleat on the wall at the foot of the bell tower and rang the bell for morning break. When I walked into the entrance hall Joseph, a tall, skeletal figure with a sharp Roman nose, was talking to his sister and Ruby the caretaker.

"An odd thing happened this morning in the High Street," he said.

"What was that?" asked Vera.

"Stan Coe *smiled* at me," said Joseph.

"Flippin' 'eck!" exclaimed Ruby and put down her galvanized bucket with a crash.

"Oh dear," said Vera.

"Why do you say that?" asked Joseph.

Vera shook her head. "This is Mr *Coe* we're talking about, Joseph — the man who has been a thorn in our side for years."

"Yes, I take your point, but perhaps he's finally seeing sense," said Joseph innocently.

"And pigs might fly, Joseph," said Vera firmly. "Can the Ethiopian change his skin, or the leopard his spots?"

"Jeremiah thirteen, verse twenty-three," murmured Joseph.

Vera nodded. "Exactly."

"Y'reight there, Mrs F," added Ruby. "Y'know what they say . . . a leopard never changes its stripes."

"Quite right, Ruby," agreed Vera defiantly, wisely choosing not to correct her mistake.

It was just before school lunch when Vera finished typing letters to the four teachers who had been shortlisted for the new post commencing next January. She passed a copy to me.

"Thanks, Vera," I said. "Let's hope we find the right person."

"And so it begins," she said quietly as she put the first letter in an envelope.

During lunch Anne was sitting at a table next to Kylie Ogden, who was a week away from her fifth birthday. Kylie hadn't been provided with any cutlery.

"Ah wanna fok-an'-knife," she shouted.

Anne assumed she had used a serious swear word. "Oh Kylie!" she said, looking horrified.

"No, Mrs Grainger," intervened Mrs Critchley, the dinner lady, "she jus' wants these." She put down a knife and fork in front of the red-faced child and Anne blushed and returned to her ham salad.

After lunch we gathered in the staff-room and Vera served tea.

"I heard from Ruby that Joseph said he saw Stan Coe *smiling*," said Anne.

"Yes, curious isn't it?" said Vera.

Sally looked up and grinned. "There was a young lady of Niger," she quoted, "who smiled as she rode on a tiger. They returned from the ride with the lady inside and a smile on the face of the tiger."

"Very appropriate," said Vera.

"Edward Lear I think . . . although I recall there's some dispute," added Sally for good measure.

At the end of school the children in my class had put their chairs on their desks, recited our end-of-school prayer and hurried out to collect their coats before going home.

Vera tapped on the door of my classroom. "Mr Sheffield," she said, "we have a visitor." She glanced back to the entrance hall. "It's Mr Coe."

"Really? I wonder what he wants."

Vera leaned forward and whispered, "Good luck."

In the entrance hall stood a sixteen-stone Yorkshireman who stank of last night's beer. Stan had clearly been frequenting his favourite pub, The Pig & Ferret in Easington. Although his sister, Deirdre, had railed at his drunkenness over the years, Stan ignored her.

Meanwhile, he continued to be consumed by greed and his estate had grown steadily.

"Ah brought this letter t'show yer," he said, pulling an envelope from his donkey jacket. "It's from t'local plannin' office confirmin' ah can replace some of m'fencin'."

"And where would that be, Mr Coe?" I asked evenly.

"Nex' to t'cricket field where ah've got some cattle and where your kids 'ang over t'fence where ah keep m'pigs."

I was expecting another complaint about the children standing on his fence, but it didn't come. He simply stood there looking awkward.

"We received a copy of the letter," said Vera brusquely.

He rubbed his hand over his face. A web of veins formed purple tracks across his ruddy cheeks and gathered round his blackened nose. "Ah thought y'might. It's gone round to all t'neighbours."

He shuffled towards the entrance door and paused. "An' ah've been thinkin'," he said.

"Yes?" I said.

"Mebbe ah were not as s'pportive as ah should 'ave been in t'past."

There was a stunned silence. This was the last thing I had expected.

It was then that he *smiled*.

"So ah'll sithee," he said and turned to leave.

Vera and I walked into the office and watched him return to his Land Rover in the car park. "Well," said Vera, "what do you make of that?"

"One may smile, and smile, and be a villain," I said. "*Hamlet*, Act 1, Scene 5."

As Stan Coe drove away, Vera sighed. "I wonder," she mused, "I just wonder."

It was the end of a successful first day, but neither of us was smiling.

CHAPTER
TWO

The Vanity of Vera

Interviews took place today for the post of the new full-time teacher to commence January 1987.
The temporary classroom was delivered.
Extract from the Ragley School Logbook:
Wednesday, 17 September 1986

Through the leaded windows of Morton Manor, pale shafts of early-morning autumnal sunshine lit up the entrance hall as Vera prepared to leave for school. It was Wednesday, 17 September and a busy day was in store. Interviews for the new teaching post were to take place and the temporary classroom was due to be delivered.

Vera glanced at her wristwatch, checked her appearance in the hall mirror and fingered the Victorian brooch above the top button of her silk blouse. She gave a wry smile. There was only one chance at youth and that was but a distant memory. She had lived through that time and it was over. Those carefree days of her young life had been replaced by those two relentless companions, Age and Experience.

She smoothed the seat of her pin-striped business suit and picked up her royal-blue leather handbag.

Then she paused to cast a loving smile towards Maggie, her favourite cat, and then of course to her husband, Rupert . . . in that order. As she strode out purposefully to her shiny Austin Metro, a raucous cry caught her attention and she stared up into the branches of the high elms. A parliament of rooks looked back at her with beady eyes. She sighed, troubled by their relentless gaze. It was as if they were casting judgement on the discussion she had had last night with Rupert. For now it would have to remain a secret shared only by her husband.

After all, retirement was so *final*.

In Bilbo Cottage Beth and I were preparing to leave and final instructions had been left for Mrs Roberts. We were lucky to have such a caring lady looking after our son and John had smiled up at her when she walked in. It was his half-day at Temple House Nursery, a large converted manor house midway between Kirkby Steepleton and Ragley village. He loved the sand pit, Plasticine and singing games, but most of all the mid-morning banana and beaker of milk.

I held him in my arms, as Beth was the first to leave for her journey to York. It was a ten-mile drive to King's Manor Primary School and Beth was always keen to arrive before the rest of the staff.

"Goodbye, darling," said Beth, "and be a good boy at nursery."

John replied with a smile: "Banana, Mummy." It was clear what was important in his young life.

22

I walked out with Beth to her car and she kissed me on the cheek. In her floral summer dress and beige *Cagney & Lacey* coat with padded shoulders she looked both smart and dynamic — an eighties woman. She took John from my arms. "Bye-bye, Mummy," he said as she hugged him.

"Have a good day, Jack," said Beth, "and good luck with the interviews."

"Not to mention the new temporary classroom," I added.

She smiled. "Goodness knows how they will get it over the school wall."

A few golden-brown autumn leaves had settled on the sunroof of her car and they blew off as she accelerated away. "Love you," I murmured.

Then it was my turn and I set off for school in my Morris Minor Traveller.

The journey out of Kirkby Steepleton to Ragley always lifted the spirits at this time of year. I wound down the window and welcomed the sharp, clean air. It was a joy to live in this beautiful corner of what was known locally as God's Own Country. Meanwhile, beyond the hedgerows the last of the ripe barley swayed in the fields in a sinuous rhythm of russet gold.

I called in to Victor Pratt's garage and one of my old pupils, Kenny Kershaw, came out to serve me. He was training to be a car mechanic and appeared happy in his work.

"How are you, Kenny?" I asked.

"Champion, thank you, Mr Sheffield," replied Kenny. "An' ah'm in charge," he added proudly, "'cause Victor's gone off t'see Doctor Davenport."

"Oh dear, nothing serious I hope." Victor was a regular visitor to our local doctor with a series of ailments that defied medical science.

Kenny pondered this for a moment. "No, ah don't think so . . . summat about 'is bum bein' on fire."

It sounded par for the course for our curmudgeonly garage owner.

"Anyway, ah'm learnin' loads o' stuff, Mr Sheffield," said Kenny with a smile as he filled up my car with petrol. "It's good to 'ave a job an' ah'm savin' up."

I didn't ask him why. It was common knowledge that he and Claire Bradshaw, the publican's daughter, were generally regarded as "an item".

When I stopped outside the General Stores to collect my newspaper, Lillian Figgins, our road crossing patrol officer, known affectionately as Lollipop Lil', was coming out with a pack of new polishing cloths. She was dressed in her bright yellow coat, ready for duty.

"Mornin', Mr Sheffield," she said and held up the cloths. "Those pews need a good seein'-to before they get checked by Mrs F. If they're not perfec' she'll soon let y'know. So I'm off up t'St Mary's after doin' m'zebra duty."

I never ceased to be amazed by the love of the locals for our church and their willingness to support its upkeep. Lollipop Lil' was in charge of the team of church cleaners known affectionately as "The Holy Dusters". Lillian ruled them with a rod of iron: it didn't do to cross this tough Yorkshire lady.

She walked towards her Citroën 2CV, or her "tin snail" as she called it, and glowered at Stan Coe as he drove by in his filthy Land Rover. There was no love lost between these two adversaries. To her surprise, he attempted a smile and she looked after him, puzzled by his reaction. Margery Ackroyd and Betty Buttle, two local gossips, were standing on the pavement and had also witnessed Stan's unusual behaviour.

"Well now ah've seen it all," said Lillian in surprise.

"'E's a wolf in cheap clothin' is that one," warned Betty ominously.

Lollipop Lil' nodded in agreement. 'Ah wouldn't trust 'im as far as ah could throw 'im.

"An' 'e's allus flashin' 'is 'orn," added Margery with feeling.

"'E's up t'summat," said Betty. "Y'can allus tell when a man's up t'summat. They pretend t'be nice. My 'Arry bought me some flowers once."

Margery and Lillian both nodded knowingly.

There's nowt so queer as folk, thought Lillian as she drove to school to pick up her stop sign.

When I arrived in the car park Joseph Evans was collecting some papers from the boot of his white Austin A40.

"Good morning, Jack," he said. "Just some notes for the interviews. All four candidates look promising."

"Yes they do," I agreed, "and Vera has all the arrangements in hand."

"I'm sure she has," said Joseph wistfully. He stared up at the office window and reflected on a time when his sister had had all *his* arrangements in hand. That was when they had lived together in the vicarage. Life had been simple then, more straightforward and peaceful. With a deep sigh, he followed me into school.

Vera was busy in the office when we walked in and it was clear she had started work earlier than usual. She had typed a letter on a Gestetner master sheet and smoothed it carefully on the rotating drum. It was to the parents of Morton School inviting them to send their children for an introductory visit to Ragley on Tuesday afternoon, 7 October. The event included a guided tour and an opportunity to meet the teachers.

"Excellent," I said, picking up one of the letters. It was perfect. There was no doubt that Vera was an expert at using our unpredictable duplicating machine. Everyone else created an inky mess.

"I have to agree," said Vera immodestly. "There is a particular technique and I've honed it to perfection over the years."

"Really?" said Joseph, a little surprised at his sister's lack of modesty.

"Oh, good morning, Joseph," said Vera. "I see from the diary you're taking assembly this morning."

"Yes, that's right."

"And what is your theme?" asked Vera.

Our vicar gave a meaningful stare. "Vanity," he said simply and walked out to the hall.

Vera returned to her duplicating and for a moment she was troubled . . . *How will they cope without me?*

★　★　★

At nine o'clock Tom Burgess rang the bell to announce the beginning of a new school day. Ruby was standing by the office door. She had put down her dustpan and was leaning on her broom. "Ah'm off in a few minutes, Mrs F."

Vera looked up at her dear friend and smiled. "I hear you have been seeing more of Mr Dainty," she said. "How is he?"

Ruby pondered this for a moment. "Well, as y'know, Mrs F, 'e's allus been gen'rous an' kind. If y'recall, 'e took me to t'Queen's 'Otel in Leeds for t'Annual Fish Fryers' Lunch an' we' ad a lovely time."

Before returning to live in Ragley, George Dainty had made his fortune in Alicante in Spain with his fish-and-chip shop, The Codfather.

"I remember it well," said Vera, "and you wore a lovely dress."

"Yes ah did, an' then 'e bought me a special gift an' it cost a fortune."

"And what was that, Ruby?" asked Vera tentatively.

"A top o' t'range deep-fat fryer, an' it meks chips a real treat."

"It sounds wonderful," said Vera, but without conviction.

"An' las' Saturday 'e took me to a posh do." Ruby fished a leaflet out of the pocket of her overall and passed it to Vera.

It read:

BATTLE OF BRITAIN DANCE
Leeds Town Hall

Saturday 13th September
Dancing to the sound of the Lloyd Allen Big Band.

"Tickets were four poun' fifty," said Ruby, full of excitement.

"Did you enjoy yourself?" asked Vera.

"Yes, ah did." Ruby picked up her dustpan to carry on with her cleaning. "An', ah mus' say . . . 'e's a proper little twinkletoes, is my George," she added proudly as she walked off to her store cupboard.

My George, thought Vera, and she smiled. Her friend had definitely moved on with her life.

It was time for morning assembly and Anne cleaned her LP record of the *Peer Gynt Suite*, placed it carefully on the turntable of our music trolley, lowered the stylus on to the correct track and adjusted the volume. Soon the familiar strains of Edvard Grieg's "Anitra's Dance" filled the hall as the children walked in quietly and sat cross-legged on the polished woodblock floor.

Joseph Evans, a slightly stooped, angular figure, took the lead and introduced the first hymn.

There were times when Vera, a devout Christian, slipped out of the office for a few minutes to join in our act of daily worship, if only to share in the Lord's Prayer. She would stand by the double doors that led to the entrance hall and by leaving the office door open she could respond to a call on the telephone.

However, this morning was different. She had been rankled by Joseph's barbed criticism and had crept quietly into the hall to hear his sermon. She sat in the seat next to mine, clasped her hands and listened intently.

Joseph told a story about a vain crow who thought he was better than the other crows. He wanted to join the peacocks, but eventually he was abandoned by his own fellows and went on to lead a lonely life. Then he opened his Bible and began to read: "Do nothing out of selfish ambition or vain conceit."

Vera leaned towards me. "Philippians, chapter two," she whispered.

Joseph glanced across at his sister and continued to read: "Rather, in humility value others above yourselves, not looking to your own interests but each of you to the interests of others."

"Verses three and four," murmured Vera.

Deep in thought, she got up quietly and returned to the office and I wondered if Joseph was making a point.

As Vera sat at her desk the telephone rang. "Ragley School," she said briskly.

"Morning," said a gruff voice. "County 'all building works 'ere."

"Oh yes," said Vera.

"Y'big 'ut is on its way."

"Hut?" replied Vera. "Surely you mean our new classroom?"

"Well, we call 'em 'uts," said the voice.

"Correct use of the English language is very important, young man," she said. "Do keep that in mind. You're referring of course to the new temporary classroom. So what time can we expect it?"

"Yer 'ut, ah mean classroom, is on its way. We've jus' loaded it . . . so mebbe an 'our."

"I see," said Vera. "Well we shall look out for it."

"G'bye," said the voice and rang off.

Vera was making a neat shorthand note on her spiral-bound pad when the telephone rang again.

"Ragley School," she said.

"It's me, my dear," answered Rupert.

"What are you doing ringing me at school?"

"I was wondering if you had thought any more about what we discussed."

"Yes, I have, but I shall pick the right moment to progress it. As you know I have concerns about the person who might one day replace me — and what will happen then to the school?"

There was a sigh from Rupert. "You'll recall we agreed to spend more time together."

"The thing is, Rupert, I've created systems here that work perfectly and it will be difficult to find someone who could sustain them."

"We are not indispensable, my dear, not even you." Rupert spoke quietly but with gravitas.

"I don't think you know what the job entails and what is going through my mind," said Vera.

"I think I do," replied Rupert. "In fact I recall Robert Oppenheimer once said that genius sees the answer before the question."

"Oh dear," said Vera, "how *vain*."

"Exactly, my dear."

Vera considered this for a moment before saying she needed to get on with her filing. She replaced the receiver.

Vera had bought a jar of Nescafé Gold Blend from the General Stores for the staff-room, plus a packet of custard creams. At morning break when the staff walked in she had heated milk in a pan for our morning coffee and had served camomile tea to Joseph to calm his nerves following a fraught lesson with Class 3.

Sally was sipping her hot drink while trying hard to ignore the fresh supplies in the biscuit tin. She had bought a *Daily Mirror* for 17p and was showing Pat a front-page photograph of Sarah Ferguson under the headline "Fergie's Secret Naughty Nibble."

"It says here," said Sally, "that the Duchess of York was caught buying chocolate in a baker's shop. Apparently the young assistant thought it was someone in fancy dress until she caught sight of the bodyguard."

"Well, a little chocolate won't hurt," said Vera, our loyal royalist, "and she has a superb figure."

Sally's politics were far removed from those of Vera. "You'll like this, Vera," she continued. "Next Sunday there's to be a so-called *intimate insight* from Highgrove into the private life of Charles and Diana along with their two sons."

Vera's face lit up. "That should be fascinating, because they lead such demanding lives."

"Yes," muttered Sally, "it must be tough with all those nannies, butlers, chauffeurs, maids and lots of holidays."

Vera retired quietly to the sink. *A lack of knowledge is a dangerous thing*, she thought.

The staff-room emptied until only Vera and Joseph remained. Vera ran some hot water to wash the mugs.

"I'll help you with that," offered Joseph and picked up Vera's favourite Flowers of the Forest tea towel.

"No, Joseph," she said sharply, "you never do it properly."

He put down the tea towel and shook his head. "Vanity of vanities, saith the Preacher, vanity of vanities; all is vanity."

Vera was a little irritated. She hated to be lectured by her younger brother. "Yes Joseph," she retorted testily. "Ecclesiastes, chapter one, verse two. I know it well."

Joseph smiled. "Your memory was always remarkable," he said softly and kissed her gently on her forehead as he left.

It was 11.30 a.m. when Rufus Snodgrass announced, "Big crane's 'ere, Mr Sheffield." All the children looked out of the window. A large crane was parked outside school and a group of villagers had gathered to watch the proceedings. The local bobby, PC Julian Pike, had appeared on his bicycle, apparently in charge of crowd control but mainly concerned with the close proximity of his new girlfriend, Ruby's daughter Natasha, who was taking a break from Diane's Hair Salon.

"Come on, boys and girls," I said. "Let's go outside."

We lined up at a safe distance near the school entrance while a group of workmen fixed long chains to something that resembled a giant green shoebox. The temporary classroom was in two halves and each half had to be lifted over the school wall and lowered on to the brick base. It was achieved with ease by the experienced crane driver, to the accompaniment of cheers from the children. The classroom was placed on the brick towers to raise it off the ground and ensure it was perfectly level.

Sadly, there was no running water in the new room, but we had been told it was the best accommodation on offer in the present economic climate. I wondered how long it would remain there or if it would become a permanent feature. It looked out of place next to our classic Victorian building, but I guessed we would get used to it. Even so, the space inside appeared generous, with a cloakroom, a large rectangular classroom space and a store cupboard.

When the operation was complete the teachers gathered on the playground. "Well, what do you think?" I asked.

"It will have to do, I expect," said Anne.

"It's pretty basic," sighed Sally. "The lack of running water inhibits art activities and hand-washing."

"Plus an extra twenty-eight children using the toilets in the main building," added Pat.

Meanwhile, our regular supply teacher, Miss Valerie Flint, had arrived to teach my class for the afternoon. Valerie, at sixty-four, had smiled when asked if she would apply for the new post. "Too long in the tooth, Jack," she said. "I enjoy my freedom too much."

★ ★ ★

It was just after school lunch and the workmen had driven away when the candidates began to arrive for the afternoon interviews. There were two men and two women and all of them were primary-school teachers in Yorkshire. They included a lady in her forties with extensive experience in primary education; a young woman who had completed three years' teaching in a Northallerton primary school; a man in his forties who had entered the profession late in life; and, finally, a young man who had recently completed his probationary year in North Yorkshire.

All of them were given a tour of the school accompanied by a member of staff while the children looked on curiously.

Shortly before one o'clock the members of the interviewing panel gathered in the school office. Joseph Evans, as chair of governors, had walked down the Morton Road from the vicarage; Major Rupert Forbes-Kitchener, also a governor, arrived in a chauffeur-driven classic Bentley; and our senior primary adviser, Richard Gomersall, roared up the drive in his six-cylinder Jaguar XJ6.

Rupert, in a tweed jacket, cavalry-twill trousers, lovat-green waistcoat, regimental tie, crisp white shirt and brown leather brogues polished to a military shine, looked his usual immaculate self. Richard Gomersall, as always, made sure he was the height of fashion with his long, wavy, carefully coiffured reddish-brown hair, a bright pink linen jacket with padded shoulders, rolled-up sleeves and baggy trousers. Cuban-heeled leather boots with pointed toecaps completed the ensemble, and Rupert eyed him curiously.

Although Joseph was officially the chair of the interviewing panel, it was our senior primary adviser who took the lead and confirmed the official arrangements for the amalgamation of the two schools. According to his records, twenty-eight children were to transfer from Morton. They were mostly five- to eight-year-olds, plus three ten-year-olds — two girls and one boy destined for my class.

I confirmed we had a list of the children and we would determine their friendship groups when they attended their preliminary visit next month. The intention was to place each child in a class with a friend to ease the problems of transfer. Richard appeared happy with this and the interviews began.

We saw the candidates in alphabetical order and the questioning followed a familiar format as we discussed their background, experience and interests. Richard Gomersall introduced topical issues, including the fact that last May Kenneth Baker had become Secretary of State for Education and it was clear he intended to make his mark.

As it emerged, three of the candidates were disappointing in an interview situation. They had appeared very promising on paper, but stumbled through their responses. In complete contrast, the young male candidate, Mr Marcus Potts, stood out from the rest.

It was 3.30p.m. and decision time.

"So, what do you think, Jack?" asked Richard.

"I think Mr Potts is an outstanding candidate. He's bright, articulate and has many of the skills we need in the sciences."

"I agree," said Richard.

"And so do I," added the Major. "A fine young man."

Joseph hesitated. "We are a Church of England school," he said, "and I remain unclear about his faith." There was a pause. "However, it is clear he is the strongest candidate, so I'll concur with the majority view."

Marcus Potts was thrilled to become the successful applicant and I shook his hand. He was twenty-three years old, no more than five feet seven inches tall, with a mop of long, wavy black hair. Trained in Cambridge, he had secured his first teaching post in a tiny North Yorkshire school that had been designated for closure, so it came as a relief for him to secure this appointment. His particular skills were in the sciences and computer studies.

"Thank you," he said. "You won't regret it."

When the bell went for the end of school I was walking with Marcus through the cloakroom area where two nine-year-olds, Ted Coggins and Charlie Cartwright, were rushing to put on their coats.

"Are you in a hurry, Ted?" I asked.

"Yes, sir," said Ted.

"We're goin' 'ome t'play Kerplunk," revealed Charlie.

"Or mebbe Operation," added Ted.

"I like Operation," said Marcus. "You need a lot of skill."

"Y'right there, sir, an' we've got plenty," confirmed the eager Ted.

The confidence of youth, I thought.

Marcus looked relaxed as he was introduced to the rest of the staff and I showed him the newly erected temporary classroom that was to be his base. I walked with him to the car park and we paused next to his rusty red Mini.

"When the furniture has arrived, can I come in from time to time to prepare?" he asked. His enthusiasm was obvious and infectious. I had a good feeling about this young man.

"Of course. Simply telephone first and make an arrangement with Vera," I said.

"Vera?"

I smiled. "Yes, our secretary, Mrs Forbes-Kitchener. You'll find her very helpful."

In the office Vera was sharing a few thoughts with Rupert.

"I'll discuss it further with Mr Sheffield," she promised.

"That's good," said Rupert simply.

"Out of pride, I believed no one could do the job better than myself."

Rupert smiled. "That's the thing about women."

"And what is that?"

"They're like bindweed." Rupert gave a wry smile.

Vera was not impressed. "Bindweed? Convolvulus? What has that to do with women?"

He took her hand gently in his. "My dear, I mean it well. Bindweed is unconventional. It climbs anti-clockwise ... against the grain, so to speak. Unexpected — just like you."

Vera looked out of the window and sighed. "I see."

"You never cease to surprise me," said Rupert, and he kissed her on the cheek and left.

A few minutes later Ruby called in to the office to empty the wastepaper bin.

"I've seen t'new teacher," she said. "Looks t'be a lovely young man."

"I do believe he is," said Vera.

"They're few an' far between, good men," said Ruby quietly.

"So, Ruby, what's the latest with Mr Dainty?"

"I'be 'onest, Mrs F, 'e's allus gallivantin' about, is George," said Ruby. "'E's never still."

"Well, he's an active man."

"'E is that," agreed Ruby with a smile.

The school was quiet now. The teachers had returned to their classrooms and I was in the office checking some paperwork. Vera sat at her desk. She appeared thoughtful.

"What is it, Vera?"

"Jack, I have something *confidential* to share with you."

I remained silent. It was unusual for Vera to use my first name and the significance didn't escape me.

"I'm considering retirement."

"I see."

"It will have to come some time," she continued.

"Vera," I said quietly, "you know what you mean to our school and how much I appreciate the support you have given to me over many years."

She smiled gently. "I know . . . but I've been talking it over with Rupert and he's keen we should spend our retirement years together — sooner rather than later."

"I can understand that."

"Well, I passed my sixty-fourth birthday during the summer holiday," she said with a sigh. "I'm not getting any younger, I'm afraid."

"You're still as sharp as when we first met, Vera."

"Perhaps."

"So when were you thinking of?"

"I would prefer to do another academic year after this one, up until 1988, but Rupert wants me to leave at the end of the summer term next July."

"You know I'll support whatever you prefer and we could leave a final decision until the end of the spring term. Then we can secure a replacement for you during the summer. But if you wish to continue for another academic year, so be it."

Vera steepled her fingers as if in prayer. "Yes, I see," she said quietly. Then she looked around our shared office, at the photographs on the wall of countless generations of Ragley children, and bowed her head. There was a long silence.

Finally she spoke up again. "Both Rupert and my brother feel I've been a little *vain*," she said suddenly. "You see, I wondered who would replace me."

"That would be very difficult, Vera, but, as always, we shall do our best. We are not irreplaceable."

Vera smiled. "Yes, that's what they said."

"So how would you like to resolve this?"

"I should like to keep it to ourselves for now."

"I understand."

She stood up, buttoned her coat, checked that her desk was left in its usual tidy state, picked up her handbag and walked to the door.

"Thank you, Jack," she said.

The room was quiet once more and only the ticking of the clock disturbed the silence.

It occurred to me that I was the guardian of secrets . . . and it was a heavy burden.

CHAPTER
THREE

Ruby Tuesday

Children from Morton School visited during the afternoon session.
Extract from the Ragley School Logbook:
Tuesday, 7 October 1986

It was a pale autumn morning on Tuesday, 7 October and I stared out of the leaded windows of Bilbo Cottage. The distant hills were shrouded in a blanket of mist and the trees were spectres in a ghostly dawn. At their feet, fallen leaves, amber and gold, lay like scattered souls. The hedgerows were rich with wild fruits awaiting nimble fingers and a future feast of jams and jellies. Goldfinches pecked at the ripe seeds while robins claimed their territory. The season was changing and wisps of wood smoke hovered above the pantile roofs of Kirkby Steepleton.

On the council estate at 7 School View, Ruby was also looking out of her bedroom window, but she was not appreciating the wonders of nature. Our caretaker had endured a troubled night with occasional tears while she recalled her life with her late husband, Ronnie. He had been habitually unemployed and what little money he had was spent on beer, cigarettes, the bookmaker and his racing pigeons. In consequence, Ruby, now approaching her mid-fifties, had endured a hard life.

However, beyond the untidy front garden and the bedraggled privet hedge was a sight that made her smile. Parked by the kerb stood a faded, harvest-gold 1970 Austin 1100, a gift from George Dainty, and it filled her with pride. Despite rust on all the doors, it had been described as "a good runner" and so it had proved. During the summer holiday, thanks to George's tuition, Ruby had passed her driving test at the first attempt, followed by a grand celebration in The Royal Oak. She was now a familiar sight driving down the High Street towards York to visit her four-year-old granddaughter, Krystal Carrington Ruby Entwhistle. Little Krystal was due to start school next summer and Ruby spent as much time as she could with the joy of her life.

Downstairs, after a hurried breakfast of a mug of tea and a Lion bar, she put on her threadbare winter coat and headscarf as the weather was turning chilly again. She picked up the heavy bunch of school keys, shouted goodbye to Natasha and set off for her least favourite day of the week. It was when she gave the toilets her extra special deep-clean and checked the ageing boiler.

"Ah 'ate Tuesdays," murmured Ruby, looking down at her arthritic fingers, " 'speshully t'day."

However, unknown to Ruby, it was destined to be a Tuesday she would never forget.

Vera glanced up from her desk. Ruby was polishing the brass handle of the office door, a sure sign she had something on her mind.

"Hello, Ruby," she said. "How are you?"

Ruby looked down and pulled tufts from her polishing cloth with her work-red fingers. "Ah've been frettin' all morning, Mrs F."

"What about?" enquired Vera.

"This an' that, Mrs F," mumbled Ruby.

Vera replaced the top on her fountain pen and closed her late-dinner-money register. "Come in and shut the door, Ruby," she said gently, "and tell me about it."

Ruby stuffed her polishing cloth into the copious pocket of her overall and sighed deeply. She closed the door and sat down in the visitor's chair. "It's our 'Azel — ah waved 'er off yesterday."

"Waved her off?"

"Yes, Mrs F," explained Ruby, "she's gone t'Paris in France on a school trip."

"But that's wonderful," said Vera.

"Yes, she were right excited," said Ruby, "but ah jus' want 'er t'stay safe."

"The teachers at Easington School have an excellent reputation for their school trips," said Vera with a reassuring smile, "and she'll learn so much."

Ruby nodded thoughtfully. "She will that, Mrs F, an' she's a quick learner, is our 'Azel. In fac', ah reckon she'll be effluent in French when she comes 'ome."

"I'm sure she will," agreed Vera with a knowing smile.

Ruby stood up to resume her work. "Well, thank you f'list'nin'," she said quietly.

The perceptive Vera could see that Ruby had been crying. "Ruby ... was there anything else that you wished to talk about?"

Ruby looked a little sheepish. "Well, ah still think back t'my Ronnie ... an' there's George Dainty, o' course ... but that'll keep for another day." She opened the door, paused and looked back. "An' summat, well, *personal* ... but that'll keep an' all."

Vera smiled after her as Ruby walked out, picked up her mop and galvanized bucket and trotted off to the children's toilets. There was more to discover, but all would be revealed in time. Finally, Vera unscrewed the top of her fountain pen again, checked the register, opened her notepad and wrote a note to herself to remind Mrs Longbottom to send her long-overdue dinner money.

At 9.15a.m., on her way home, Ruby decided to call in to the General Stores. On the forecourt Edna Trott was loading her groceries into the basket of her Rascal Electric Supertrike. Many years ago, Edna had been the caretaker at Ragley School before Ruby. She was now eighty years old and her mobility scooter helped her retain her independence.

"'Ello Ruby," Edna greeted her. "'Ow's that old boiler shapin' up? It were on its las' legs when ah worked at t'school."

"Ah've jus' checked it, Mrs Trott," said Ruby, "an' it'll probably las' me out."

"An' 'ow's that young man ah keep seein' you with?" enquired Edna with a secret smile.

Ruby's cheeks flushed. "E's fine, is George, thank you — a lovely man."

Edna climbed on her scooter and nodded thoughtfully. "Grab y'bit o' 'appiness while y'can, Ruby. Life's too short for mopin' abart all day."

Ruby looked after her as she drove off. *Per'aps she's right*, she thought.

When Ruby walked into the General Stores, the bell above the door rang merrily and she joined the queue. Prudence Golightly was serving Maurice Tupham with a large sack of potatoes. Prudence had used the huge weighing scale on the floor that, in a bygone age, had been used to weigh sacks of grain on a local farm.

Mrs Ogden was in the shop with her daughter, Kylie, before taking the little girl to the dentist. Kylie stepped on to the scale. "How much do I cost, Mummy?" she asked and was puzzled when all the grown-ups laughed.

Finally it was Ruby's turn.

Prudence Golightly, in her mid-sixties, had known Ruby for most of her life and had a soft spot for the hard-working caretaker.

"Good morning, Ruby," she said, "and how are you?"

"Fine thank you, Prudence, an' 'ow are you?"

"Couldn't be better," said Prudence brightly. "Companionship is a wonderful thing." She glanced up at Ragley's favourite teddy bear, dressed in his autumn ensemble of brown cord trousers, green jacket and a bright mustard scarf. "I've had Jeremy Bear for many years, but now I've got my Trio and he is such a loyal friend." Trio was a three-legged cat that Prudence had collected from the Cat Sanctuary in York. "You really can't beat a good friend."

"Y'right there," agreed Ruby with emphasis. She looked around the well-stocked shelves.

"So, what's it to be?" asked Prudence.

"Jus' a box o' that daft cereal what our Duggie likes, please, Prudence, an' a sliced loaf." Ruby rummaged for her purse. "Oh 'eck, ah've jus' remembered . . . an' a tin o' corned beef, please. Ah'd be losin' me 'ead if it weren't screwed on."

Prudence smiled. "Easily done, Ruby."

"Mebbe so," said Ruby, "but, mind you, ah'm not as bad as that Emily Cade." Emily was in her sixties and her mother, Ada, was Ragley's oldest inhabitant at ninety-eight.

"Really?"

"Well, she's gettin' *real* forgetful," confided Ruby.

"Forgetful?"

"Yes, she left 'er mother in t'Co-op las' week. Poor ol' sod were there f'two 'ours afore she remembered."

"Oh dear," said Prudence.

"It's a shame," said Ruby. "Emily were allus a good cook — in fac' she were good at gravy, an' y'can't say fairer than that."

Prudence nodded in agreement. In the pecking order of Yorkshire culinary expertise, excellent gravy was right up there.

At morning break I was on playground duty, so I collected a mug of coffee from the staff-room and walked outside. As usual, the boys dominated the wider spaces of the playground, playing football and leapfrog, while the girls huddled in corners deep in conversation.

Eight-year-old Jeremy Urquhart, a thoughtful, freckle-faced little boy, looked up at me. "Do you like being a teacher, sir?"

I was used to direct questions. "Yes, I wanted to be a teacher from being very young." I studied the little boy's eager face. "So, what about you, Jeremy? What would you like to be when you grow up?"

Jeremy considered this for a moment. "Taller," he said and ran off.

Ask a daft question, I thought.

I joined a circle of children by the school wall under the shade of the avenue of horse chestnut trees, where Stuart Ormroyd and Tom Burgess were playing conkers. A group of five-year-olds, including Ryan Samson, Gary Spittall and Walter Popple, were watching with fascinated interest.

"Ah wish ah could play conkers," said Ryan.

Stuart looked down at the three younger boys. "Well, y'need a friend t'play with."

Ryan looked at Gary. "Well, Gary's my friend," he said.

Walter looked forlorn. "Ah wish ah 'ad a friend — a *real* friend."

Stuart stopped playing conkers and looked down at the little boy. "What d'you mean, Walter . . . a *real* friend?"

"Well," said Walter, "y'know — one wi' chocolate," and he wandered off.

When the bell rang for the end of break I called in to Pat's classroom. She was busy with our school computer, a BBC Micro, purchased for £299 and, according to Pat, it contained a huge 16KB of RAM.

"The problem is, Jack," she said, "many of these children go home to a ZX Spectrum or a Commodore 64. We're not keeping pace."

"I'll keep trying, Pat, but the school budget is tight. We're educating these children on a few pence per child per day, and without PTA support we wouldn't have this."

Pat smiled. "No problem, Jack, just thinking out loud."

Ruby was back in school after putting out the tables for our daily Reading Workshop, when parents and grandparents were invited in to hear children read.

Six-year-old Alison Gawthorpe was sitting at a table with her reading book and her mother was encouraging her to read the first page. "Come on, Alison, shape y'self and get readin'," she said sharply. "An' wipe that snot off y'nose."

Alison was not impressed. She stared up at her mother. "What were you like when you were young, Mam? 'Cause Gran says you used t'be nice."

"Oh, did she?"

"An' she said when you married Dad y'didn't 'ave y'thinkin' cap on."

"Well, she's no business t'say that," said Mrs Gawthorpe.

Alison shook her head. "Well I'm not gettin' married," she declared.

"Why not?"

"Well, you'd 'ave t'share y'toys."

Ruby had called in to the office with an unexpected announcement. "Ah were thinkin' o' slimmin', Mrs F," she declared.

Vera put down her fountain pen. *Now this is a surprise*, she thought.

"Really?"

"Yes, ah were thinkin' ah'd let m'self go a bit."

"You're fine, Ruby," said Vera cautiously. "Is this something to do with Mr Dainty?"

Ruby's cheeks flushed. "Well, mebbe a bit."

"Has he mentioned this?" enquired Vera.

"No, Mrs F," said Ruby hurriedly, "but ah jus' thought George might prefer me if ah weren't such a big lass."

"I'm sure Mr Dainty prefers you as you are, Ruby, never fear," Vera assured her with a gentle smile. It was clear to everyone that George Dainty worshipped the ground that Ruby walked upon.

Ruby looked down at her triple-X overall, stuffed her chamois leather in her pocket and ran her hands over her hips. "Mebbe so, but ah were jus' thinkin' o' losin' a few pounds. 'Avin' said that, ah don't want t'be jus' skin an' bone an' look emancipated like them models."

It was late morning when Ruby walked out to the village green. A bench had been positioned outside The Royal Oak under the welcome shade of a weeping willow tree and next to the duck pond. A brass plaque screwed to the back of the bench commemorated the life of Ronnie. It read:

In memory of
RONALD GLADSTONE SMITH
1931–1983
"Abide With Me"

Ruby sat down and thought of her children. Thirty-five-year-old Andy was a sergeant in the Army; thirty-three-year-old Racquel was the mother of Ruby's pride and joy; and thirty-one-year-old Duggie was an assistant to Septimus Flagstaff, the undertaker. Twenty-six-year-old Sharon had moved in with her long-term boyfriend, Rodney Morgetroyd, the local milkman, with the Duran Duran hairstyle. Natasha, now twenty-four years old, worked part-time at Diane's Hair Salon, with occasional babysitting as a sideline. Meanwhile, the baby of the family, thirteen-year-old Hazel, was in her third year at Easington Comprehensive School.

Maurice Tupham walked by on his way to the Post Office. "How are you, Ruby?" he asked, raising his flat cap.

"Fair t'middlin', Maurice," said Ruby.

He stopped and looked at her. "Y'look miles away."

"Ah were jus' thinkin' 'bout m'granddaughter. Our Krystal's growin' up quicker than your rhubarb," said Ruby proudly.

Maurice Tupham's prize-winning forced rhubarb was famous in North Yorkshire and his life was devoted to the creation of perfect *Rheum rhabarbarum*. However,

50

success had come at a cost and his marriage had suffered. Maurice's wife had left him long ago, as he spent more time in his forcing sheds than in their bedroom. She had run off with a man who worked for Bird's Custard. Consequently, every time she sat down to a pudding of rhubarb crumble and custard she reflected on the two men in her life.

"Y'look troubled," observed Maurice.

Ruby sighed. "Sometimes ah feel ah can't do right f'doin' wrong."

"It'll be right as rain, never you fear," Maurice reassured her and crossed the road to the village Pharmacy.

Betty Buttle suddenly sat down next to Ruby.

"'Ello, Ruby," she said. "What y'doin'?"

"Ah were jus' thinkin' 'bout Ronnie."

"Well, like m'mother allus used t'say," said Betty, "your Ronnie were as much use as a choc'late teapot." Betty never minced her words.

"An' she were right," agreed Ruby.

"An' now you've got that lovely Mr Dainty," continued Betty. She squeezed her friend's hand gently. "Things are lookin' up for you."

Ruby smiled. "Y'right there, Betty, there's light at the end of t'funnel."

Betty set off for Diane's Hair Salon and Ruby was left alone once again.

Her daughter Natasha had arrived for her shift at the hairdresser's and the local bobby, PC Julian Pike, was waiting to greet her.

Ruby saw them and smiled. *Young love*, she thought. It was good to enjoy their budding romance.

Julian was a mere five feet eight inches tall, but with double insoles, an extra heel of shoe leather and his policeman's helmet he cut a fine figure. Natasha had fallen in love with his moustache, fashioned on Robert Redford's Sundance Kid. It tickled when she kissed him.

"It's good of you t'wait f'me, Julio," she said.

Julian blushed as he always did when she called him by his new nickname. On their first night out at the local Berni Inn, Julio Iglesias had sung his hit record "Begin the Beguine" in between their melon boat starter and their main course of gammon steak, chips and peas. By the time the Black Forest gateau arrived Natasha had decided Julian was the one. Meanwhile, as he sipped Irish coffee and nibbled an After Eight mint, Julian knew his card would be stamped that night. Next day, for the first time, the usually punctual police constable was late for duty.

"It's a busy day," said Julian adoringly, "but I shall *always* find time for you."

Natasha sighed deeply. Like her mother, she was completely unaware of her affinity for mixed metaphors. "Well y'know what they say, Julio — a rollin' stone is worth two in the bush," and she didn't need to stretch up to peck him on the cheek. She remembered it was agreed that kissing on the lips was not permitted when he was on duty.

During lunch break in the staff-room, Vera was thinking about Ruby.

"Sally," she said, "Ruby needs cheering up. She has a lot on her mind."

Sally looked up. "What was it you were thinking of, Vera?"

"Do you still go to Weight Watchers?"

Sally blushed slightly. "You know I do."

"Well, I was thinking . . ."

Up the High Street in Diane's Hair Salon, Betty Buttle was pleased with her recent purchase, the latest issue of *Cosmopolitan*.

"Ah've brought this posh magazine for you to 'ave a look," she said to Diane. "Y'get some really good articles." She held it up at a page with the heading "Vivat Vagina".

"Bloody 'ell!" said Diane. "Ah see what y'mean."

Betty was pleased with the reaction. "It sez 'ere, '*Every woman owes it to herself to be on good terms with her vagina*', an' y'can't say fairer than that."

It occurred to Diane that she had never even been on *bad* terms with her private parts, but decided to light up another cigarette and seek refuge in her box of giant rollers.

In The Royal Oak George Dainty was having a drink with Deke Ramsbottom.

George was a short man in his early fifties with ruddy cheeks and a ready smile. Beneath his flat cap he had a balding head. He had left the village many years ago as a teenager and his fish-and-chip shop, The Codfather in Alicante, had turned him into a millionaire, thanks in part to the quality of his famous batter but largely because of his capacity for hard work and honest toil.

"Y'must 'ave 'ad a good fish-an'-chip shop, George," said Deke.

"It were t'best," agreed George. "Ah 'eard there's a new fish-an'-chip shop in Easington."

Deke shook his head and frowned. "Ah don't go there since Big Bad Bob took over."

"'Ow come?"

"Well it put me off when ah saw 'ow 'e tests t'see if 'is oil is 'ot enough."

"What does 'e do?"

"'E spits in it. If it bounces back, then it's ready. 'E never were into 'ygiene, were Big Bad Bob."

"Ah see what y'mean."

Deke pointed at his *Sun* newspaper. "'Ave you 'eard, George?"

"What's that?"

"Littlewoods 'ave said t'jackpot will go up to one million pounds in November."

"That's a lot of money."

"Y'not kiddin'," said Deke. "Only thing is, t'cost for a full perm for eight draws from ten picks is goin' up from thirty-six pence to forty pence."

"That's not much," said George, not wishing to dampen the enthusiasm of Ragley's favourite cowboy.

"Jus' think," mused Deke, staring into space, "ah could be a millionaire an' 'ave anything ah want."

Not everything, thought George. He was thinking of Ruby.

Behind the bar, Don Bradshaw, the publican, turned up the volume control on the television. Diego Maradona was giving an interview. The little Argentinian footballer insisted he did not handle the ball for his infamous "Hand of God" goal against England in Mexico.

"Turn it off!" yelled Deke. "Cheatin' little bugger."

Don switched channels quickly, turned down the sound and smiled. He was pleased it had had the desired effect as the men in the tap room supped their pints and resumed their secret thoughts of Angela Rippon's long legs.

The highlight of the afternoon was the arrival of the children from Morton School.

It was only for an hour but the visit went well and twenty-seven children attended. The only absentee was George Frith, one of the ten-year-olds due to join my class. That apart, all the children enjoyed meeting the teachers, seeing their classrooms and making new friends with the Ragley children.

They left during afternoon break and several Morton parents stayed to talk to Anne and Pat, as they were to receive the majority of the new intake.

In the office, Joseph had called in to see his sister.

"I've just been talking to Albert Jenkins," he said. Albert, as well as serving as a local councillor for more than twenty-five years, had been a trusted governor when I first arrived at Ragley. He had also been instrumental in removing Stan Coe from the governing body.

"Oh yes?"

"Albert said he had heard that Stan Coe was up to no good."

"That doesn't surprise me," said Vera. "Do we know what it is?"

"Something to do with buying land."

"Oh dear." Vera stared out of the window. "Whoever sows injustice will reap calamity, and the rod of his fury will fail."

"Proverbs twenty-two, verse eight," murmured Joseph, almost to himself.

"Quite right, Joseph," said Vera. "I'll mention it to Rupert — he may know something."

"I wonder Stan bothers," mused Joseph. "There are better things to do with our time."

"Very true, Joseph," agreed Vera. "Man is like a mere breath; his days are like a passing shadow."

Joseph hesitated.

"Psalm a hundred and forty-four," Vera informed him with a smile.

"You always were better than me in our Bible studies," he muttered.

The bell rang for the end of school and there was excitement in the cloakroom area. Stuart Ormroyd and Tom Burgess were hurrying to collect their coats. "Sir, me an' Tom are meeting 'is big brother. We're off apple scrumping and then 'e says we're going t'stand outside the fish-and-chip shop in Easington for a free bag of scraps."

"Does your mother know?" I asked.

56

Mrs Gawthorpe was standing nearby with her daughter, Alison, and had overheard the conversation. "It's all right, Mr Sheffield, I've just seen their mothers at t'school gate."

"Thanks, Mrs Gawthorpe," I said.

She looked down at her daughter. "So why do you want t'go t'your friend's 'ouse? Is it because she 'as a computer?"

"No, Mam," said Alison, "it's 'cause 'er 'ouse is cleaner than ours."

Mrs Gawthorpe blushed and looked at me. "Out of the mouths of babes, Mr Sheffield."

George had called in at the village Pharmacy and was speaking to *Star Trek* fan Eugene Scrimshaw.

"Eugene, ah'm a bit worried about Ruby," he confided. "She's lookin' a bit run down t'me, y'know — proper peaky. Ah think she's workin' too 'ard."

Eugene smiled. "Ah've got jus' the thing, George." He rummaged in a box behind the counter. "'Ere it is," and he put a packet on the counter. The label read Carnation Buildup. "Jus' add some milk an' it's a proper tonic — proteins, vitamins an' minerals, it's got the lot. Gets y'back on y'feet in no time."

"Thanks, Eugene," said George, "ah'll tek it."

Eugene's wife, Peggy, had overheard the conversation. "She's a lovely lady, is Ruby," she said. "Good to hear someone is looking after her after all this time." She gave George a stern look. Peggy wasn't a woman to mess with.

George paid quickly, nodded gratefully and walked out of the shop.

The school was quiet now and I was alone in the office. A busy night lay ahead. It was my second evening class at Leeds University. In three years' time it would lead to a Masters Degree in Educational Management. The course comprised two years of weekly modules to be followed by a final year devoted to completing a dissertation.

I rang Beth at her school.

"So what is it tonight?" she asked.

I glanced down at my notes from last week. " 'The Education Acts of the Twentieth Century'. Tonight it's a history of educational legislation."

My tutor, Evan Pugh, was an elderly, grey-haired man in a bright bow tie and waistcoat. He was a walking encyclopedia of dusty facts and somehow brought it all to life. I had noticed I appeared to be one of the older students in the group and reflected on my career path so far. Perhaps Beth was right and I ought to think beyond being a village school headmaster. It just happened to be the job I loved.

Last week's discussion had been dominated by the more recent changes in education. Dr Pugh believed we were entering a time of "seismic change" with a common curriculum for all our children on the near horizon.

"I've got some property brochures," said Beth suddenly.

It was a quick change of subject but, as always, her ideas refreshed me like spring water.

"I thought we had decided to improve Bilbo Cottage," I said.

"Yes, we did, Jack . . . but there's no harm in looking."

"Fine, see you later tonight," I said.

"Love you," she said and ended the call.

As usual, Beth had added a scattering of stardust.

I climbed into my car and switched on the radio. The number-one record, "Don't Leave Me This Way" by the Communards, was playing and, as I drove down the High Street, I hummed along.

It was early evening and George Dainty and Ruby were sitting on Ronnie's bench.

"Ah got this for you from t'chemist," said George.

"What is it?" asked Ruby, looking suspiciously at the packet.

"It's chocolate flavour, Ruby, an' ah know y'like chocolate."

"Mebbe too much, George — ah'm gettin' a bit on the 'eavy side."

"Y'look fine t'me," said George graciously. "It's got proteins an' stuff t'give you a bit of extra get-up-an'-go, so t'speak."

"Ah could do with that, George," acknowledged Ruby. "Ah've 'ad t'do that boiler t'day an' clean toilets an' polish that ol' piano. Ah 'ate Tuesdays."

There was a pause as if George were searching for the right words. "Ah've been thinkin', Ruby . . . in fac' ah've been thinkin' a lot these days."

"'Bout what?" asked Ruby.

"You an' me, Ruby."

Ruby paused and looked up at the branches of the willow tree above their heads. They swayed in the rhythm of the gentle breeze. "So what's on y'mind, George?"

"Ah'm in love," said George.

"Oh 'eck," said Ruby.

"Ah've been in love since ah were seventeen years old . . . wi' a girl what was t'village May Queen. She's allus been light o' my life an' she's sittin' 'ere right next t'me."

"Them's nice words, George."

"So ah've got a question — an important question."

"Well, y'better ask it," said Ruby quietly.

George stood up from the bench and got down on one knee. He took Ruby's hand in his and said, "Ruby, my love, will you marry me?"

And Ruby smiled.

Perhaps Tuesdays weren't so bad after all, she thought.

CHAPTER
FOUR

Every Loser Wins

School closed today for the half-term holiday and will reopen on Monday, 10 November. The new furniture arrived for the temporary classroom. There was a meeting of the governing body at 7.00p.m.
Extract from the Ragley School Logbook:
Friday, 31 October 1986

It was a perfect autumn morning and bright sunshine lit up the trees as I drove towards Ragley village. Around me russet leaves swirled across the road and bared their fragile skeletons. Now was the time of the gathering of leaves, a time for reflecting on misty memories. The season was changing and in the hedgerows teardrop cobwebs shivered in the sharp breeze.

The number-one record, "Every Loser Wins" sung by the *EastEnders* star Nick Berry, was on the radio once again. The BBC soap opera was Ruby's favourite programme. I recalled she had told me that the song was performed by Nick Berry's character, Simon "Wicksy" Wicks, along with his backing group, The Banned. It had dominated the charts and I listened to the words as I drove along.

On the council estate Nellie Robinson was washing up the breakfast pots as her husband, Big Dave, got ready to leave in his bin lorry to collect Little Malcolm.

"Ah'm off t'see Dorothy this mornin'," she shouted after him. "She's not 'erself."

Big Dave grunted a reply. He had his own problems. "Neither is Malc'," he said. "'E's been a pain in t'bum this las' week."

His diminutive cousin was definitely out of sorts and he didn't know why.

"Well, ask 'im what's up," said Nellie firmly. "You've known 'im long enough."

Big Dave looked puzzled. He had never been into *emotions* — that was for women. "Ah don't like," he said.

"Men!" muttered Nellie. As she turned off Nick Berry on the radio she prayed that his message *every loser wins* applied to ordinary young women like her best friend Dorothy. She picked up her coat and set off for Nora's Coffee Shop.

I pulled up on the High Street by the General Stores. The sign outside read:

GENERAL STORES & NEWSAGENT
"A cornucopia of delights"
Proprietor — Prudence Anastasia Golightly

The bell above the door rang as I walked in. Betty Buttle and Margery Ackroyd were being served.

Prudence put a bottle of Sanatogen wine and a *TV Times* on the counter.

Betty held up the bottle. "M'mother swears by it, Prudence. She says it's 'er brain tonic."

"It's certainly a powerful pick-me-up," said Prudence, "although I heard the Australians didn't trust it. In fact they banned it during the First World War."

"Well that's flippin' Australians for you," retorted Betty. She held up her *TV Times*. "In fac' there's even a new soap from Australia called *Neighbours*. We've got enough soaps, so I don't know why we want another one, speshully from them down under."

Prudence nodded politely. She had a very dear aunt who lived by the sea in Wollongong in New South Wales and didn't feel inclined to damn the whole of Australasia.

"It'll never catch on," added Margery for good measure as they walked out.

As always, Prudence had my morning newspaper ready for me. "Good morning, Mr Sheffield," and the petite shop-keeper moved up on to the next wooden step behind the counter to be on a level with me.

"Good morning, Prudence," I said and glanced up, "and good morning to you, Jeremy."

Her dearest friend was sitting on his usual shelf next to a tin of loose-leaf Lyons Tea and an old advertisement for Hudson's Soap and Carter's Little Liver Pills. Prudence always made sure her teddy bear was well turned out. Today he looked smart in a checked lumberjack shirt, brown cord trousers and a bright blue bobble hat.

"Oh dear," said Prudence glancing at the front page article. "There's more about Jeffrey Archer, I'm afraid."

The politician and popular novelist had stepped down from his role as deputy leader of the Conservative Party at the start of the week following reports that he had paid a prostitute, Monica Coghlan, to leave the country so that she wouldn't be questioned by the police about his involvement with her.

"Yes, I heard about the photograph," I said.

The previous Sunday's *News of the World* had published a photograph of an intermediary sent by Archer handing over the money at Victoria station and his downfall was swift.

As I turned to leave, Prudence looked around the shop — at that moment there were no other customers. "Mr Sheffield," she said, "I hear things here in my shop and, as you know, I'm not one for trivial gossip."

I was curious. "Of course."

She lowered her voice. "Two men were in earlier today talking about Mr Coe. I was in the back room seeking out some Castella cigars for one of them and I heard the word 'revenge'. It really sounded quite unnerving."

"Intriguing," I said. "Perhaps it was nothing," I added, not wishing to alarm Prudence. Secretly it occurred to me that Stan Coe had probably collected many enemies over the years. I paid for my newspaper and walked out to my car. The local refuse wagon trundled past and Big Dave Robinson gave me a cheery wave. Sitting alongside him was his cousin, Little Malcolm Robinson, head down and deep in thought. It appeared all was not well.

As I drove towards the school gates I was surprised to see a dark blue Ford Transit parked under the horse chestnut trees by the school wall. It sported the words "Junk & Disorderly — E. Clifton of Thirkby" painted on the side in gold letters. I recognized the tall figure of Edward Clifton. He was the keen amateur astronomer and David Soul lookalike who had given an excellent talk to the children last year concerning the arrival of Halley's Comet. He was in earnest conversation with Anne Grainger and I presumed our deputy headteacher was arranging another visit.

I parked my car, picked up my old satchel from the passenger seat, took a deep breath and set off to face another school day. It was destined to prove eventful.

In the office Ruby was talking to Vera.

"So what did you say, Ruby?"

"Well, ah said ah'd 'ave to ask m'children first an' 'e said 'e understood. 'E really is a lovely man, Mrs F, 'e were so patient."

"I'm so pleased for you, Ruby," said Vera with a smile. "Mr Dainty is a very fine man." She stood up and gave her a hug. "I presume this is confidential for the time being?"

Ruby nodded. "Ah need t'pick m'moment, speshully wi' our 'Azel. She took Ronnie's death the 'ardest an' ah don't want 'er upset."

"Of course," said Vera. "I'm sure there will be a good time."

"'E wants t'buy me a ring but ah've said we need t'wait 'cause of m'children."

Vera closed the door. "Ruby, if you married Mr Dainty would you want to stay on as caretaker?"

"Dunno, Mrs F," said Ruby, staring out of the window. "Ah'd miss m'job, an' t'children . . . an' you o' course."

Vera smiled at her dear friend. "That's a kind thing to say, Ruby."

"Thing about *retirement*, Mrs F, is that my mother says there's nothing t'do all day an' all day t'do it in. So ah'd prob'bly carry on working, but mebbe part-time."

"Are you absolutely certain?" asked Vera.

Ruby thought hard and then nodded. "Ah'm certain, Mrs F, absolutely certain . . . an' wi'out any fear o' contraception."

Vera smiled gently at her friend. "Well you can't be more certain than that," she said.

Meanwhile the refuse wagon had reached the leafy road to Morton and Big Dave was becoming tired of his cousin's downcast mood. "C'mon, Malc', y'not 'xactly a bag o' laughs this mornin'. What's up?"

Little Malcolm sighed deeply and shook his head. "Ah'm a *loser*, Dave," he said mournfully.

Big Dave glanced across at his diminutive cousin and changed down a gear. "'Ow come, Malc'?"

Little Malcolm sighed. "Well ah'm jus' a bin man what can't get things right."

Big Dave realized this called for action and he pulled into a layby. "But we're t'best bin men i' Yorkshire," he said proudly. "Ev'ryone says so."

66

"Ah know that," conceded Little Malcolm, "but it's my Dorothy. Ev'rythin' ah say . . . she bites me 'ead off."

Big Dave switched off the engine. "So what's up wi' Dorothy?" he asked. "Ah mus' say ah've noticed she's been a bit quiet lately, but my Nellie goes like that sometimes. It's 'cause they 'ave 'ormones."

"But she's gettin' real mardy — sort of *irritated*," lamented Little Malcolm, "an' ah think she said summat abart seein' Doctor Davenport."

"That's what women do — they're allus goin' to t'doctor's wi' all them *feminine* things."

"Ah s'ppose," admitted Little Malcolm glumly.

"Jus' tek 'er out," advised Big Dave, "that's what ah do wi' Nellie. Ah tek 'er to t'pub an' then mebbe tell 'er ah like 'er 'air."

"Ah've tried that an' it dunt work," said Little Malcolm mournfully.

"Well, tell 'er she's lookin' slim," suggested Big Dave knowledgeably. "That never fails. They all love that."

Little Malcolm considered this for a moment. "Mebbe you've got summat there, Dave, 'cause ah've noticed she 'as been gettin' a bit on the 'eavy side."

"It's all *psychological* wi' women, Malc'," said Big Dave, tapping his forehead with a grubby forefinger. "You 'ave t'keep 'em 'appy."

Little Malcolm settled back in his seat. He knew Big Dave was doing his best to make him feel better, but he still felt like a five-foot-four-inch loser. "OK, Dave," he said, resigned to his fate. "Let's c'llect some bins."

Big Dave smiled: it was another problem solved. He crashed the wagon into first gear and they drove off.

In the school office I had barely hung up my duffel coat and scarf before I sensed the atmosphere. Vera had opened the morning mail and was sitting white-faced with anger. "I don't believe it," she said and thrust the letter in my direction.

It was from the School Governor Services Department at County Hall confirming our revised list of governors for the new amalgamated school of Ragley & Morton, commencing January 1987.

The list looked the same apart from two names. One was Mrs Rebecca Parrish, a senior lecturer in education at the college in York, who had become our new parent governor. This was positive news. Her nine-year-old daughter Katie had just moved up into my class and Mrs Parrish's expertise would prove a welcome addition to the governing body.

However, the final name on the list was a bombshell. It was the only remaining ex-governor of Morton School — a certain Mr Stanley Coe.

"Oh no!" I groaned.

Vera had composed herself. "I'll speak with Joseph," she said quietly. "Perhaps something can be done."

"Let's hope so," I said. "I wonder if that's why he was smiling."

With a weary tread I set off for my classroom.

It was a few minutes before morning break when our mathematics lesson was interrupted. "Big van comin' up t'drive, Mr Sheffield," announced Stuart Ormroyd without appearing to look up from his School Mathematics Project workcard and the properties of equilateral triangles.

A large truck was reversing into the school car park and a man in blue overalls was waving his arms to direct the driver. The sign on the side read "COUNTY OFFICE FURNITURE SUPPLIES". The tables, chairs and storage units for the temporary classroom had arrived.

"Is it t'furniture for t'new classroom, Mr Sheffield?" asked an excited Hayley Spraggon.

"An' can we watch, sir?" put in Barry Stonehouse as all heads turned towards the windows.

"Yes, I'm sure you can," I said, "but you need to make sure you don't get in the way." I sent a message to Anne, who was on playground duty, to make sure the children kept well back from the procession of furniture.

Meanwhile, Ruby had arrived to put out the dining tables in preparation for our daily Reading Workshop in the school hall. Twirling her bunch of keys, she then set off for the temporary classroom to unlock the double doors. She stood inside, determined all the furniture should arrive in good order.

On the other side of the school wall, the two village gossips, Betty Buttle and Margery Ackroyd, had stopped to watch the unloading of the furniture.

"Looks posh," said Margery.

"Ah wonder who's goin' in there?" murmured Betty.

"Mebbe all t'new uns from Morton," suggested Margery.

Betty pondered this for a moment. "No, ah think Mr Sheffield'll want t'put 'em all t'gether. Y'know, Ragley an' Morton, so they don't feel left out an' can mek friends."

Margery nodded and stared at Anne Grainger, who was in animated conversation with the children.

"You'll never guess what ah saw when ah went t'Thirkby market las' Saturday," confided Margery.

"What's that then?" asked Betty.

"Only Mrs Grainger," said Margery, nodding towards our deputy headteacher.

"So what's t'do about that?" asked Betty.

Margery looked left and right to ensure they would not be overheard. "Well, she were comin' out o' that antiques shop where that big good-lookin' man works."

"Y'mean 'im what gave a talk about that comet?" queried Betty.

"That's the one, Betty, an' 'e looks spittin' image o' David Soul."

"Oooh yes," said Betty, going weak at the knees. "But mebbe she were jus' shoppin'."

"It were more than shoppin'," said Margery conspiratorially. "They looked all lovey-dovey t'me."

"Well who would 'ave thought, an' 'er a teacher an' all," said Betty.

"Mebbe so, but 'e could 'ang 'is coat on my bedroom door any day of the week," added Margery.

They both sighed and for a moment imagined an afternoon of hot passion with the handsome antiques

70

dealer. The chiming of the church clock up the Morton Road disturbed their lurid thoughts and with a sigh they went their separate ways.

After checking with Vera to see if there were any important messages, I collected my mug of coffee and went out to help Anne supervise the children. A large crowd had gathered, all showing interest as two burly workmen proceeded to unload the new furniture. Slowly but surely it was neatly piled in the temporary classroom to Ruby's satisfaction. I looked inside. There were smart new rectangular tables with grey Formica tops and trays for the children's books and pens. The chairs were modern and stacked easily, and the bookcases and the teacher's desk smelled of new wood. Finally, a huge chalkboard and a collection of large noticeboards were carried in and propped up under the windows, waiting to be fixed to the walls by the next team from County Hall.

When the bell rang for the end of playtime Anne went over to stand with the children in her class. This was an excellent opportunity for language development, so she gathered her children around her and encouraged them to describe the events taking place.

As they walked back inside, Anne looked down at little Walter Popple's outdoor shoes. "Your shoes are on the wrong feet, Walter."

Walter was puzzled. "No, they're not, Miss — they're on mine!"

Anne smiled, but the smile quickly disappeared as, beyond the school wall, she saw a familiar Ford Transit driving slowly past the village green and the driver giving her a hesitant wave. There were decisions to make in her life and some of them were difficult.

At lunchtime we gathered in the staff-room, where Vera had prepared a pot of tea and laid out a plate of her home-made oat crunch biscuits. She poured the tea and, to her dismay, noticed that Sally Pringle was reading the *Guardian*.

"Makes for dismal reading," observed Sally. "Average house prices have shot up to almost forty thousand pounds, a gallon of petrol is now one pound eighty-nine and the rate of inflation is now three point four per cent.

"Oh dear," said Anne.

"We'll never afford our own home at this rate," said Pat reflectively.

"Life is getting more difficult under Maggie," added Sally pointedly.

Vera kept quiet and wiped the draining board.

Sally looked across to her. "And there's a report about something called 'mad cow disease' . . . but never fear, Vera, I don't think they're referring to our Prime Minister."

Not worth a reply, thought Vera as she dried the cups with her favourite tea towel.

Everyone sank into their own thoughts.

Pat was marking some of her children's writing and trying to decipher six-year-old Dallas Sue-Ellen Earnshaw's writing. It was clear that Dallas was still using her own version of phonics. She had written "arwentart afta me metantatipi" and Pat deduced it meant "I went out after my meat and potato pie".

At least she's trying to write, thought Pat as she carefully printed out the correct sentence.

During afternoon school the children in my class continued with their history project. I was helping Sigourney Longbottom to use the index in the back of one of the reference books we had borrowed from the mobile library. It was then that I noticed her answer to one of the questions. In response to "In which battle did King Harold die?" Sigourney had written, "His last one." I decided to discuss this with her after conceding that, technically, she was correct.

As I walked away I overheard Claire Buttershaw lean across the desk and say, "Sigourney, your hair's all messy. Do you want t'borrow my brush? I've got one in my bag."

"Thanks," said Sigourney and she ran her fingers through her spiky, unkempt hair. "Ah learned a long time ago that when yer mam's mad at you, don't let 'er brush yer 'air."

Very true, I thought.

At afternoon break Vera was busy preparing a note for parents confirming the half-term holiday dates and the arrangements for the Parent Teacher Association bonfire.

I was on duty, so I collected a mug of tea and walked out on to the playground. Two seven-year-olds, Billy

Ricketts and Sam Whittaker, were talking about girlfriends.

"'Ave you got a girlfriend?" asked Billy.

"No, ah don't like girls," said Sam. "So, 'ave you got one?"

"No, ah don't like 'em, they're all soft an' can't play football."

"Y'right there," agreed Sam.

"But my big brother 'as got a girlfriend," said Billy. "'E went out wi' 'er for t'first time las' night. 'E said it were a date."

"A *date*?"

"Yes, that's what 'e said it were."

"Is 'e seein' 'er again?"

"Dunno," said Billy. "But 'e *knows* about girls. 'E said if y'tell 'em enough lies, y'get a *second* date."

"Oh, ah see," said Sam . . . but he didn't.

"Ah think 'e's in love," added Billy knowingly.

"What's love?" asked Sam.

"M'brother says it's when y'buy a girl some flowers 'cause if y'don't y'get told off."

Sam considered this for a moment until something caught his attention on the other side of the playground. "Alfie Spraggon's got a spider in a matchbox."

"Cor!" said Billy. "Let's go," and they ran off to investigate another of life's mysteries.

It was "Story Time", the last lesson of the day, and I was reading *Dragon Slayer: The Story of Beowulf* by Rosemary Sutcliff, an inspirational author who had spent most of her life in a wheelchair. The children

74

were spellbound as the Anglo Saxon epic unfolded, and it was at times like this I remembered why teaching was the best profession in the world. Also, on occasions, it could be the most amusing.

When the bell rang for the end of school I dismissed the children and walked through the cloakroom area towards the office. Ted Coggins, the burly farmer's son, was in excited conversation with Charlie Cartwright about Trick or Treat night. He was in such a hurry he bumped into me in the corridor. "Steady on, Ted!" I cried, a little winded by the collision. "You shouldn't run in school."

Quick as a flash Ted replied, "Mr Evans told us about t'Ten Commandments, Mr Sheffield, an' it didn't say anythin' 'bout runnin' in school."

He walked off at great speed and with a big smile on his face, as if he were in an Olympic time trial. "'Ave a good 'oliday, sir," he shouted over his shoulder.

I didn't reprimand him for shouting. I guessed that wasn't included in the Ten Commandments either.

When I walked into the office Vera handed me the telephone receiver. "It's Beth," she said in hushed tones and resumed tidying the private domain that was her four-drawer filing cabinet.

"How's it going?" asked Beth. "Have you got the new furniture?"

"Yes, it looks terrific."

"So, are you getting a bite to eat before the governors' meeting?"

"Yes, I'll walk over to the Oak," I said, "although I feel like drowning my sorrows."

"Really? Why is that?"

"You'll never guess who is on the list of new governors."

There was a moment's silence. "Not that dreadful man again?"

"I'm afraid so."

"Oh dear — will he never go away?"

"Well, wish me luck."

"Must go, Jack. I'll be home in good time to give John his tea — so see you later tonight."

I wanted to say "Love you", but Vera was at the other desk so I refrained.

Joseph had called in to the office to check all was well for the meeting. "I'll come back in good time," he said.

"And the agenda is prepared," said Vera.

"Thanks," I said. "It should be an interesting meeting."

"And we shall have Mr Coe to cope with once again," added Joseph.

"I have the feeling he's up to something," I said, "and, no doubt, it will be something to do with money."

"The love of money," quoted Vera, "the root of all evil."

"First Letter to Timothy, chapter six," murmured Joseph and Vera gave an imperceptible nod.

★   ★   ★

It was six o'clock and the orange lights of The Royal Oak were a welcome sight as I walked out of school and across the village green. Sheila Bradshaw was behind the bar and gave me a cheery welcome. She was wearing a sparkly boob-tube that left little to the imagination and a black leather mini-skirt.

"Evenin', Mr Sheffield, what's it t'be?" I looked up at the Specials board. Tonight there was a choice of Chicken in a Basket, Corned Beef Hash or a Sheila Salad.

"I've got a meeting in school, Sheila, so nothing too filling," I said.

"Well, we've got a nice mushroom salad if y'want summat light."

"Thanks, that's fine," I said. "A salad and better make it a soft drink."

Old Tommy Piercy, our local butcher, was in his usual seat at the bar next to the signed photograph of Geoffrey Boycott, or "Sir Geoffrey" as Old Tommy called him.

"A salad!" he said. "What's t'world comin' to? Mark my words," he added prophetically, "man can't live by veg alone."

There was a celebration going on behind me, and Little Malcolm and Dorothy were sitting on the bench seat under the dart board, flanked by Big Dave and Nellie and most of the Ragley Rovers football team.

Sheila smiled as she served up my orange juice. "It's a special night f'Dorothy," she confided. "She's jus' found out she's pregnant."

"That's wonderful news," I said. "Put a couple of drinks behind the bar for them from me," and I handed over a ten-pound note.

I walked over and shook Little Malcolm's hand. "Congratulations to you both," I said.

"Ah'm feeling ten feet tall, Mr Sheffield," he said. For our vertically challenged bin man, this clearly was something special.

Big Dave had his arm around Little Malcolm's shoulders and was whispering something in his ear. I didn't know what it was, but Little Malcolm nodded to his giant cousin while I noticed Nellie looked a little wistful. Meanwhile, Dorothy was simply glowing.

I sat alone eating my salad at the table in the bay window. On the juke-box Nick Berry was singing "Every Loser Wins" and, as Little Malcolm smiled sheepishly up at his giant cousin, it seemed appropriate.

The governors' meeting took place in the staff-room and Vera, as the secretary, had placed an agenda on each chair. At seven o'clock Joseph welcomed everyone and said it was to be a short meeting, intended to welcome the new governors and confirm arrangements prior to the new school opening in January.

"First of all, we welcome two new governors — Mrs Rebecca Parrish, as parent governor, and Mr Stan Coe from the Morton governing body."

Vera made a note in the book of governors' minutes and sighed deeply.

78

Ragley's existing governing body was reappointed *en bloc*, along with Stan Coe as the only surviving member of the Morton governing body. All the other Morton governors had resigned.

In contrast Mrs Parrish was a most welcome addition. She appeared relaxed and happy with her new life after a difficult time last January when she had separated from her husband, Simon, a lecturer at the University in York. His affair with one of his students had come to light and Mrs Parrish had acted swiftly. I recalled meeting the arrogant Simon Parrish, who had boasted to me of his 1985 "C" Saab 900i with its distinctive cochineal-red metallic paintwork. Now it was simply £10,000 worth of motor car that meant nothing to him. Today he would have willingly given up all he owned to spend time with his talented daughter. The relationship with his former student was over; she had found a younger man and a less complicated lover. Rebecca Parrish had closed the door and was getting on with her life.

Stan Coe said very little except he was pleased to be back supporting his local community once again. There were a few sceptical looks from Major Forbes-Kitchener as Stan gave a forced smile through nicotine-stained teeth.

We discussed the arrangements for the official opening of the new school and confirmed that Miss Barrington-Huntley, the chairman of the Education Committee, would be the guest of honour. We also confirmed the allocation of the children into five classes instead of the present four.

The meeting was about to close when Rebecca Parrish raised the issue of new homes in the area. "I did hear about some new executive homes being built further down the York Road."

"Yes, it was mentioned by our Primary Adviser, Mr Gomersall," I said. "There are a lot of computer programmers working at the chocolate factory in York and more in the Unilever offices on the Leeds northern ring road. They need homes, but they're likely to be closer to York and not in our catchment area."

Vera looked across to Rupert, who took the hint. "I know there's been talk of building in the village," he said.

"I think it's just gossip at present," said Anne, the teacher representative on the governing body. Up to then she had been very quiet. There was clearly something on her mind and it wasn't anything to do with bricks and mortar.

Meanwhile, Stan Coe shuffled in his seat, gave a wintry smile and said nothing.

After the meeting closed everyone walked out to the car park and I stood in the entrance hall with Joseph and Vera.

"Thanks for your support," I said.

Vera watched our local pig farmer get into his Land Rover. "What is a man profited, if he shall gain the whole world, and lose his own soul."

Joseph smiled grimly. "Mark chapter eight, verse thirty-six," he said quietly and they walked out into the darkness.

I locked up the school and drove home.

Under the vast purple sky over the plain of York and beneath a blizzard of stars, I reflected on their words.

Stan Coe didn't mind losing his soul if it meant that in the end he would win.

CHAPTER
FIVE

The Last Firework

*The annual PTA bonfire on Saturday, 8 November
raised £206.45 for school funds. Mr Marcus Potts,
our newly appointed teacher, visited school today
to work in his classroom and attend a staff meeting.*
Extract from the Ragley School Logbook:
Monday, 10 November 1986

It was an iron-grey morning. A reluctant light spread
across the land and a cloak of mist shrouded the silent
fields.

I was listening to The Pretenders as I drove on the
back road to Ragley. It was Monday, 10 November and
even the church bells of St Mary's sounded mournful
as I pulled up on the forecourt of Victor Pratt's garage.
Liquid rainbows reflected in the pools of oil and
rainwater as he ambled out to greet me.

"How are you this morning, Victor?" I asked, but
without conviction. Victor usually had a medical
problem and today was no exception.

"Not good, Mr Sheffield," he replied, giving his
ample backside a rub. "Ah'm off t'see Doctor
Davenport again this mornin'."

"Oh dear," I sympathized.

"Yes," said Victor mournfully, "ah've got them 'aemorrhoids an' they're a right pain in the neck."

"Yes, I suppose they are," I said. It was clear he was suffering significant discomfort even though its location was open to interpretation.

I paid him and he nodded in appreciation. "Good bonfire t'other night," he said.

"Yes, the PTA always do a good job."

"And t'fireworks were t'best ah can recall," he added.

"Spectacular," I agreed.

"Mind you, our Nora said she thought t'guy looked a bit like Maggie Thatcher."

"Oh did she?" I decided not to pursue the point, particularly as it was Sally, our ardent socialist, who had put the finishing touches to the traditional guy prior to its being seated on a broken chair on top of the bonfire. The straw hair and sharp cardboard nose certainly had the appearance of the Prime Minister. Also, I couldn't imagine Guy Fawkes wearing a blue dress with a delicate bow at the neck.

As I pulled away from the garage I noticed a green Citroën that I had never seen before in the village. It was parked on the other side of the road on a patch of gravel in front of the five-barred gate that led to Stan Coe's farm. As I drove by I glanced in my rear-view mirror and caught sight of a tall man in a black raincoat.

The High Street in Ragley was coming to life and a few figures emerged like wraiths in the mist. Heathcliffe

Earnshaw had finished his paper round and Rodney Morgetroyd trundled by on his milk float. On the village green the Robinson cousins, Big Dave and Little Malcolm, were collecting old firework cases, rocket sticks and used sparklers as part of their annual clean-up operation. Both gave me a cheerful wave as I turned right at the top of the High Street and into school.

Two days ago, on Saturday evening, the weather had been dry, cold and calm — a perfect evening for a bonfire. Hundreds of villagers had lined the fence at the back of the school to join in the celebrations. The Parent Teacher Association had provided the best chicken soup I had ever tasted, and John Grainger's spectacular firework display had rounded off a successful evening. Sadly, Anne had left the event early saying she had a headache. The following morning the village had settled back into its usual routine, with our thoughts turning towards Christmas.

When I pulled up in the car park next to Vera's smart Austin Metro, a rusty red Mini was already parked there. It would have been a style icon in the 1960s, but now in the 1980s it had clearly seen better days.

Suddenly, Ted "Postie" Postlethwaite pulled up on his bicycle beside me.

"Morning, Mr Sheffield," he said.

Our postman was regular as clockwork, regardless of the weather. "I'll take in the mail if you like, Ted," I offered.

"Thanks," he replied and handed over a thick wedge of letters held together with a rubber band. "Have a

84

good day, Mr Sheffield," he called out as he cycled away.

I reflected on this sparky village character who never seemed to age. Ted lived in the flat above the Post Office with his new wife, the postmistress Amelia, following their low-key wedding in the summer. According to local gossip, they were blissfully happy in their world of parcels, letters, stamps and frequent sex.

Ruby was in the entrance hall carrying a stack of paper towels when I walked in. "That new teacher 'as come to visit, Mr Sheffield," she informed me, "an' Mrs F put 'im in t'staff-room . . . very p'lite young man."

"Thanks, Ruby," I said. "Yes, he's got the day off for a preliminary visit and to check out his new classroom."

"Well, 'e'll do f'me," said Ruby with a note of approval and she wandered off to replenish the paper-towel dispensers in the children's toilets.

In the school office, Vera was talking to Mrs Jackson, mother of the twins Hermione and Honeysuckle. Pippa Jackson was also our newly appointed chair of the PTA and had called in with the grand sum of £206.45 raised at the bonfire evening.

"Thank you, Mrs Jackson," said Vera, "that's exact to the penny," and she deposited the coins in her metal money box. "I'll bank it later today." Mrs Jackson smiled and Vera looked up. "Good morning, Mr Sheffield," she said brightly. "Mr Potts is in the staff-room and I've given him a cup of coffee."

"Thank you, Vera," I said, "and thank you, Mrs Jackson, for all your support."

"A pleasure, Mr Sheffield, and please call me Pippa."

Vera frowned. This was a little too familiar for our straight-laced school secretary.

"Well, yes, of course," I replied after a brief hesitation. I glanced across at Vera. "Perhaps in private conversation," I added and headed quickly for the staff-room.

Marcus Potts was staring out of the window when I walked in. "Hello, Marcus," I said, "and welcome to Ragley. I'm so pleased you could make it."

"Thanks for the invitation. I'm looking forward to getting stuck in."

"I'm sure you'll like your classroom. The new furniture has arrived and Ruby has removed all the protective wrapping and given the floor and windows a good clean. Also, the chalkboard and display boards have been fixed to the walls — so you've got a flying start."

He gave me a boyish grin from under his mop of black wavy hair. In a cord suit, denim shirt, old school tie and polished shoes, it was clear he had made an effort to smarten himself up. "Thanks," he said. "It gives me a chance to settle in and make my mark. In fact, I was hoping to come in each week after school if I may to ensure I'm ready for January."

"Good idea." I was impressed by his commitment. "Let's go, shall we?"

We walked out to the playground, climbed the wooden steps and stopped outside the door of the temporary classroom. It was locked, and with great ceremony I gave him his own duplicate key. Vera had arranged for a spare one to be cut at Pratt's Hardware Emporium and she had attached it to a large brass ring. On it was a cardboard luggage label with "MR POTTS" written on it.

Marcus stared at it as if it marked a profound moment in his life. "My own classroom," he murmured quietly. "May I?"

I nodded and he unlocked it almost reverentially.

We stood there and looked around. Ruby had made a good job of cleaning, while Anne and Pat had been in to arrange the furniture to leave space for a book corner, a wet area complete with plastic buckets, and a display table. It was a welcoming sight and he drank it all in. "Wonderful," he said. "Simply perfect."

He was thrilled and I was moved to see his reaction.

Pat suddenly arrived carrying our BBC Micro computer. "Hi, Marcus. You said you would be bringing in some new software, so you might as well keep this here for the rest of the day. I've brought a spare extension lead so you can set it up wherever it suits."

Marcus looked as though all his Christmases had come at once. It occurred to me that Pat and Marcus were the teachers of the future, and the new technology of the eighties was something they had both adopted with ease.

"Thanks, Pat," he said. "I've got some software in the car, so I'll load up the programs and we can check them out later." He looked across at me. "If that's fine with you, Jack."

"Yes, by all means," I said. "Pat will appreciate the support." I didn't mention that Anne and I had been left behind in terms of working with our computer, although we were trying hard.

He looked around at the bare walls and empty display boards. "Well . . . perhaps I'll begin by putting backing paper on the noticeboards, and I've got some terrific posters of the planets of the solar system."

"I've got a spare staple gun you can have," offered Pat and hurried off to her classroom.

"Well," I said, "I'll leave you to it. Everything you need should be in the stock cupboard, but check with Vera regarding basic equipment for your desk, such as pens and pencils. In the meantime, see you later for morning assembly at ten fifteen."

I left him staring in admiration at his pristine new teacher's desk.

At the end of morning assembly, including a rousing rendition of "When a Knight Won His Spurs" followed by the Lord's Prayer, I invited Marcus to stand up and tell the children something about himself. He was relaxed as he recounted his early life in Cambridge, where he went to school and university, along with his interests in computers, insects, cycling, classical music and amateur dramatics. I saw the reaction from the teachers as well as the children. It was clear we had appointed a remarkable young man.

Unwittingly, he asked the children if they had any questions and many hands shot up.

"'Ow old are you, sir?" asked Sigourney Longbottom.

Marcus smiled. "I'm twenty-three."

"Are you married, sir?" asked Julie Tricklebank.

"No, I'm not," he replied cautiously, "but perhaps one day . . ."

"An' d'you like spiders, sir?" Charlie Cartwright wanted to know.

"Yes, I like all sorts of creepy-crawlies."

"An' would y'like to 'ear me whistle?" added Ted Coggins for good measure.

"Perhaps later," said Marcus, "on the playground."

Good answer, I thought.

Marcus took all the questions in good spirit and rounded it off by saying how much he was looking forward to coming to Ragley.

During morning break I telephoned home. Beth's parents, John and Diane Henderson, had come up from Hampshire to stay for a few days during the half-term holiday and had joined us for the school bonfire. However, as usual, there were occasional tensions. Diane seemed to want to "control" her daughters — Beth here in Yorkshire and her younger sister, Laura, apparently enjoying life in Australia. In many ways she was reminiscent of Maggie Smith's portrayal of Charlotte Bartlett, the conventionally English chaperone from E. M. Forster's *A Room with a View*. Beth had reacted, and it was one of the key reasons that, last year, she had rejected the opportunity to secure a headship in Hampshire. The thought of her mother on the doorstep each day was not something she wished to endure.

Conversely, John, a tall, weather-beaten sixty-three-year-old, was much more laid back and I always felt relaxed in his presence. He was never happier than when he was playing with John William or busy with his voluntary work rebuilding steam engines on the Watercress Line near their home. In complete contrast to Diane, he was always supportive, and we had formed a positive bond over the years. I saw him more as a friend than a father-in-law.

It was John who answered the telephone and reassured me that all was well. Apparently, he had purchased a large wooden train from the Habitat catalogue.

"A bargain, Jack, at ten ninety-nine," he said, "and young John is really enjoying himself. I think we may have another train enthusiast here."

I smiled. That would certainly please my train-buff father-in-law. "I may be late home, John," I said. "The new teacher has arrived and I wanted to spend a little time with him after school."

"That's fine," he said. "See you later."

In the background I heard my son chanting, "Choo-choo," before I replaced the receiver.

It was shortly before lunchtime when Stuart Ormroyd glanced up from his spelling test and announced, "Major's 'ere, Mr Sheffield."

The test comprised a list of spellings beginning with the letter "A" and all the children were trying hard.

"In 'is big posh Bentley," added my best reader, Michelle Gawthorpe, who had a column of perfect answers including "action", "anoint", "appliance" and "awkward".

A familiar large, shiny, chauffeur-driven classic black Bentley purred into the car park and parked with precision. Rupert, in a three-piece tweed suit, strode into school and knocked gently on the office door.

"Vera, my dear," he said with a smile, "I do hope I'm not disturbing you."

Vera looked up from her desk and smiled. "An unexpected pleasure," she replied.

"I came in to meet Mr Potts," he said. "I thought it was important we made the young man welcome."

"How thoughtful, Rupert."

He looked around the office at Vera's desk with the photograph of her three cats; the well-organized noticeboard and school timetable; the calendar of term dates and the carefully labelled filing cabinet. Finally he looked back at Vera. "I was wondering, my dear, if you have had further thoughts about . . . *retirement?*"

Vera looked out of the window to where the children were playing on the school field, happy in their secure world of simple games and fleeting friendships.

"Yes, Rupert," she said quietly, "I think about it frequently and I shall know when the time is right. However, for now, there is much to do and I'm needed here."

Rupert nodded and remained silent. He would bide his time.

At lunchtime in the staff-room Sally was reading her November issue of *Cosmopolitan* magazine and smiled

approvingly at the article "Fatness is not a problem —
other people's attitudes are".

I am a large lady, she thought ... *in fact,
Rubenesque is the graceful way of putting it.* However,
she was eyeing the tin of custard creams when the
Major walked in with Marcus and Rupert began to
question him as if he were seeking to attend
officer-training school. Fortunately Marcus was not
overawed.

On the playground seven-year-old Billy Ricketts was in
conversation with Scott Higginbottom. "My dad uses
t'f-word," said Billy.

Scott looked puzzled. "So does mine," he said.
"What does it mean?"

Billy considered this for a moment and shook his
head. "Dunno ... but ah thinks it's summat t'do wi'
sex an' y'say it t'people y'don't like."

Scott surveyed the playground. "Dallas Earnshaw
said you were smelly this morning."

Billy frowned. "Well, let's go say it to 'er," and they
ran off.

Up the High Street in Nora's Coffee Shop, Dorothy
was reading her latest *Smash Hits* magazine. Her
pregnancy had captured the imagination of the village
and Little Malcolm felt he had achieved new status. He
really did feel he was walking tall.

Dorothy was studying a picture of her secret
heart-throb, Shakin' Stevens. His new record, "Because
I Love You", was causing some excitement as each copy

92

included a "genuine autograph". Nora was looking over Dorothy's shoulder. The front cover photograph of Ade Edmondson brandishing a chainsaw did little for Nora, but Dorothy was engrossed.

Drooling over pictures of Bon Jovi, Duran Duran, along with Spandau Ballet on their tour of Holland, had occupied a few minutes between customers for Dorothy. She held up the centre-page spread of Prince for Nora to admire.

"What d'you think, Nora?"

"Who is it?" asked Nora.

"It's Prince."

"Pwince?" queried Nora, who had never been able to pronounce the letter "R".

"Yes, don't y'think 'e looks smart?"

Prince was wearing a bright yellow suit with white buttons and what looked suspiciously like lip gloss. Nora studied the photograph. "Well, Dowothy, ah can't see my Tywone in a suit like that."

Dorothy had to agree. The thought of Tyrone Crabtree, Nora's boyfriend, looking like a giant banana in a yellow suit was a step too far.

Diana Ross's "Chain Reaction" was playing on the juke-box when Big Dave and Little Malcolm walked in.

"Ah'll get 'em in, Dave," said Little Malcolm confidently and, while Big Dave sat at their usual table, Little Malcolm approached the love of his life. He noticed that Dorothy's peroxide-blonde hair seemed to have taken on a life of its own and spiralled upwards in a mass of eccentric waves and curls.

"Yer 'air looks nice, Dorothy," he said, thinking back to Big Dave's suggestions on how to please women.

"Oooh thank you, Malcolm," replied Dorothy. Then she pursed her lips and looked thoughtful, and Little Malcolm wondered what was coming next. "Problem is," she continued, "ah couldn't mek up m'mind whether t'go for a proper glossy 'old wi' m'Shock Waves Wet Gel or go for a bit more lift wi' m'Super Firm Gel."

Little Malcolm hadn't realized the world of hairdressing threw up so many problems. Momentarily it crossed his mind that it would be preferable to have a son and not a daughter. Dorothy loaded up a tray and served them with two pork pies and two large mugs of sweet tea.

It was then that a young teenager in a polo-neck jumper and a pair of scruffy jeans walked in and stared at the pile of rock buns in the cabinet.

"Ah'll'ave one o' them," he said bluntly, "an' a coffee."

He took out a fifty-pence piece and slapped it on the counter.

Nora hated bad manners. "That's not vewy p'lite," she said.

Dorothy arrived behind the counter. "Y'should say *please*."

"An' ah'm in a 'urry," retorted the boy, pushing back his long black unkempt hair.

"Y'bein' wude," said Nora.

"An' shouldn't you be in school?" asked Dorothy.

94

"Ah've no lessons this afternoon," he said defensively, "so can ah 'ave m'coffee . . . *please?*"

Both Big Dave and Little Malcolm heard the conversation. "Be'ave y'self," growled Big Dave.

"An' say y'sorry," added Little Malcolm.

"Sorry," mumbled the boy without conviction.

Finally, as he walked out he flashed a V-sign to the two bin men and ran off down School View.

"Who were that?" said Big Dave.

"It's young Dean, Mrs Skinner's son," said Little Malcolm. "They moved into one o' them farm cottages 'round back o' Morton Road. We do their bins."

Across the road, Dean lit up a cigarette, sat on a wall and looked aimlessly around. Then he felt in the pocket of his leather jacket and pulled out a firework. It was his last one and he had saved it following last Saturday's Bonfire Night. *After all*, he thought, *a spare firework could always come in handy.*

When the bell rang for afternoon break I called in to see Marcus in his classroom.

"I've brought you a mug of tea and some biscuits," I said.

"Thanks, Jack. I'm just loading up the computer with some of the educational software I've brought in."

"And here are the up-to-date class lists for next January when we move to five classes."

I handed over the lists and looked around the classroom. It was impressive. Stimulating posters covered the display boards and the beginnings of a book corner had emerged. I left him in there checking the list of new pupils who were to arrive next term from Morton School and learning their names.

We finished the day with a brief staff meeting and Vera served tea. We began by welcoming Marcus to the team and he thanked everyone for their support. Sally took the lead on the next item.

"The retirement home has got back to us," she said, "and confirmed arrangements for our visit there on Saturday morning, twentieth December. It's when the school choir will be singing Christmas carols."

Vera read out a letter from Miss Barrington-Huntley, the chair of the Education Committee in Northallerton, confirming she had accepted the invitation to attend the official opening of the newly amalgamated school on the first day of the spring term. She added that she would be accompanied by her assistant, Miss Cleverley.

Anne outlined a few ideas for the Christmas party on Friday, 19 December, the last day of term, and Pat enthused about the success of our netball team. It was a relaxed beginning to the new half-term.

As everyone drifted back to their classrooms to do some final tidying up, I settled down to some paperwork. Marcus said he would be working in his classroom so we agreed to meet later. Gradually the staff went home, Ruby swept all the classrooms and I battled with a questionnaire from County Hall concerning "Health & Safety in the Workplace". It occurred to me that if we followed all the recommendations we would never go on another school trip or permit children to play any of our team sports.

An hour later the temperature dropped as the old school boiler rumbled to a halt. Suddenly it was chilly in the office and the windows began to rattle as the wind moaned through the cracks in the wooden casements.

I had just written in the school logbook, "*Mr Marcus Potts, our newly appointed teacher, visited school today to work in his classroom and attend a staff meeting*" when the church clock up the Morton Road chimed six. It was time for some refreshment, so I locked up the school and collected Marcus from his classroom. We crunched over the fallen leaves on the village green towards The Royal Oak. Across the road, Ted Postlethwaite was at the front door of the Post Office and gave us a wave as we walked in. The warmth was a blessing.

At a corner table in the lounge bar, Claire Bradshaw, the landlord's daughter, and Anita Cuthbertson, two twenty-year-olds who had been in my class when I first arrived in Ragley, were sipping orange juice and smoking cigarettes.

"'Ello, sir," said Claire while Anita eyed up Marcus.

I noticed that Anita had adopted a Gothic look. The ensemble comprised long, back-combed hair, pale skin, dark eye shadow and lipstick, black nail varnish and a spiked dog collar. It was perhaps a blessing that her long black gabardine raincoat covered her leather corset. She had left behind dreams of a night of passion with Shakin' Stevens and discovered new interests in Siouxsie and the Banshees, The Cure and The Cult.

Meanwhile, Claire had purchased *The Smash Hits Yearbook 1987* for only £2.95 and, for these two young women, life seemed complete.

Anita was studying a Phaze advertisement for a pair of so-called bondage trousers in black or tartan, complete with zips and D-rings. With no change out of £20 it was a significant purchase, but for Anita image was everything and Claire let her cut out page 86.

At the bar Sheila Bradshaw came to serve us and I saw Marcus react when he witnessed North Yorkshire's finest cleavage. Perhaps I should have warned him.

"What's it t'be, Mr Sheffield?" asked Sheila, simultaneously fluttering her false eyelashes at Marcus.

"Just a half of Chestnut for me, please, Sheila. We're not staying long."

"And the same for me, please," added Marcus.

"This is our new teacher, Mr Potts," I said. "He starts next January."

"Pleased t'meet you," said Sheila. She leaned forward provocatively. "An' ah 'ope you'll come back t'try one o' my *Specials*."

Marcus blushed slightly, but to his credit retained his composure.

I pointed up to the Specials board. "Sheila does some lovely food, Marcus," I explained.

We took our drinks to a table by the bay window and relaxed while the regulars drifted in. Derek "Deke" Ramsbottom arrived at the bar with two of his sons, Shane and Clint.

Clint was wearing a baggy, slouch-shouldered, red leather jacket with puffy sleeves, black leather pants and

98

sunglasses. In contrast, Shane was still part of punk sub-culture with ripped jeans, a Sex Pistols T-shirt and a denim jacket decorated with safety pins. The letters H-A-R-D tattooed on the knuckles of his right hand caught the eye as he lifted his tankard, and they took their drinks to a battered table in the tap room and lit up their cigarettes.

Sheila reached up to remove Deke's tankard from the shelf above the bar while Deke nodded towards his sons. "'E's a good lad, is our Clint," he said quietly in Sheila's ear. "'E can't 'elp bein' a big girl's blouse."

Sheila merely shook her head as she pulled Deke's pint of Tetley's bitter. She knew that in the singing cowboy's world this was as close as he could get to accepting Clint's sexuality.

Marcus and I chatted amicably about school and life in general. We finished our drinks and stood up to leave.

It was then that it happened.

Ted Postlethwaite suddenly burst in, rushed up to the bar and looked frantically around. "FIRE!" he shouted. "FIRE!"

Everyone stared at Ted and put down their tankards.

He looked across to the bay window and saw me. "Mr Sheffield," he yelled, "come quick!"

I hurried towards him. "What is it, Ted?"

"A fire at t'school . . . it's that new classroom . . . it's going up in flames!"

CHAPTER
SIX

Judgement Day

The headteacher attended the magistrates' court in York during afternoon school to give evidence concerning the fire that damaged the temporary classroom. Miss Flint provided supply cover.
Extract from the Ragley School Logbook:
Friday, 5 December 1986

It was Friday, 5 December and the first snow of winter had fallen. A world of silence awaited me as I looked out of the bedroom window of Bilbo Cottage. The distant land was covered in a white shroud that curved gracefully across the ploughed fields and muted the sounds of the countryside. I could only hope that Deke Ramsbottom would clear the back road to Ragley before I set off. Ahead of me was a difficult journey.

Also, later in the day, my first visit to the local magistrates' court in York was in store. It was judgement day for Dean Skinner and I wondered what the outcome would be.

In Bilbo Cottage Beth had risen early and was sitting at the kitchen table completing some notes for her Christmas concert. It was the day of her reception class

100

Nativity play and Beth was keen that all the preparations would go smoothly.

When I came downstairs with John it was just after 6.15 a.m. and on the small portable television on the worktop Anne Diamond and Geoff Meade had introduced *Good Morning Britain*. They were cranking up the excitement towards Christmas, while Wincey Willis tended to dampen our enthusiasm with a freezing weather forecast.

Beth was too preoccupied to join in with the opportunity to "shape up with Lizzie Webb", preferring to check the dates for her forthcoming meetings with the governing body and the PTA. I turned down the volume and gave our hungry son a bowl of porridge topped with sliced banana. Somehow John managed to get most of it over his face as he watched Popeye the Sailorman eating his spinach on the morning cartoon. As I was wearing my best suit, I kept my distance. I had learned from bitter experience — our lively son had been known to hit the far wall of the kitchen with a handful of mushy peas.

Mrs Roberts arrived and Beth and I left for work. The journey to Ragley on the winding country road was slow and arduous in spite of Deke's snow plough clearing the worst of the drifts. Far beyond the frozen hedgerows the high moors loomed ominously with the threat of more snow, while the chattering sound of grouse crying "go-back, go back" was a warning. On my car radio the number-one record, Europe's. "The Final Countdown", seemed prophetic. I pulled up outside the General Stores and the bell rang as I walked in.

Mrs Ricketts was in front of me in the queue. She had bought a packet of cigarettes, an aniseed-flavoured Black Jack for her daughter, Suzi-Quatro, and a *Daily Express* for 20p. It was while she was admiring a photograph of Sarah Ferguson under the headline "Fergie Meets Santa" that Suzi-Quatro announced, "Santa's comin' to our 'ouse, Miss Golightly."

"I wonder what he might bring?" replied Prudence with an encouraging smile.

"Dunno," said Suzi-Quatro. "Mebbe another doll."

Mrs Ricketts looked down sharply. "*Another* doll?"

"Yes, Mam, jus' like the one hidin' under your bed."

"What were y'doin' under my bed?" asked Mrs Ricketts crossly.

"Playin' 'ide an' seek wi' our Billy."

"Don't you go there again," said Mrs Ricketts firmly. "Play *downstairs* in future."

"OK, Mam," said the little girl cheerfully as she began to chew her Black Jack and the colour of her tongue changed from pink to black. After all, why should she mind if her mother went to bed to play with dolls of her own?

Prudence moved up to a higher step to serve me. "Here's your newspaper, Mr Sheffield," she said, "and it sounds as if that politician with the greasy hair is trying to make a name for himself."

Beneath the headline "Baker Unfolds Far-reaching School Reform" it read: "Plans to introduce the biggest changes in schools for more than 40 years were outlined yesterday by Kenneth Baker, Secretary of State for Education & Science."

I sighed. "Yes, more changes ahead it would seem." I always felt it prudent to be cautious, as I knew the other shoppers might repeat my comments.

As I drove up the High Street, a distinctive green Citroën passed me, heading towards Coe Farm and the back road to York, and I tried to recall where I had seen it before. The school car park was a welcome sight and I locked my car with frozen fingers. A bitter wind brought tears to my eyes as I hurried towards the entrance porch.

"Good luck in court t'day, Mr Sheffield," shouted Ruby from the far side of the playground. She walked over to the entrance porch, clearly not feeling the freezing wind as I did. "Ah 'ope it gets sorted, but t'way it's goin' it could snowball into a right can o' worms."

Regardless of mixed metaphors, I knew that Ruby was right — it could. I was entering a new world of cross-examinations and important judgements.

The warmth inside school was a relief as I walked into the office.

"Good morning, Mr Sheffield," said Vera. "Valerie called to say she will be here at lunchtime to cover for you this afternoon."

Valerie Flint always helped us out in an emergency and I knew my class would be well looked after during my absence.

"Thank you, Vera," I said, as I hung up my old college scarf and duffel coat. She noticed I was dressed in my best grey three-piece suit.

"And very smart indeed, if I may be so bold," she added with a twinkling smile. Vera was trying to boost my spirits on a difficult day. "Also, there's a letter from County Hall saying the replacement furniture for the temporary classroom will arrive next week. Then, no doubt, Mr Potts will have to start all over again. The poor man . . . all that work."

"Yes, thank goodness it wasn't worse," I said, thinking over the events of that fateful evening.

It had been a frightening few minutes after Ted Postlethwaite raised the alarm. Marcus and I had run out of The Royal Oak, followed by Deke Ramsbottom and his sons, with Don the barman close behind. As we dashed across the village green I saw that one of the temporary classroom windows was broken and smoke was pouring out. Flames could be seen where Marcus had prepared his book corner. Moments later, Deke Ramsbottom had located the hosepipe next to Sally's classroom and sprayed water in through the broken window, and this had an instant effect. Fortunately, Amelia at the Post Office had alerted the emergency services and within minutes they arrived, so Marcus unlocked the door and stood back.

The firemen from Easington had taken control in a calm, well-rehearsed manner. Everyone seemed to know their job and the fire was quickly extinguished. Then they sprayed the shell of the Portakabin with powerful jets of water from long hoses, while dark pools of water spread across the tarmac playground and the crowd looked on. The sound of their siren had attracted many villagers out of their homes, including Ruby with her son Duggie and daughters Natasha and Hazel.

PC Julian Pike had arrived on the scene quickly and cordoned off the area. He had taken charge of crowd control and, in the eyes of Natasha Smith, he was a hero. Soon his uniform was soaked and covered in ash. Finally, when the firemen were satisfied all was safe, they secured the building and I was left talking to PC Pike and the fire officer. They said they would return in the morning to continue their investigations.

"You were lucky," said the chief fireman. "We caught it early."

"Looks deliberate," said PC Pike, pointing at the broken window.

"We think it was a firework," added the fireman.

Fifteen-year-old Billy McNeill, once a Ragley pupil, had approached us out of the crowd. "Ah saw who did it, sir. It were that Dean Skinner from Morton. 'E's in my class, but 'e didn't come in today."

PC Pike looked at me and raised his eyebrows. He took Billy to one side and began to write in his notebook. Later that evening, Dean Skinner was taken to the police station in York with his mother and admitted to the charge of arson. "Ah were jus' bored," he told the investigating officer.

The following day my friend Sergeant Dan Hunter, who had been best man at my wedding, had arrived from the station in York with another colleague. Their uniformed presence was reassuring. Dan wanted a quiet word. "You'll have to go to court, Jack," he said, "but don't worry, they just need to know the extent of the damage."

For the rest of the week there were various visits from County Hall officers. Industrial cleaning of the smoke-blackened walls was arranged, followed by a complete redecoration, while the damaged furniture had to be replaced. For me, the saddest memory was sifting through the fire-damaged classroom with Marcus and seeing all his hard work destroyed.

That was over three weeks ago and, after the sound of the school bell, the children in Anne's class had other things on their mind. Class I was a hive of activity, with parents arriving with rolled-up curtains, tea-towel headdresses and assorted sandals in preparation for our forthcoming Nativity play.

Mrs Buttershaw had wrapped up three boxes for the Kings' presents for baby Jesus. These included an empty bottle of Johnnie Walker Black Label Whisky covered in silver foil, an empty packet of Kellogg's All-Bran wrapped in red Christmas paper, and a box of multi-wormer (for cats with roundworm and tapeworm) beautifully wrapped in gold tissue paper. They looked very impressive, particularly the whisky bottle with its silver bow.

Anne gave me that "Here we go again" look and sat down with a group of children to make a large star from thick cardboard and gold foil.

At morning break Vera heated a pan of milk, opened a new jar of Nescafé Gold Blend and we settled down for a welcome cup of coffee.

Anne was sitting next to the gas fire and staring out of the window.

"Penny for them," said Pat, and Anne looked up guiltily, making us wonder what might be on her mind. From the way she reacted, it didn't appear to be the Nativity. That morning she had exchanged sharp words with her DIY-obsessed husband about the hours he spent creating unwanted wooden constructions. Anne felt her life was drifting away. She wanted excitement and new experiences instead of boring routines. It was only in her teaching that she retained her zest for life. She had smiled while decorating the Christmas tree when Kylie Ogden said, "I like being a girl, Miss, but sometimes I wish I was a fairy."

At lunchtime Valerie Flint arrived. She was our "safe pair of hands". A tall, slim lady dressed in a familiar trouser suit, Valerie was very experienced and a close friend of Vera's.

As usual she approached me with confidence. "I'm well prepared for the afternoon, unless there's something in particular you want me to progress."

We discussed the current topic work and the opportunities to stretch some of the most able children. Miss Flint took all this in her stride. The saying concerning *old dog* and *new tricks* crossed my mind, but I didn't dare repeat it.

After a lunch of Spam fritters, mashed potatoes and carrots, followed by jam roly-poly and the thickest custard known to man, I walked out to my car. The A19 was busy and I passed the local chocolate factory and the hospital in a queue of traffic on my way to the magistrates' court. I thought of Marcus and hoped the whole sorry incident would be resolved if only for our new teacher. He had been a regular visitor since the fire and it was encouraging to see his reaction when the classroom was painted again. The smell of smoke had disappeared and his bright posters once again filled the display boards.

I parked and, entering the building, followed signs for the courtroom and was directed towards a waiting room. In the corridor outside I spotted Dean Skinner. He was dressed in his best suit and tie and I presumed it was his mother standing beside him. She glowered at me, then returned to berating her son.

Shortly before 2p.m. I was summoned and I walked into a courtroom for the first time. It was a new and strange experience. I was asked to stand and repeat the oath, then a kindly old judge explained that I would be required to answer a few questions. Opposite me, on the other side of the room, stood Dean Skinner. He looked nervous. The youngster was definitely out of his comfort zone and all the false bravado had gone.

I was asked to describe briefly the damage and the cost of refurbishment. I explained that the furniture had been new and that tables and chairs plus two eighteen-drawer storage units had had to be re-ordered. Also, the classroom had been redecorated and County Hall had informed me by letter that the costs would be in the region of £800.

Following a brief cross-examination, it was over in a few minutes. The judge summed up quickly and stated that he had taken the family's financial situation into account. With a severe look at Dean Skinner, he declared the boy's parents would have to repay the costs at the rate of £20 per week for the next forty weeks.

When I walked out of the court towards the car park I saw a man in a shabby suit sitting on a bench with his head in his hands. He was rocking forwards and backwards in clear distress.

"What's the matter?" I asked. "Can I help?"

He looked up at me. "You're that teacher what got 'is classroom set on fire."

"Yes I am," I replied, wondering where this conversation was going.

He sighed deeply. "It were my stepson what did it."

"I see," I said.

"Twenty quid a week for best part of a year," he moaned, "an' all 'cause of 'er stupid boy."

"You seem to have taken this very hard," I said, trying to offer some sympathy.

He was shaking his head in disbelief. "Y'not jokin'," he said. "Ah only married 'is bloody mother six weeks ago."

I didn't know whether to laugh or cry.

When I reached the car park I looked back to see that his new wife had arrived with her teenage son and they were in animated conversation. As I drove out of York and back up the A19 it struck me that sometimes life simply wasn't fair.

That evening at seven o'clock Ruby and George were in George's luxury bungalow watching Bruce Forsyth's *Play Your Cards Right*.

"Mr Sheffield said that boy got sentenced in court t'day an' 'is mam an' dad will 'ave t'pay for all t'damage."

"That'll set 'em back," said George as he sipped on his cup of tea. His mind was on something else.

"Ah'll 'ave t'get back after this," said Ruby. "Natasha got tea ready for our 'Azel an' Duggie, but she's goin' out and our Duggie's still seein' that *mature* woman so our 'Azel'll be on 'er own."

George sighed. He loved it when Ruby shared his sofa and they watched television together. "OK, Ruby, ah'll tek y'back."

"That's all right, George, ah'm used t'walkin'."

"No, it's freezin' out there, luv, an' t'pavements are slippy. Ah'd never forgive m'self if y'fell."

Ruby smiled. It was good that there was someone to care.

George held her hand. "Ah was wond'ring if you'd made up y'mind about, y'know . . . *us*."

Ruby thought *it's now or never.*

"Yes, ah've spoken to our Andy on t'telephone an' 'e said 'e jus' wants me t'be 'appy . . . an' our Duggie said t'same."

"An' what about y'girls?" asked George.

"They all think you're a lovely man, George, 'xcept for our 'Azel."

"Bloomin' 'eck," said George. "What about 'Azel?"

110

"She took it 'ardest of t'lot of 'em when my Ronnie died, so it's a matter of pickin' t'right time. She's only a little lass . . . but ah do know she likes you."

They stood up and George kissed her gently on the cheek. "Well, ah've waited this long, Ruby. A bit longer won't mek a lot o' diff'rence ah s'ppose."

When they pulled up outside 7 School View, Hazel heard the car and was staring out of the window. It occurred to her that her mother looked happy — and, finally, she understood why.

It was Saturday morning and in her Coffee Shop Nora was reading her *Woman's Weekly* magazine.

"Dowothy," she said, "there's an article 'ere on bweast-feedin' an' it looks int'westin'."

"What's it say, Nora?" asked Dorothy.

"Well, it says this formula milk pwovides all t'nutwition a baby needs an' at six months y'can go on t'cow's milk."

Dorothy shook her head in a determined fashion. "No, Nora, ah want t'give our baby proper *nat'ral* milk. It'll only 'ave t'best . . . so ah'll be *breast* feeding."

Nora looked at the young woman who had become her dearest friend and knew how much this baby meant to her. Then she sighed and wondered what it was like to be a mother. As she closed the magazine and began to load up the display cabinet with fruit scones, it occurred to her that, in her own way, she had been a parent of sorts since Dorothy was eighteen years old. So perhaps she had experienced the next best thing.

I had taken the opportunity to drive to Easington market to buy some Christmas gifts while Beth looked after John. The market square was busy when I arrived. Music from two loudspeakers next to the war memorial boomed out "Take My Breath Away" by Berlin. It had topped the charts during November and the shoppers hummed along.

I saw Mrs Gawthorpe buy a Cabbage Patch Baby for £15.87, complete with a nappy and blanket plus its birth certificate and adoption papers! Dolls had certainly come a long way in the eighties.

At Shady Stevo's stall I joined a large crowd. Clint Ramsbottom had just purchased some Carlton-style heated curling tongs amid general laughter. "It's a top-quality styling brush," said Stevo, "wi' a non-stick barrel for easy stylin'. Y'girlfriend'll love it." Stevo was on a roll. "Wi' change out of four pound, y'lookin' at a bargain."

Clint didn't mention it was a gift for himself.

Stevo waved a large box in the air. "Now 'ere's y'chance f'summat special an' a perfec' gift for Christmas," he shouted. "In Hoxford Street down in London this state-of-the-art Transformer Metroplex is selling for twenty poun'. It can change from a city into a battle station and then a giant robot." Stevo could see interest was growing. "It's sellin' like 'ot cakes all over t'country — but am ah askin' fifteen? No, ah'm askin' only twelve poun'. So who's first t'spot t'best bargain on t'market?"

On impulse I raised my hand. It looked like a toy John and I could enjoy, although I wasn't sure about

Beth's reaction to encouraging our son to build a battle station. I passed over the money to Stevo's lady assistant and relaxed in the thought that John would have something special for Christmas.

Big Dave and Little Malcolm had arrived and each of the intrepid duo had £10 to spend. Little Malcolm was looking for something sophisticated for Dorothy and Big Dave wasn't too fussy so long as he didn't spend more than his allocated sum.

"'Ow's this for a bargain?" asked Stevo. "In them posh shops that southerners go to, this would set y'back twelve quid. It's a Clairol Beauty Line Ladyshave. Y'can use it wet or dry, an' it's ideal for them close shaves, ladies. Ah'm even throwin' in free batteries."

The anticipation was mounting. "Ah'm not askin' ten, an' ah'm not askin' nine." You could almost hear the roll of the drums. "So, who fancies a bit a quality for only eight poun'?"

Dave's hand shot up, followed by more laughter among the ladies in the crowd.

Undeterred, Big Dave handed over his £10 note and collected his box plus change. *Christmas sorted*, he thought.

Shady Stevo knew his customers and eyed up Little Malcolm. He held up a set of Ultra-Glow Super Duster Make-Up Brushes. "Now then, 'ere's a bit o' 'igh class for a *sophisticated* lady — an' only six quid," he said. "An' t'mek a perfec' matchin' pair, 'ow about a genuine Mary Quant toilet bag for three poun'?"

Little Malcolm took out his £10 note and stared at it ... decision time. Stevo decided to deliver the final *coup de grâce*. "Y'can 'ave both of 'em for eight poun'."

"A deal," shouted Little Malcolm and he passed over his £10 note, collected the carrier bag and stared at his change. "Enough for a bacon butty, Dave, an' a mug o' tea," he said triumphantly. For the bin men of Ragley their Christmas shopping was completed and it had been ten minutes well spent.

On Monday morning at break we gathered round the gas fire in the staff-room. Sally was on playground duty and I shared the news with Anne and Pat about the Transformer for John. The response wasn't as enthusiastic as I had hoped.

"So what about you, Anne?" asked Pat. "What have you got for *your* John?"

Anne sighed deeply. "Not very exciting, I'm afraid, although I'm sure he will be in seventh heaven. I spent thirty-one pounds on a Black and Decker Orbital Sander."

I was impressed. "I've seen them and they're really good."

Anne and Pat gave me that familiar "boys' toys" look.

"Perhaps it will smooth some of his rough edges," mused Anne. She had hidden it in her wardrobe for wrapping at a future date. However, it was a different future date that was on her mind. She had arranged to bump *accidentally* into Edward Clifton at next week's Easington market.

★　★　★

After lunch Vera served tea in the staff-room. It was a quiet gathering as we were all immersed in our own tasks, marking books and checking proposed acquisitions in the Yorkshire Purchasing Organization catalogue, while Pat scanned my morning paper.

She looked up and broke the silence. "Did you watch the *Weekend World* interview with Kenneth Baker?"

Suddenly there was a flurry of interest and everyone stopped what they were doing. It had been compulsive viewing. We all nodded with the exception of Sally. Her weekend had been dominated by her daughter's high temperature.

"Yes," said Anne, "Matthew Parris certainly asked the right questions and the Education Secretary sounded very determined."

"He certainly did," I said. "Beth and I watched it and I remember Kenneth Baker saying that the present system was seriously flawed. He wants to move to something called a 'national curriculum'."

"National curriculum," mused Anne. "That could catch on."

"He said he would lay down what every child should learn in primary and secondary schools," said Pat. "Sounds very far reaching."

"Unlikely," retorted a determined Sally, "and the government would have to win the next election to push it through."

Vera looked up sharply but decided to say nothing. She didn't want to rouse the determined Sally any more than was necessary.

Anne was scanning the article. "It says here that they would set attainment targets so that teachers, parents and pupils would know exactly what should have been learned in each subject at specific ages."

"Impossible," murmured Sally as she reached for another custard cream. This wasn't the moment to adhere to her diet.

"Oh dear," said Anne shaking her head. "It says they might vary teachers' rates of pay."

"Surely not!" exclaimed Pat. "Think of the upset that would cause."

"Pie in the sky," said Sally. She munched on her biscuit and headed for the door. "Time for my recorder group."

"More tea anyone?" asked Vera and we settled down again to our various tasks. The proposed national curriculum would keep for another day.

At the end of school I was in the entrance hall talking to Joseph and Vera about the progress made in the temporary classroom since the fire when Ruby arrived with her galvanized bucket and mop.

"'Ave you 'eard?" she said. "There's been a right shoutin' match on the 'Igh Street. Everybody 'eard it."

"Oh dear," sighed Joseph.

"Stan Coe 'ad offered to buy some of Maurice Tupham's land and Maurice wasn't int'rested."

Ruby set off to clean the classrooms.

"A public row on the High Street," I marvelled.

Vera shook her head. "So much for our smiling school governor."

116

"But I say unto you," quoted Joseph, "that every idle word that men may speak . . ."

Vera smiled up at him and continued,". . . they shall give account thereof in the day of judgement." She squeezed his arm affectionately. Brother and sister had always enjoyed exchanging familiar quotations from the King James Bible. "Matthew twelve," added Vera, "verse thirty-six."

Joseph nodded. "It will come to us all one day," he said, "and certainly to Stan Coe," and he walked out to his car.

Vera looked up at me with a wry smile. "Until we reach the final judgement day," and she followed her brother out to the car park.

It was a lowering sky and darkness had fallen, a time of bare branches and frosty nights. The light and dark of a forthcoming festive season was a special time of the year. Christmas in school would be followed by a family Christmas with crackling log fires and twinkling stars.

However, I reflected on Vera's words as I drove home.

A Judgement Day in court had come and gone but there was another on the horizon . . . and not just for Stan Coe.

CHAPTER
SEVEN

A Carol for Christmas

School closed today for the Christmas holiday with 105 children on roll and will reopen on Monday, 5 January 1987. The children in Classes 1 and 2 rehearsed their Nativity play to be performed in the Crib Service at St Mary's Church on Wednesday, 24 December. The school choir will visit the local retirement home tomorrow, Saturday, to sing a selection of Christmas carols to the residents.

Extract from the Ragley School Logbook:
Friday, 19 December 1986

Her name was Eileen Kimber and she was alone.

For the most part it had been a solitary life and now she was a resident at the Hartford Home for Retired Gentlefolk or, as she preferred to call it, "God's Waiting Room".

She stared out of her bedroom window at the winter world beyond. A fresh snowfall covered the tall yew hedge and the distant fields. Wisps of smoke rose from the high chimney pots of Ragley village and floated in diagonal pathways towards a wolf-grey sky. She smiled

118

grimly. The world outside resembled her heart — cold as iron, still as stone.

Her walking frame squeaked on the polished floor and she looked down at its pair of aluminium legs. Mobility was more difficult now. It was thirty years since she had read George Orwell's allegorical novella *Animal Farm*, but she recalled a famous line, "Four legs good, two legs bad", and she grimaced. Once again she would eat breakfast in her own room and not in the communal dining room.

Only the rattling of the letter box when Ted the postman delivered the morning mail or the clatter of bottles when Rodney Morgetroyd arrived on his milk float had become familiar sounds of her morning routine. Her belief in the old adage that time was a healer had faded long ago. The silent days had become weeks of solitude while time merely ticked on remorselessly. There was no respite from a never-ending anguish — no respite from a pain that was always there in the core of her being.

At first she had savoured the peace and privacy, but widowhood had proved a heavy burden. For more than forty years she had kept her late husband's flat cap as an affectionate reminder of his presence. Finally she had moved into the retirement home but found it difficult to make friends. Solitude and silence were her companions in this private space.

Destiny, however, moves in mysterious ways.

It was early morning on Friday, 19 December and, unknown to Eileen, her world was about to change.

In Bilbo Cottage Beth and I were both at the kitchen table writing a last-minute memo for our final day of term while John was enjoying a hearty breakfast of juice, cereal and buttered toast soldiers. There was much to do, with parties, letters to parents followed by, in my case, final preparations for the amalgamation of Morton and Ragley. There was also a rehearsal of our Nativity play to be performed at the Crib Service in St Mary's Church on Christmas Eve. John was polishing off his breakfast while the current top of the pops, "Caravan Of Love" by The Housemartins, was playing on the radio and the disc jockey wondered if it would be the Christmas number one.

The road to Ragley was a blue thread of crystal and the hedgerows were rimed with frost. Soon the sun broke through the mist and lit up the sprinkling of snow on the branches of the bare trees. In the sharp sunshine they resembled a charcoal and chalk drawing by a small child. Holly berries sparkled in the diamond light and a crust of frost had settled on each fleur-de-lis on the school railings. Ragley School looked like a scene from a Victorian Christmas card as I drove up the cobbled drive.

When I walked into the entrance hall Vera and Ruby were standing together staring out of the window. "The north wind doth blow an' we shall 'ave snow," recited Ruby.

"And what will poor robin do then, poor thing?" continued Vera.

They both looked up. "Well, ah'd best get on," said Ruby and she hurried off with her brush and shovel.

120

Vera nodded towards the office. "Miss Cleverley has arrived *unannounced* from County Hall, Mr Sheffield," she said. It was clear that Vera did not approve of our visitor. "She is sitting at *my* desk and checking the list of children who are coming here from Morton." Miss Cleverley was assistant to the chair of the Education Committee, Miss Barrington-Huntley, and had been a dominant force last July on the interviewing panel for the Ragley and Morton headship.

When I walked in she didn't look up immediately but rather continued to check the list in front of her. I recalled her manner at our earlier meeting and wondered about the purpose of her visit. I hadn't seen her since that day, when she had been abrupt, analytical and unpleasant. I was soon to learn that little seemed to have changed in the interim.

Finally she spoke. "I knew the last day of term would be busy for you, Mr Sheffield," she said, "so I thought I should meet with you before the start of school." She gestured towards my desk. "Do sit down."

For the next thirty minutes she reviewed our arrangements for the amalgamation of the two schools. We discussed safety, transport, communication with parents and the role of the governing body. Then she looked at her wristwatch. "Must go," she said, "time is precious."

The class timetable on the noticeboard caught her eye and she tapped it with a perfectly manicured fingernail. "I must point out to you that Kenneth Baker's national curriculum will improve this overnight." With that she strode out, ignoring Vera, and hurried to her brand-new Ford Sierra 2.0i GLS. She turned on the four-speaker sound system to full blast, flicked on the tailgate wash/wipe, made a minute adjustment to her remote-control door mirrors and roared off.

"What an unpleasant lady," remarked Vera.

"Miss Cleverley is certainly very forthright," I said with a fixed smile.

Vera shook her head. "If that's the future of education I want no part of it. The thought of her succeeding Miss Barrington-Huntley is a great worry. She lacks the human touch. It is very disappointing."

I decided to leave it at that. It concerned me that Vera spoke of possible retirement more frequently these days and I wondered if she had made a final decision.

In the school hall Anne and Pat were busy with a few supportive mothers preparing for the forthcoming Nativity play.

Five-year-old Kylie Ogden was proud to be holding a bamboo cane with a large cardboard star fixed to the top. She had covered it in kitchen foil and was pleased with the result.

"This is my star, Mr Sheffield," she said.

"It's lovely, Kylie."

"It's that big star that comes out ev'ry Christmas."

"Is it?"

"An' Cheyenne, Joe an' Dylan 'ave t'follow me with their presents for Jesus."

"That's wonderful."

"An' when we go t'church we'll 'ave a proper Jesus."

"A *proper* Jesus?"

"Yes, Mr Sheffield, 'cause we've only got Emily's Cabbage Patch doll t'be goin' on with."

I looked at the appropriately named Madonna Fazackerly who was playing Mary. She was holding the Cabbage Patch doll with great tenderness and wrapped in so-called swaddling clothes — namely, a grubby M&S tea towel.

When I called in to Pat's class she was gathering the children in the school entrance hall to post their cards to Father Christmas in our cardboard postbox.

Six-year-old Alfie Spraggon had a tendency to reverse his letters and numbers. Pat Brookside was trying hard through regular practice to help this friendly little boy to correct this familiar anomaly with left-handed pupils, and he had worked hard to produce a classic that read:

> Dear Santa, Please can I have a yo-yo and no sprouts.
> Thank you, your friend, Alfie Spraggon.

The letters to Santa from other six-year-olds were all priceless and included:

> Dear Santa, I can't find my list so anything left over will do.
> Karl Tomkins

> Dear Santa, Mummy won't let me bring straw into the front room so what shall I leave for

Rudolph?
Love Hermione Jackson

Dear Santa, Daddy has just put in a burglar alarm. The code is 2346. Hope this helps.
Love Honeysuckle Jackson

Dear Santa, Just one of everything please.
Best wishes, Emily Snodgrass.

I followed the queue of children waiting to put their cards in the postbox and made sure the letters from the Jackson twins were redirected to their mother.

It was morning assembly and Joseph had reminded the children of the Christmas story.

"So, boys and girls," he said encouragingly, "what do you think Mary and Joseph were thinking when the innkeeper kindly offered them room in his stable?"

Hermione Jackson's hand shot up at the same moment as her twin sister's. The girls lived in one of the most luxurious and expensive houses on the Morton Road.

"Yes, Hermione?" asked Joseph.

"Has it got a downstairs toilet?" suggested Hermione.

"That's what I was going to say," added Honeysuckle for good measure.

Joseph ground his teeth. "Good try," he said without conviction, "but has anyone else got a suggestion?"

"Ah felt a bit sorry f'Jesus, Mr Evans," said eight-year-old Scott Higginbottom.

"And why is that, Scott?" asked Joseph, pleased at the obvious compassion shown by this freckle-faced little boy.

"'Cause 'e didn't get any *proper* presents . . . jus' a bit o' gold an' that other stuff."

Joseph sighed and wondered if he should have chosen a different career . . . maybe a librarian; after all he *understood* books.

At morning break we gathered in the staff-room. Sally had spent 64p on a *TV Times* Christmas & New Year Double Issue. There was a dramatic picture of Torvill and Dean, the world's most exciting ice dancers, on the front cover advertising their "Fire and Ice" spectacular.

Vera said she would be watching Aled Jones, her favourite boy treble, on Christmas Eve, while I earmarked the Christmas Day Disney film *Dumbo* to share with young John. Pat was determined to watch the James Bond film *The Spy Who Loved Me* on Boxing Day, with the suave Roger Moore and co-starring Barbara Bach as a Russian agent. Sally went for Jools Holland's new year's eve show and a bottle of Baileys. We all agreed she had made the best choice.

On Friday afternoon the children were excited. It was time for the end-of-term Christmas party.

By half past one they were sitting on their chairs around the edge of the hall. We played Statues and Musical Chairs, danced to records and, when the children looked suitably exhausted, we sent them out to play while Ruby came in and supervised the arrangement of the dining tables for our party tea. Members of the PTA had called in to help Shirley and Doreen in the kitchen and soon the tables were covered in bright red crêpe paper. Plates piled with crab-paste sandwiches, sponge cakes, jammy dodgers and mince pies were arranged, while Shirley and Doreen wheeled out a trolley with enough jelly and ice cream to feed an army.

By three o'clock the food had been devoured, sticky fingers and faces wiped and the tables put away. The afternoon ended with the children sitting next to the Christmas tree while Sally played a selection of Christmas songs on her guitar, including "Frosty the Snowman" and "Rudolph the Red-Nosed Reindeer". Parents drifted in to collect their children along with a small gift of sweets from Ruby, a balloon and a Christmas card.

It was a weary but happy group of teachers that gathered in the staff-room for a final cup of coffee.

In the entrance hall Ruby was talking to Vera.

"Ah've med up m'mind at last, Mrs F," she said with a tired smile. "In the end it were our 'Azel who asked if ah were goin' t'marry Mr Dainty."

"And what did you say, Ruby?"

"Ah said ah'd allus love her Dad . . . but ah were 'appy wi' George an' ah loved 'im in a *diff'rent* way. She gave me a kiss an' said 'e'd mek a lovely new dad."

Vera took Ruby's hand and smiled at her friend. "That's wonderful news, Ruby."

"So we're goin' into York tomorrow t'buy an engagement ring."

"How exciting. Can we go and tell the rest of the staff? They will be thrilled."

We gathered with Ruby in a crowded staff-room and, while we had to imagine the orange juice was Bucks Fizz, it was a wonderful celebration.

On Saturday morning the carol singing event at the Hartford Home for Retired Gentlefolk was due to begin at eleven o'clock. Beth and I secured John in his child seat and drove into Ragley.

When we pulled up outside the General Stores, Karl Tomkins and Jimmy Poole were both out with their dogs. Karl had a French poodle named Flossie and hated taking it for a walk.

"D'you want t'swap, Jimmy?" he asked, staring in admiration at Scargill, the lively Yorkshire terrier.

Jimmy, now aged thirteen, still had his familiar lisp. "No thankth, Karl," he replied. "Thcargill ith my friend."

"Mebbe they could play together," suggested Karl.

Jimmy looked down at the perfectly coiffured little poodle, sporting a bright pink bow, and then at his lean, hungry and occasionally savage terrier, the scourge of our local postman. "Ah don't think tho," he concluded. "Thcargill geth exthited," and Karl wandered off.

Jimmy, with his ginger curls and black button eyes, smiled up at me. "'Ello, Mr Theffield, would y'like t'thee my Tharp Thientific calculator?"

New technology had changed his life. Complicated mathematical conundrums were suddenly easy to solve. His fingers sped across the buttons with well-practised familiarity and it made me reflect on my insistence on teaching mental arithmetic each morning and learning tables by rote.

"It's excellent, Jimmy," I said, while keeping my distance from Scargill's jaws.

"Thankth," he said, "an' a 'appy Chrithmuth," and he ran off with an eager Scargill yapping at his heels.

We called in to Nora's Coffee Shop for a coffee and some hot milk for John. On the juke-box was "Reet Petite" by Jackie Wilson, a strange choice for a Christmas number one but it had caught the imagination of the public and reminded me of a Glenn Miller big band sound.

Nora Pratt was excited. Her Christmas present for her fact-loving boyfriend, Tyrone Crabtree, had arrived. She had seen David Bellamy advertising the *Encyclopaedia Britannica* and had purchased thirty-two magnificent volumes. As we approached the counter, she had just served Felicity Miles-Humphreys, artistic director of the Ragley Amateur Dramatic Society. With an extravagant gesture Felicity pointed towards the large poster advertising the annual village pantomime. Rehearsals were now well advanced for *Sleeping Beauty*.

"I do hope to see you there," said Felicity.

"Of course," I said.

Dorothy appeared behind the counter in her dangly Christmas-tree earrings and a baggy elf suit. "Ah'm one o' Santa's 'elpers, Mr Sheffield," she said with a grin.

"And I hear you've got a part in *Sleeping Beauty*," said Beth.

Dorothy glowed with pride. "An' so 'as my Malcolm."

"He's a born thespian," announced Felicity.

Dorothy was puzzled. She thought only women could be thespians . . . however, undeterred, she served up two frothy coffees and a cup of hot milk.

Shortly before eleven o'clock we arrived at the retirement home and paused in the entrance to admire a beautiful winter display of poinsettias.

It was clear the staff worked hard for the benefit of all. They were kind and caring in all they did, and appeared always to have time to check on the wellbeing of their elderly residents. I was welcomed by the senior carer, Janet Ollerenshaw, who was in conversation with Vera. Janet, a tall, confident young woman in blue jeans and a Cambridge-blue polo shirt with the Hartford oak tree logo, shook my hand.

"Thanks for coming, Mr Sheffield."

"A pleasure."

"Everyone is looking forward to it," she said.

"It's our Christian duty," added Vera.

The choir had assembled and parents and residents were taking their seats. Coffee was being served by Stella Fieldhouse, a popular sixty-one-year-old volunteer helper, who came in every Saturday morning. In recent years Stella's coffee mornings had become an important and popular social event for the residents.

As a young teenager during the Second World War, Stella had been evacuated to a cottage in the countryside near Brooklands in Surrey. In 1940, aged fourteen, she was on her bike riding home when the bombs fell, killing a hundred people. She had never forgotten the horror of that day — it had a huge impact on her and from then on she determined to value life and help others in need. Later Stella became a wages clerk at the local factory and eventually she married an engineer who went to work on Concorde. Following his sad death, Stella had moved north to live with her sister on the Morton Road, where her zest for life continued unabated.

Stella was the one person who took time to talk to Eileen and she took a cup of coffee to her room. When she walked in Eileen was ironing a set of antimacassars. "Hello, Eileen, here's a hot drink for you."

Eileen was eighty years old and had shared the story of her life with Stella. She was the only daughter of a grocer in a lovely village called East Tittleham. In 1933 she met David Kimber, a handsome man from West Tittleham on the other side of the River Tittle, which formed the boundary between the two villages. They would meet on the bridge over the river and there they would spend happy hours talking about their hopes and aspirations. They married in 1935 and the following year they moved to Hull, where David worked on the docks and Eileen gave birth to a daughter, Mary. At the outset of the war David joined the Army and left, saying they would have a happy life together in the years to come.

Then it happened.

The Luftwaffe dropped a huge bomb.

It killed fifty people, including Mary. The little girl was due to be evacuated to Lincolnshire but it was too late. She was four years old. In an old suitcase Eileen had kept her daughter's favourite pinafore dress plus a faded copy of the *Yorkshire Post* dated Thursday, 5 June 1941. The headline read "Heroism in Hull Air Raids".

The following spring, David Kimber was among a party of soldiers that attacked the port of St-Nazaire in German-occupied France. The intention was to prevent any large German warship, such as the *Tirpitz*, from having a safe haven on the Atlantic coast. The raid, which took place on 28 March 1942, was successful, but David was killed in action and decorated posthumously.

For many years Eileen's home felt like a prison, close and oppressive. She had lost everything that was dear to her and longed for the open fields and fresh air of her youth. In consequence, Ragley village seemed to be a good place to retire.

I came here to forget and be forgotten.

"I was hoping you would come to the common room, Eileen," said Stella, "because I know you love singing." She was encouraged by Eileen's look of interest. "The children from the school are here," she continued, "and there's a little girl called Rosie. She was the one on television two years ago and she's going to sing 'Silent Night'. It would be lovely if you could hear her."

There was a moment's silence. "I used to sing," said Eileen quietly.

131

"I know," said Stella. She put her hand on her arm. "Come on, Eileen, maybe it's time to leave grief behind and move on with your life."

"Perhaps," said Eileen. She had been attracted by the thought of the little girl singing. She stood up and rested on her walking frame. "Stella," she said almost to herself, "in my mind's eye my Mary is always a girl . . . forever young."

The children in the choir were at their best and, as Sally accompanied them on her guitar, the residents loved every moment. Eileen sat in the back row and there were tears in her eyes when Rosie sang "Silent Night". Her solo was captivating and the applause went on for many minutes.

The children had been encouraged to speak with the residents at the end and Rosie approached Eileen.

"Hello, I'm Rosie Appleby. I'm pleased to meet you."

Eileen looked intently at the polite little girl. "I used to have a daughter like you and she liked to sing."

"My mummy says singing is like a cosy fire," said Rosie. "She told me to think of rainbows and not thunderstorms."

Eileen smiled softly. "Your mummy is quite right and your singing was wonderful. I was in a choir once just like you and I used to sing 'Silent Night' in German."

"I can sing it in German as well," said Rosie. "Well, just the first verse." Then, quite naturally, she began to sing: "*Stille Nacht, heilige Nacht, Alles schläft; einsam wacht.*"

132

On impulse, Eileen joined in: "*Nur das traute hochheilige Paar. Holder Knabe im lockigen Haar . . .*"

Stella was watching and beckoned to Vera. Rosie's eyes were wide as the two voices blended beautifully. "*Schlaf in himmlischer Ruh,*" they sang, "*Schlaf in himmlischer Ruh!*"

"That was splendid," said Stella.

"Do you know," said Eileen, "I do believe I had forgotten what *happiness* feels like."

Vera smiled. "I have an idea," she said.

It was Christmas Eve and Beth and I had driven to Easington Market before going to the Crib Service.

Once again Gabriel Book from the local Rotary Club was dressed up as Father Christmas in his little wooden hut. Kylie Ogden was standing next to him while Mrs Ogden looked on proudly.

"So, what would you like for Christmas?" asked Gabriel.

"Ah'd like some Mickey Mouse slippers please, Santa."

Her mother looked surprised. This was unexpected. "Let's put them on your Christmas list," she said cautiously.

Kylie looked indignant. "No, Mummy, I want them on my *feet*."

The realization of the logic of very young children was shared in a moment by both Gabriel and Mrs Ogden.

Soon it was John's turn.

"Have you been a good boy, John?" asked Gabriel.

133

He had been well briefed by Beth regarding this question and nodded vigorously. "Yes, Santa."

"That's good," said Gabriel, "and what would you like for Christmas?"

"Presents please, Santa," said John. Our son was a happy and contented little boy but, as we were about to discover, also very *logical*.

"And what sort of presents?"

John replied in an instant. "*Christmas* presents please, Santa."

Ask a silly question, thought Gabriel while Beth and I shared a secret smile.

At the retirement home Eileen put on her best dress, then wrapped up warm and prepared to leave for the Crib Service. She looked around and recognized that her surroundings were tranquil and peaceful. It was a time for reflection. Her silent world had been replaced by new friendships and music.

A special minibus had been provided and Eileen, with her "fellow inmates" as she called them, set off. Wood smoke hovered in a purple sky as they approached the church.

At half past two crowds of parents and grandparents were also making their way towards St Mary's with an assorted collection of tiny angels, shepherds, kings and Roman soldiers. This was one of the most popular of all the Christmas services and we followed the crushed ribbon of scumbled footprints into the haven of the church. The work of the ladies in Vera's flower-arranging team was there for all to see. Tall white candles surrounded by green variegated holly with bright red berries had been arranged on the wide ledges of the stone pillars. As I admired the flower arrangements, refracted light from the stained-glass windows touched the ancient walls with an amber hue and lit up the choir stalls where the children waited patiently.

Joseph was standing next to the model crib filled with its hand-painted clay figures. The service was about to begin and gradually silence descended on the congregation. Elsie Crapper, the organist, after taking her much-needed Valium, launched into her version of "Little Donkey".

John, dressed as a shepherd, sat on my knee and waited for his moment in the limelight. The choir sang "Away In A Manger" and Beth dabbed away a tear as John joined in while acting out the timeless story.

Then, to everyone's surprise, Rosie Appleby went to stand next to a chair by the pulpit where Eileen Kimber was sitting. Vera stepped forward and helped Eileen to stand up, supported by her walking frame. The old lady looked down at the smiling face of the little girl as Elsie played the opening bars of "Silent Night".

So began a duet that would never be forgotten. They sang the first verse in German and the next two verses in English. It was a special moment and many members of the congregation shed a tear when Eileen sat down and squeezed Rosie's hand. Little did we know it, but it was the beginning of a strong friendship.

It was then that Eileen reflected that she had lived her life in a dark and silent retreat, a melancholy shadow in a place of despair. There had been no relief until the arrival of the unexpected — a Christmas gift that began with the face of a child and ended in a song of hope.

"Thank you, Mrs Kimber," said Rosie. "Did you enjoy that?"

Eileen knew her life had changed. "Yes, Rosie," she whispered, "we shared a carol for Christmas."

The following evening, after we had put John to bed, Beth and I settled down with a glass of wine in front of a roaring log fire to watch the Christmas Day episode of *EastEnders* along with over thirty million other viewers. The drama lived up to expectations when Den Watts, played by Leslie Grantham, told his wife, Angie, played by the volatile Anita Dobson, that he wanted a divorce. While peace on earth and goodwill to all men were not in evidence in Albert Square, it was lively entertainment.

At the end, Beth got up to check on John after his exhausting day of presents and games. It was time for bed and I knew my restless soul had found peace in her presence. A firmament of stars danced over the spectral grey earth, while clouds drifted towards an endless horizon.

I lay there within our solitude of secrets and reflected on our life together. Since meeting Beth the tapestry of my life had been woven with golden thread. Our love had begun like a summer storm nine years ago, tempestuous and with the power of lightning. In a world of vanishing certainties, it had been a love forged in fire and shaped in creation. Now, with the passing years, it rested in silence within the heartbeat of our lives.

Beth stirred next to me. "By the way, who was that lovely lady who sang with Rosie?"

"Her name is Eileen Kimber."

"She looked tearful after the carol," murmured Beth.

"Yes," I said, "she used to be lonely . . . but not any more."

CHAPTER
EIGHT

Sleeping Beauty

*The new school sign was delivered this morning
and Mrs Smith supervised. The headteacher checked
school security and collected mail. 20 children are
cast members in the village pantomime, Sleeping
Beauty, to take place in the village hall this evening.*
Extract from the Ragley School Logbook:
Wednesday, 31 December 1986

Nora Pratt switched off her sewing machine and
sighed. *It will have to do*, she thought.

She held up her Alpine corset and examined the
strips of leather she had inserted down each side. Nora
had purchased the perfect foundation garment from
Ambrose Wilson, Britain's No. 1 Corsetry Catalogue,
and she slipped it on, stood in front of the mirror and
considered her expanding waistline. Then she added
the leather corset and, after fastening the toggles, she
breathed in and out slowly. Finally she smiled. *It
worked*. No one would notice it wasn't quite the
identical corset she had worn in all the previous
productions of the Ragley Amateur Dramatic Society.
Nora's big day had arrived and as Princess Aurora, the

star part in *Sleeping Beauty*, she was determined to look her best.

It was Wednesday morning, 31 December, and a Ragley pantomime that would never be forgotten was only a few hours away.

In Bilbo Cottage, Beth's parents, John and Diane Henderson, had arrived on Boxing Day for a one-week holiday over the remainder of the festive season and into the New Year. As usual they had risen early to help look after their grandson and young John was enjoying all the attention.

The previous day had been cold, clear and sunny and my father-in-law had spent time in our garden pruning and tidying. He had worked in the border by our south-facing fence and cut back the old blackberry canes that were now bleached of colour and life. It was the time to cut out the old and encourage new growth, and the symbolism was not lost on me as I considered the dying embers of 1986 and the coming dawn of 1987.

Diane had brought Laura's Christmas card with her from Hampshire and when I walked into the kitchen she was deep in thought as she read it once again. Beth's younger sister had left suddenly to pursue her career in Australia and had taken the Sydney fashion scene by storm.

Diane scanned the letter that had arrived with Laura's card. "Apparently the *latest* boyfriend is a rich Sydney banker," she said, shaking her head in disapproval and with emphasis on the word "latest". She glanced at me to judge my reaction. There was history between Laura and myself.

139

John was washing his hands at the kitchen sink and, as always, he kept his thoughts to himself. His daughters had always been very different in their outlook on life and Laura had been the one to give him the most sleepless nights.

By mid-morning Diane and Beth had settled down to watch the feature film *Oklahoma!* on ITV, starring Gordon MacRae, Shirley Jones and Rod Steiger, while young John played with his Christmas toys on the floor.

I looked at the clock. "Time to go," I said. There were a few jobs in school and I had volunteered to assist in some last-minute painting of the scenery for the village pantomime.

John looked relieved to have an opportunity to get out of the house. "I'll come with you," he said, striding out to the hallway to collect his coat and scarf. "Let's use my Land Rover."

The sun was breaking through the mist with a sharp bright light as we drove towards Ragley. The frozen fields were shrouded with snow and the bare trees cast sharp grey shadows across the road. When we drove into Ragley High Street the hedgerows were capped with a fresh snowfall and the dark ivy was rimed in sparkling frost.

"John, I've got a few things to do in school, so why don't you call in to the Coffee Shop and I'll see you there."

I knew John was partial to Nora's hospitality and lively conversation with the locals. "Excellent idea," he said with a broad grin.

I pulled up on the High Street behind Big Dave and Little Malcolm's refuse wagon and John got out of the car, crunched across the frozen forecourt and hurried into the warmth of the Coffee Shop.

I drove on, then turned right at the village green towards the school gate, where Ruby and Vera were in conversation with a workman wearing blue overalls and a York City bobble hat. He was fixing a large metal plate to one of the stone pillars by the gate. It was a new sign that read:

RAGLEY & MORTON CHURCH OF ENGLAND PRIMARY SCHOOL
North Yorkshire County Council
Headteacher: Mr J Sheffield

I parked under the avenue of horse chestnut trees, climbed out and joined in the excited conversation.

"G'mornin', Mr Sheffield," said Ruby. "This is Vernon from Thirkby an' 'e's mekkin' a good job." Vernon nodded in shy acknowledgement at this very direct assessment of the quality of his work and continued to fix the final screw. Ruby was animated and pointed in the air. "Ah told 'im *pacifically* t'put it 'igh up where ev'ryone could see it." I smiled and presumed Ruby was referring to the sign and not her engagement ring, which sparkled in the sunshine.

"Thank you, Ruby," I said. "It's perfect."

Vera touched my arm. "I simply had to see the new school sign, Mr Sheffield," she said with a smile. "A special day." Vera was already in a good mood because

141

her favourite actors in the *Yes, Prime Minister* series, Paul Eddington, who played Jim Hacker, along with Nigel Hawthorne as the cunning Cabinet Secretary Sir Humphrey Appleby, were both to receive CBEs in the New Year Honours List.

"A new era," I mused.

"Changing times," murmured Vera and her mind seemed elsewhere for a moment.

Meanwhile, Vernon collected his tools and we stood back to appreciate the significance of the new name for our village school . . . each of us with our own private thoughts. I left Vera and Ruby by the gate while I called in to collect the mail and check that windows and doors were secure.

A few minutes later I walked down the High Street to the General Stores, where Deke Ramsbottom was scanning the front page of his *Sun* newspaper. He was pleased that one of his favourite footballers, the Irish goalkeeper Pat Jennings, had been awarded an OBE on his retirement.

"Grand day, Mr Sheffield," said Deke, touching the brim of his cowboy hat in acknowledgement. As a hardy outdoor worker, the sub-zero weather had little effect on this son of Yorkshire. "Ah'll be up your way soon," he added, nodding towards his snow plough parked by the kerb.

"Thanks, Deke, and maybe see you later for the pantomime."

"Wouldn't miss it for all t'tea in China," he said cheerily. "Ah see Malcolm an' Dorothy 'ave got parts

142

again. 'E were t'star turn las' year," and he wandered off to clear the back roads of North Yorkshire.

After collecting my newspaper I decided to join John in the Coffee Shop for a hot drink. When I walked in the Christmas number-one record, Jackie Wilson's "Reet Petite", was playing. John was sitting at a corner table and reading a spare copy of the *Daily Mail*. He was admiring a photograph of a smiling Bruce Forsyth, who was cuddling his seven-week-old son, Jonathan Joseph, before flying out of London to spend New Year in the sunshine of Puerto Rico with his wife, former Miss World Wilnelia Merced.

"Another coffee, John?" I asked.

He gave me a thumbs-up and I approached the counter.

"Two coffees please, Nora."

"Comin' up, Mr Sheffield," shouted Dorothy from the far end of the counter. She looked happy and excited at the prospect of the special day ahead.

"She's like a cat wi' two tails, Mr Sheffield," said Nora, "an' she's twied weally 'ard wi' all 'er lines for t'panto. She's kept 'er eyes to t'gwindstone."

I guessed she meant *nose*, but this was Nora's big day of the year and it was important to show support. "I'm looking forward to it," I said.

"Would y'like a pwogwamme, Mr Sheffield?" offered Nora. "It's fwee."

She handed over a folded A4 sheet with "SLEEP-ING BEAUTY" printed on the front and a list of cast members inside. It read:

Princess Aurora (Briar Rose) — Nora Pratt
Maleficent, the evil witch who curses Princess Aurora
    — Deirdre Coe
King Stefan, Princess Aurora's father — Peter
    Miles-Humphreys
Queen Leah, Princess Aurora's mother — Elsie
    Crapper
Prince Philip — Rupert Miles-Humphreys
Flora, the Red Fairy — Dorothy Robinson
Fauna, the Green Fairy — Claire Bradshaw
Merryweather, the Blue Fairy — Anita Cuthbertson
King's Guard — Malcolm Robinson
Narrator (and prompter) — Nigel Miles-Humphreys
Chorus — Children of Ragley School

"Ah'm Pwincess Auwowa," said Nora pointing to the first name on the list. Nora was always top of the bill. "An' Tywone is comin'," she added proudly. Nora's boyfriend, or as Nora called him her "gentleman companion", was a short, plump, balding man in his fifties with a Bobby Charlton comb-over. Tyrone had an important job at the local chocolate factory — he was in charge of cardboard boxes.

"An' Dowothy's playin' Flowa the Wed Faiwy," said Nora.

"An' ah know m'lines off by 'eart, Mr Sheffield," added Dorothy proudly. "Me an' Malcolm 'ave been practisin' ev'ry night."

"That's wonderful, Dorothy," I said.

"An' it should be our lucky day, Mr Sheffield. Ah'm an Aquarian an' my Malcolm is a Gemini an' in today's

144

'oroscope it says f'me 'your destiny awaits', so it mus' mean t'panto. An' f'Malcolm it says 'be prepared for t'unexpected'."

I had no idea how prophetic her words would be.

"So . . . two coffees, Mr Sheffield," Dorothy continued. Her face was flushed.

"An' we've got some Eccles cakes fwesh in," added Nora, nodding towards a towering plate behind the display case.

But when were they made? I wondered. "Go on, I'll have two please."

Dorothy suddenly disappeared into the back room and I noticed a flicker of concern in Nora's eyes. No one knew Dorothy better than our Coffee Shop owner. She had been everything a mother should be to her young assistant since her arrival at her door as a disturbed teenager. Dorothy had been a little off-colour that morning but had insisted on doing her morning shift.

"Two fwothy coffees comin' up," said Nora, "and two Eccles cakes fwesh in on Monday," she added proudly. For a moment she looked longingly at the Eccles cakes but resisted the temptation. After all, she had to look after her figure. She gave me my change and hurried into the back room to check on Dorothy.

When John and I got up to leave, Madonna was singing "True Blue" on the old juke-box and it occurred to me that Vera would have approved of the title.

Up the Morton Road, Petula Dudley-Palmer was also thinking about her figure. Her two daughters had

145

attended Ragley School and had moved on to the Time School for Girls in York at the age of eleven. Petula was reading her *Woman's Weekly* and learning that, according to a survey of six thousand readers, the average female was five feet four inches tall, wore size sixteen dresses and measured a cuddly 37, 30, 40. Apparently an M&S spokeswoman noted that they had noticed a trend towards bigger busts after checking the sales of bras.

The magazine also reported that Sarah Ferguson had been voted the girl with the most gorgeous figure, namely, "a warm, well-rounded laughing delight". Petula was disappointed that Princess Diana was in second place.

After donning her new lime-green leisure suit and Chris Evert trainers, Petula stared at her reflection and found it reassuring that her regular fitness routine had transformed her figure. She was beginning to turn heads again, including that of her husband. *It's a pity he was unfaithful*, she thought, and recalled happier days in years gone by. She glanced at the hall table. There were three tickets for the evening pantomime, for herself and her two daughters, and she sighed. There used to be *four* tickets.

On the Crescent Anne Grainger was about to leave to help with preparations for the pantomime. She had arranged to meet Pat and Sally at the village hall to go through a rehearsal with the group of children who had volunteered to be in the chorus line. The producer, Felicity Miles-Humphreys, had insisted on a simple dance routine to the accompaniment of the Bangles' "Walk Like an Egyptian". However, much to her dismay, two of the five-year-olds, Cheyenne Blenkinsop and Kylie Ogden, had both been blessed with two left feet.

"I'm going now, John," shouted Anne from the hallway.

There was no answer, just a hammering from the garage. Anne's DIY-fanatic husband had begun a new project, a cumbersome wine rack that Anne hoped would stay out of sight. She popped her head round the garage door and John looked up.

"Will you be coming with me to the pantomime?" she asked.

John shook his head. "I want to finish this."

"But you said you would come."

John rubbed his bearded face. Flecks of sawdust drifted down from his curly, unkempt beard. "No thanks — there's better things to do."

Too right, thought Anne and slammed the door as she left.

It was then she decided that on the way to the village hall she would use the public telephone outside the Post Office. She was in need of a sympathetic ear and possibly companionship.

When John and I left the Coffee Shop, Claire Bradshaw and Anita Cuthbertson gave me a wave. "See you at the panto, sir," called Claire.

It was rumoured that Claire was now *engaged* to Kenny Kershaw. Apparently it was supposed to be a secret, but in a close-knit village such as Ragley it had quickly become common knowledge.

"Good luck," I said, waving the programme. "I see you're in it."

"We're a couple o' fairies," said Anita with a grin.

John looked back at me and raised his eyebrows.

"Come on," I said, "we've got an hour to finish painting King Stefan's castle." He didn't appear full of enthusiasm. "Or you could go back to Diane and pick me up later."

"No thanks," he said quickly, "I'd rather paint a castle."

An hour later John and I had not only painted a reasonably convincing representation of King Stefan's castle but also, on another sheet of hardboard, a dense, dark forest as a backdrop for the evil fairy Maleficent. We stood back to admire our efforts and, as we put on our coats, the dress rehearsal began.

As usual, it wasn't going to plan, with the added complication that Dorothy wasn't feeling well and had gone back to the Coffee Shop to lie down. "I need someone to read the part of first fairy," announced Felicity in a strident voice. For a moment she stared expectantly in our direction as John and I headed for the door. However, common sense prevailed and Felicity decided against it. "Everyone, please take your places for the opening number and I'll read Flora's part." As we hurried out, Nora was singing "Lady in Wed", which, sadly, bore little relation to Chris de Burgh's number-one hit.

It was 2.15p.m. and in Morton Manor Vera switched the television to BBC2 and settled down in her favourite armchair to enjoy an afternoon of peace and contentment.

The Bolshoi in the Park was about to start, with highlights from *Sleeping Beauty*, *Les Sylphides* and other ballets. It occurred to Vera that the elegance of this particular production of *Sleeping Beauty* was a world away from the one in store that evening in Ragley village hall.

Two hours later in Bilbo Cottage, John, Diane and Beth were settled on the sofa in front of a crackling log fire watching *Skating '86*. It featured Robin Cousins, who had been joined by other international skating stars to raise funds for famine relief. Meanwhile, I was on my hands and knees with young John, playing with his train set in the hallway.

Eventually, we gathered round the kitchen table and, after a warming meal of Diane's home-made leek and potato soup with crusty bread, Beth and I set off in her VW Golf for Ragley's cultural treat of the year — the annual pantomime.

Tickets were 50p each and we took our seats. Timothy Pratt turned out the lights, switched on the single spotlight and the pantomime began. It followed the usual format, with some dreadful acting and lively audience participation. Deirdre Coe would have been booed even if she had not played the part of Maleficent. While the three fairies and Little Malcolm were cheered to the rafters, the highlight was

149

undoubtedly the small children doing their dance routine. Uncoordinated and out of step it may have been, but this was a Ragley village audience and the standing ovation was well deserved.

For once the storyline was a familiar one and easy to follow. Felicity's younger son, Nigel, was the official narrator and was dressed as a cross between the American singer P.J. Proby and a medieval minstrel. He kept appearing at the side of the stage, hitching up his baggy green tights and describing the next scene. "The young Princess Aurora is cursed by the evil fairy, Maleficent," he recited. This was followed by boos and hisses as the decidedly unpopular Deirdre Coe clumped around the stage and waved her magic wand in the direction of Julie Tricklebank's doll. Fortunately the doll was rescued by the three good fairies, Claire, Anita and Dorothy, to raucous cheers from the audience.

Soon Nigel was on his feet again, explaining that sixteen years had passed and Princess Aurora had grown into a beautiful young woman. It was then that Nora made her first appearance, to enthusiastic applause.

"She dunt look sixteen," commented Stevie "Supersub" Coleclough from the back row. The rest of the football team nodded in agreement.

"An' she's bustin' out o' that corset," added Shane Ramsbottom.

Vera turned from the third row and frowned and the comments died down. Then Nora launched into the Berlin hit record and sang "Take My Bweath Away". There was suppressed laughter from the football team at the back of the hall, quickly drowned out by vigorous applause led by Tyrone Crabtree in the second row.

"And the young princess fell into a deep sleep," announced Nigel.

Nora flopped down on an old sofa, watched over by three distressed fairies.

"Only true love's kiss can awaken the princess from her enchanted sleep," proclaimed Nigel with gravitas.

Big Dave Robinson was sitting with Nellie on the third row directly behind Tyrone Crabtree. Nora's boyfriend was awestruck, staring up at the woman of his dreams. Big Dave leaned forward, tapped Tyrone on the shoulder and whispered in his ear, "You should give her one."

Tyrone flushed profusely.

"'E means give Nora a kiss, Tyrone," added Nellie gently.

She gave her huge hulk of a husband a look he knew so well, and Big Dave settled back in his seat suitably chastened.

"The handsome Prince Philip arrived on his sturdy steed," continued Nigel in a loud voice. Behind the curtain, Felicity's other son Rupert, the lanky six-feet-four-inch supermarket shelf-stacker and would-be actor, suddenly began to bang together two halves of a coconut and ran on to the stage. Unfortunately he was still holding the coconut as he delivered his opening line: "Behold, who is this fair young maiden?"

"It's grab-a-granny time," shouted Chris "Kojak" Wojciechowski, the Bald-Headed Ball Wizard, from the back row, followed by laughter.

151

Undeterred, Rupert hid the coconut behind his back, knelt down and gave Nora a hasty and unconvincing peck on the cheek.

Nora awoke and sat up quickly. "Oooh, a handsome pwince," she said. "'Ave you come to wescue me?"

Beth whispered, "I thought he was supposed to be captured by Maleficent."

"That's coming next," I said knowingly. "I painted the dragon's cave."

We looked back to the stage. "Yes, I have," said Rupert boldly, "but first I have to do battle with Maleficent."

"Told you so," I said and Beth gave me a dig in the ribs.

Nigel stood up and read from his script: "Prince Philip rode off to the castle of Maleficent."

Rupert looked down at the coconut and pranced off to huge cheers, tapping his shells together.

The curtains closed as Nigel walked to the centre of the stage and made a dramatic announcement.

"Prince Philip is a prisoner in Maleficent's castle, where the evil fairy descends to her cave and transforms herself into a fire-breathing dragon."

There were noises behind the curtain as my sheet of eight-by-four hardboard was dragged on to the stage by Felicity and her son.

Undeterred by the sound of Rupert shouting, "Oh Mother, you've laddered my tights," Nigel pressed on.

"Prince Philip is forced to face her in mortal combat."

The curtains opened and Rupert, holding up his shredded tights in one hand and a plywood sword in the other, struck a pose to face the fierce dragon — Deirdre Coe wearing a cardboard dragon's head.

It was then that a strange commotion began backstage. The curtains were closed abruptly and a few moments of silence followed.

Suddenly, on the steps leading from the side of the stage, Felicity appeared with Malcolm. "Turn on the lights," she shouted to Timothy. Between them they were helping Dorothy into the auditorium and heading for the exit. A coat had been thrown round her shoulders and she was clutching her stomach, clearly in a lot of pain.

Alarm spread through the audience like wildfire.

Nora was just behind them. "Tywone," she shouted, "go out an' get y'car. We 'ave t'get Dowothy to the 'ospital."

The pantomime had stopped and actors, children and the audience had begun to mill around in confusion. It was clear that something was seriously wrong, but York hospital was only twenty minutes away.

"Malcolm, Malcolm!" cried Dorothy.

"Come on, luv," said Malcolm. "We'll sort it."

Nellie reacted quickly. She grabbed Big Dave's elbow. "Dave, come on, we 'ave to 'elp," and they both rushed out.

Beth and I hurried to the exit, where Nellie shouted in my direction, "Mr Sheffield, Malcolm's got t'car keys. Can y'give me an' Dave a lift?"

153

Beth's car was parked immediately outside the village hall and she gave me the keys. "You take them, Jack. I'll get a lift home. Stay with them for as long as it takes."

It made sense for one of us to get home and I could see the concern in her eyes. "Thanks," I said.

Tyrone had driven off at speed with Nora next to him and Malcolm doing his best to comfort Dorothy in the back seat. Meanwhile, Nellie was almost dragging Big Dave out on to the pavement. Like Malcolm, he looked stunned, as if he couldn't take in everything that was happening.

I opened Beth's car. "Get in," I said. Big Dave and Nellie jumped into the back seat and in a few moments we were speeding down the A19 towards York.

An hour later we were sitting in a corridor. Dorothy had been taken into one of the wards and Little Malcolm had been told to wait outside. There was a hot-drinks machine and I approached Big Dave and Little Malcolm and offered them two beakers of sweet tea. Big Dave gave a nod of thanks and urged Little Malcolm to take a reluctant sip.

Nora and Tyrone sat together on the other side of the corridor. Nora was white-faced with anxiety. Time ticked by as we waited for news.

Finally, just before midnight, a nurse spoke quietly to Little Malcolm and ushered him into the ward. It seemed to take an age, but finally he reappeared and sat down with his head in his hands.

"We've lost our baby," he said in almost a whisper.

Nellie was holding his hand. "What about Dorothy?" she asked.

He looked up, tears streaming down his cheeks. "Doctor said she'll be all right." Nora burst into tears and walked away, while Tyrone tried to comfort her.

"Can we see 'er?" asked Nellie.

Little Malcolm shook his head. "She's sleepin' now . . . an' she looks beautiful."

Big Dave, too upset to speak, wrapped his cousin in a giant embrace and held him tight.

We sat there, uncertain what to do next. Eventually, the doctor came out to speak to us all and said that Dorothy needed rest. He advised us to go home but would understand if Malcolm wanted to stay and there was a comfortable private room nearby.

"You go 'ome now, Nora," said Nellie. "Y'can't do owt 'ere. Get some rest."

Tyrone held Nora's hand. "Nellie's right," he said softly.

"You too, Mr Sheffield," said Nellie, "an' thanks for 'elping."

"What about you?" I asked. "Shall I take you home?"

Nellie looked back at her husband trying to comfort his cousin. "There's no way Dave'll leave Malcolm now. 'E'll sit wi' 'im as long as it teks an' ah'll stay an' look after 'em."

Nellie was gradually taking charge and I admired this tough lady for her resilience and clear thinking.

I followed Nora and Tyrone down the corridor and paused to look back. Little Malcolm stood there with Big Dave's arm around his shoulders while Nellie spoke to them both in hushed tones. The diminutive bin man was in despair, lost in an eternal sorrow within the shelter of his grief. Ahead of him was a black night of broken dreams while the cracked bones of his spirit cried out without hope. For this tough Yorkshireman there was only a closed door and a chilling heartache while he waited for his sleeping wife to awake.

As I drove home I thought about the enormity of what I had just witnessed and my chest felt tight with the depth of sorrow. It was a silent, lonely journey, while above me the tattered shreds of cirrus clouds dimmed the light of a gibbous moon.

It was then I realized . . . a new year had dawned.

CHAPTER
NINE

Footprints in the Snow

School reopened today for the spring term with 133 children on roll. The official amalgamation of Ragley and Morton schools began today with the arrival of 28 children from Morton. Mr Marcus Potts began his appointment as full-time teacher with responsibility for Class 3 in the temporary classroom.

Extract from the Ragley & Morton School Logbook:
Monday, 5 January 1987

It was a dark winter morning when I set off for the first day of term and a heavy snowfall during the night made for a difficult journey. It was Monday, 5 January and the land was silent and still while the creatures of the countryside sought refuge. I called in at the General Stores and even the bell above the door sounded muted as I walked in. It appeared the village had been in mourning since the news of Dorothy losing her baby.

"A sad start to the New Year, Mr Sheffield," said Prudence. "I pray that Dorothy will recover."

"It will certainly take time," I said.

"Well, she's a strong young woman . . . and she has a loving husband," Prudence added wistfully.

I could barely imagine the effect this would have had on Little Malcolm. He worshipped Dorothy.

"Something for the staff-room, Mr Sheffield?" enquired Prudence. "Reduced after Christmas." She took a box of Sarah Bernhardt Butter Cream & Fondant Fancies from behind the jars of Seven Seas Castor Oil on the shelf at the back of her and placed it on the counter. "These for a treat and perhaps . . . a packet of Brontë Biscuits." She lowered her voice, "A gift for your staff."

"That's very kind, thank you, Prudence," I said. "They will be appreciated."

"You're very welcome," replied Prudence, "and a Happy New Year."

"And to you too — and Jeremy, of course."

It was very early and I expected I would be the first member of staff to arrive. The newcomers from Morton were due to attend for their first full day at Ragley, along with our new teacher, Marcus Potts.

I paused for a moment to take in the sight. The playground had a new covering of fresh snow, and frost coated the fleurs-de-lis on top of the metal railings. The clock tower looked frozen in time and the new temporary classroom blended in with its blanket of whiteness. In the hedgerow blood-red berries were bright against the snow.

Meanwhile, a bitter malevolent wind cut through my duffel coat and I shivered as I picked up my old leather satchel, locked my car and set off towards the school

158

entrance. It was then that I spotted them . . . *footprints in the snow*. Someone had arrived even earlier and headed towards the old cycle shed.

I set off to investigate.

A short, stocky ten-year-old boy in blue jeans, thick woollen jumper and an old green anorak was leaning against the wall. He had straight black hair with a severe fringe and an engaging smile.

"Good morning," I said. I guessed he was the boy who had not attended the preliminary visit but had called in very briefly with his mother after school one evening. They had spoken with Anne. "It's George, isn't it? You're coming into my class."

He looked up sharply. "Yes, sir . . . George Frith from Morton."

"Do you know me?" I asked with an encouraging smile. "I'm Mr Sheffield, your new headteacher."

He considered me for a moment. "What 'appened to t'other one, sir — that Mr Timmings from Morton?"

"He moved to another school."

George considered this and nodded. He blew on his hands, which looked blue with cold.

"In weather like this pupils can go into school before nine o'clock so long as there's a member of staff there," I explained. "Then you can sit in the library if you wish. It's warm in there."

He stared at the school entrance, where Ruby had appeared with a broom and a carton of Saxa salt. "Ah like lib'ries, sir, but ah wouldn't want t'go in . . . y'know, wi' not knowin' no one."

I changed tack. "Why have you come to school so early, George?"

"'Cause ah never knew m'dad an' m'mam works the early shift, sir, at t'chocolate factory. We leave 'ome before eight an' she drops me off. At Morton ah allus 'ad t'wait outside. Caretaker didn't like me."

A sharp gust blew a flurry of snow into the cycle shed and it settled around his heavy brown boots.

"Let's go into school," I said, "and you can help me with a job."

Although his teeth were chattering, he managed a smile and we walked into the library. "George, I'd like you to select six books that you think would be good to read and we'll take them into our classroom."

He set to eagerly. "OK, sir."

I paused before going into the school office. "Who are your friends?" I asked.

For the first time his infectious smile disappeared. "Ain't got none, sir," he said, "'cause at Morton there were no other boys my age — jus' girls."

It was my turn to smile. I hung up my coat and scarf and walked into the school hall to prepare for morning assembly. I left the double doors open so I could keep an eye on him.

A few minutes later the car park was filled with new arrivals. Vera parked in her usual place and headed briskly for the school office. Pat Brookside skidded to a halt next to my Morris Minor Traveller, at the same time as Marcus Potts chugged slowly towards the space next to the cycle shed in his little red Mini. Sally had

160

collected Anne en route and they were both unloading a collection of posters.

Vera had started work in the school office and looked up with a smile when I walked in. "Good morning, Mr Sheffield," she said, "and a Happy New Year."

"And to you, Vera. It promises to be eventful."

Telephone calls had already been coming in. Vera looked down at her spiral-bound notepad. "Miss Barrington-Huntley called to say she couldn't get out of her driveway this morning and sends her apologies and best wishes. She said Miss Cleverley may call in later in the week."

"Thank you, Vera," I said. *I would have preferred Miss Barrington-Huntley*, I thought.

Vera opened the new register for Class 5. "The boy in the library — that's George Frith, isn't it? He's one of your new pupils in the top class."

"Yes, he seems a little subdued at present but I'm hoping he will make new friends."

"I'll keep an eye open, Mr Sheffield."

"You always have done," I said, "and I'm sure you always will."

Vera looked at me thoughtfully as if searching for a hidden message. "Thank you," she said simply and returned to her registers.

"Well, I'm off to see how Marcus is getting on."

Vera held up a pair of pristine registers. "I've prepared these for the new Class 3 and I've entered the children's names in alphabetical order. It's important Mr Potts gets off to a good start."

Vera's immaculate copperplate writing was distinctive.

"Thanks Vera," I said, "and good luck today. No doubt there will be a few queries from the new parents."

Vera merely smiled. Nothing could faze our reliable secretary. She had seen it all before.

I walked out to the temporary classroom. Between Christmas and New Year, a team of builders had created a substantial wooden structure providing cover from the steps outside the temporary classroom to the main building. It was reassuring that the steps would be kept safe and dry in all weathers. When I opened the door to our new building I saw that Marcus had labelled the coat pegs with the names of all the children in his care. He had also transformed his classroom. There were bright and inviting displays against the back wall and he had created an attractive reading corner and a science table filled with activities and reference books.

"Splendid, Marcus," I said. "Your classroom looks terrific."

He smiled and looked around him; it was a job well done. "I just wanted to create lots of interest for the children." He picked up a glass prism from the science display and turned it carefully in his hands to produce a kaleidoscope of colours on a white sheet of cardboard. "You know," he added with a grin, "plenty of awe and wonder."

"You've certainly achieved that," I said as I looked around, "and we finished up with a far superior temporary classroom."

"Yes," he said wistfully, "in a strange way perhaps the fire did us a favour."

162

I reflected on my conversation with Dean Skinner's stepfather about his weekly payments. "Perhaps," I said. "Anyway, here are your registers from Vera, and if you need anything, please ask."

He gave me a slightly nervous smile and placed the registers on his desk next to two pens, one red and one black, plus his dinner-money tin.

All seemed to be well, so I walked back to the hall where Sally and Pat were making preparations for morning assembly. Owing to the influx of new children, we had decided to have an extended morning assembly at ten o'clock to integrate the newcomers as quickly as possible.

"Morning, Jack," said Sally. "I'm hoping to find a few more children for my choir and recorder group this morning."

Pat glanced out of the window towards our new Class 3. "How's Marcus?" she asked. "I called in and he's worked wonders with his classroom."

I returned to the entrance hall, where Ruby had washed down the children's toilets and was putting away her mop and galvanized bucket.

"Thanks for all your work, Ruby," I said. "The school looks really clean and tidy."

"An' ah gave Mr Potts's classroom a *proper* polish, Mr Sheffield," said Ruby, her face flushed with exertion. "An' that nice safety officer from County 'All, 'im who's a bit boss-eyed wi' a gammy leg, called in yesterday an' fitted a fire distinguisher in t'entrance to 'is classroom."

I recalled the genial Mr Harry Nettles, who coped well with the setbacks in his life. "That's good to hear."

Ruby nodded towards the office door. "An' ah've got a couple more 'ours each week f'me to cover m'extra cleaning."

At 8.45a.m. William Featherstone's Reliance coach pulled up outside the school gate and eighteen children hurried excitedly up the cobbled drive. The remaining pupils from Morton had chosen to arrive by car or on foot. First up the drive was Mrs Nobbs, wife of the Morton baker, with her seven-year-old identical twin boys, Benjamin and Edward.

Anne had the majority of the new children in her class and a group of parents had arrived early to discuss arrangements with her.

"Yes, please come into the classroom at the end of school to collect your children," said Anne. "It's important I can link the children to their parents so they always leave our classroom in safety."

Anne was her usual professional self and completely at ease with the new situation. Some of the parents appeared anxious, but calmed down quickly when Anne put their minds at rest.

One parent who seemed particularly concerned was Mrs Stansfield. She crouched down next to her five-year-old daughter, Jacqui, and stroked her dark brown pigtails. "Now, Jacqui," she said quietly and held up a clean white handkerchief, "this is y'special 'anky, so remember what we said 'bout wavin' t'me at playtime if you're all right an' 'appy, 'cause ah need

164

t'know. I'll be across the road in the bedroom window at your Aunty Jean's."

In the centre of the handkerchief she had stitched a rectangle of material that she had cut from Jacqui's comfort blanket.

"So, don't forget," she said. "When y'see me waving ah want you t'wave back with this 'anky. Will you remember?"

"Yes, Mummy," said Jacqui, who, unlike her mother, was feeling quite relaxed and excited at the sight of her new classroom. There seemed to be lots of interesting things to do. She was looking forward to playing in the Home Corner. She had spotted an ironing board and a model cooker with an assortment of pots and pans.

Mrs Stansfield gave her a big hug and, with tears streaming down her face, the anxious parent hurried out into the snow. As soon as she had gone, the confident and inquisitive Jacqui ran into the Home Corner, put a pan on the stove and began to stir some make-believe soup with a plastic spoon. Another five-year-old, Zach Eccles, joined her and, within one minute of her mother's departure, Jacqui had a new friend and the beginnings of an imaginary three-course meal.

When I returned to the office Vera was busy with a new parent who appeared very agitated.

"This is Mrs Nobbs, Mr Sheffield," she said, looking up from her admissions register. "Her sons Benjamin and Edward will be going into Mr Potts's class."

"I've brought some spare clothing for Ben," explained Mrs Nobbs. "'E's the one wi' red socks, 'is brother 'as blue ones." I saw Vera make a note. "Y'see our Ben 'as this 'ffliction."

"Fliction?" I queried.

"I think Mrs Nobbs is referring to an affliction, Mr Sheffield," interpreted Vera.

"Oh, I see," I said, "and what is that?"

"Well, 'e teks after me."

"Does he?"

"'E does that."

Vera was keen to get to the point. "What exactly is this affliction?"

Mrs Nobbs took a deep breath and flushed to the tips of her ears. "'E wets himself when 'e gets nervous."

"Oh dear," I said. "Well, I'm sure we'll manage and perhaps you will be able to call in at the end of school and we'll see how Benjamin has coped."

"Thank you, Mr Sheffield."

"I'm sure all will be well," I reassured her as I got up to open the office door.

"There is one more thing, that is if you don't mind," said Mrs Nobbs, hopping from one foot to the other.

"Yes?" asked Vera.

"Can ah use y'toilet afore ah go?"

After pointing out the visitors' toilet, I walked out to the entrance hall where two ten-year-olds in my class, the library monitors Claire Buttershaw and Michelle Gawthorpe, were looking concerned.

"Sir, there's a new boy in our library," reported Claire.

"And he's collecting a pile of books," added Michelle.

"Yes, I told him to do that," I said. "So go and introduce yourselves and make him feel welcome. His name is George and he's coming into our class."

Both girls nodded politely but without conviction. They were good-hearted girls, but for them boys were a strange and distant species.

"Show him where to hang his coat and then bring him into class. Then you can help him display the books he has selected in our book corner."

The two girls gave me glassy-eyed smiles and hurried back to the library with gritted teeth.

After the bell rang for the start of school I made a point of ensuring the new pupils settled in. I gave a talk about making friends and helping the arrivals from Morton, not just in our class but throughout the school. I had placed George Frith next to Barry Stonehouse and asked them to take charge of our class book corner. "Thank you, sir," said Barry, "an' don't worry, ah'll look after George."

Many years have passed since that day long ago, but friendships often start with small steps and a lifetime of companionship had already begun. It was unknown to me then but, eight years later, the two boys were also destined to play rugby together for Yorkshire Schoolboys. However, on that freezing-cold January morning, they were simply two ten-year-olds who by chance shared a desk along with an interest in *Grange Hill*, *Masters of the Universe* and library books.

It soon became apparent that we had to get used to children from the temporary classroom having to walk into the main building to use the toilets.

At 9.45 a.m. I spotted Ben Nobbs hurrying down the steps towards the main school, so I popped my head round the classroom door. "Are you all right, Ben?" I asked.

Ben looked up at me nervously. "Jus' goin' to t'toilet, sir," he said.

"That's fine, Ben."

At least he knows the way, I thought.

At ten o'clock our morning assembly was a relaxed occasion and lacked the usual formality. We took the opportunity to introduce the teachers, plus Vera and Ruby along with Shirley and Doreen from the kitchen. Sally led us in a couple of songs on her guitar and we asked the older children to keep an eye on the younger ones during playtime.

On this occasion *all* the staff went out on playground duty while the children played in the snow. It was a happy time, during which, as adults, we were reminded that children somehow don't feel the cold when they are making snowmen. Meanwhile, we clutched our mugs of hot coffee and stamped our feet in our sub-zero corner of North Yorkshire.

After morning break our school nurse, Sue Phillips, called in to check the general health of the children. As always, she was smart in her light blue uniform with a spotless white apron. She looked every inch our school nurse with her sensible, black lace-up shoes and a navy blue belt that sported a precious buckle depicting, appropriately, the God of Wind.

The first child was five-year-old Noel Crump from Morton.

Sue checked his name on the register. "How are you, Noel?" she asked with a gentle smile.

"I'm fine thanks, Miss," said the confident Noel, "how about you?"

"Er, yes, I'm fine too," replied Sue, a little taken aback. "Now, I would like you to stand on one foot."

Noel looked down. "Which one, Miss?"

"I don't mind," said Sue, "you choose."

Noel stepped forward a short pace and stood firmly on Sue's left shoe. "There y'are, Miss," he said politely. The last thing his mother had said to him that morning was "Always do *exactly* as you're told."

Ask a daft question, thought Sue, as she looked down at her scuffed shoe.

Meanwhile, on the High Street, Betty Buttle and Margery Ackroyd were standing outside the General Stores when Petula Dudley-Palmer drove past in her Rolls-Royce.

"There she goes in 'er big car," noted Betty.

"There was a time when she wouldn't say boo to a goose," reflected Margery knowingly, "but she's changed."

"She 'as that," agreed Betty.

"An' she stands up t'that two-timin' 'usband of 'ers."

"Ah 'eard talk that she's jus' bought a continental quilt," said Betty.

"That's posh," said Margery.

"Mus' be foreign," added Betty as an afterthought.

★ ★ ★

Meanwhile, in the staff-room during lunchtime Marcus and Pat were scanning through the December issue of *Personal Computer World*. For Marcus, on a modest teacher's salary, at £1.10 it was his monthly luxury. They were staring in awe at a photograph of Apple's new state-of-the-art computer.

"It's the Mac Plus," said Marcus, his eyes wide with excitement.

"One megabyte of RAM," said Pat, shaking her head in disbelief. "Just imagine that."

Anne glanced up at me from her Yorkshire Purchasing Organization catalogue and gave me a familiar wide-eyed stare. Our younger colleagues appeared to be talking a foreign language. She smiled and returned to the price of powder paint.

"Sounds impressive," I said, keen to show interest.

Marcus nodded. "It's got a new keyboard."

"Really?"

"Yes," he replied, "with cursors and a numeric alphabet."

"How much is it?" I asked.

"The price is in dollars," said Pat. "It's two thousand six hundred . . . a bit out of our league."

Anne mumbled something under her breath as she turned the page and began her search for the cheapest HB pencils.

I walked into the entrance hall, where I was surprised to see Stan Coe leaning against the display board. His filthy oilskin coat had creased and marked Sally's arrangement of winter posters.

170

It was clear from the outset that Stan was agitated. However, he managed a fixed smile.

"Yes, Mr Coe?"

"Ah've come in as a good neighbour."

"Oh yes?"

His wellington boots were covered in slush and something that smelled a little more toxic. Ruby would not be pleased with the state of the floor, so I had no wish to invite him into the office.

"Even though ah'll be out o' pocket," he added.

"What is it you wish to discuss?" I was mindful that, regardless of whatever had gone on before, he was a member of the school governing body.

"Can ah jus' point summat out t'you?" He gestured with a grubby finger to the small window at the end of the entrance hall. From it we could look out on the school field. I followed him and we stared out. "It's your ol' bit o' fencin'," he said. "Ah'm sure you'll agree it's in a bad state."

I nodded in agreement. "It's certainly seen better days — but that's something the County Maintenance Department check on from time to time."

"That may be so, Mr Sheffield, but you'll recall ah own t'land jus' t'other side an' ah'm wantin' t'tidy it up — so ah were thinkin' a new fence would benefit us both."

I was surprised at such a charitable notion. "Well, I suppose it would, but you'd have to discuss it with the local authority. I presume County Hall would be involved, plus the local planning department?"

"Yes, ah understand all that," he said a little too quickly. "What ah'm jus' checkin' t'day is that you'd be 'appy wi' a smart new fence."

"Well, yes, I would look kindly on any improvement to the grounds that would benefit the school and the children, so long as the authorities agree."

He nodded and gave me that forced smile once again.

It appeared his business was concluded and he shuffled back to the entrance door. "Allus good t'talk, Mr Sheffield, an' good to 'ear you agree wi' t'proposal."

With that he walked out into the snow and I was left to ponder on an unexpected conversation.

During the last half hour of the school day I had just finished reading a chapter of Clive King's *Stig of the Dump* to my class when Stuart Ormroyd called out, "Billy McNeill comin' up t'drive, Mr Sheffield."

When I walked into the entrance hall, Billy was waiting for me. He had just passed his sixteenth birthday and stood there in his best suit and Doc Marten boots with air-cushioned soles that were his pride and joy. He was clutching a large envelope.

"Hello, Billy," I said. "You're looking smart."

"Thank you, sir," he said. "M'mother wondered if you'd 'ave a look at these forms for me, please."

He handed over the envelope.

"Yes, fine, Billy." I knew Mrs McNeill and remembered she had told me that her husband had left home many years ago with his "fancy piece".

"Ah want t'join the Army nex' year, sir. It says if y'get three O-levels then ah can be a Technician Apprentice an' there's good promotion prospects an' you'll get self-respect an' m'mam says they'll tek sixteen-year-olds."

He explained he had seen an advertisement in the back of one of Dorothy's old *Smash Hits* that were piled on a shelf near the door of the Coffee Shop, next to Nora's collection of *Woman* magazines.

"I'm pleased to help, Billy. Can you come back tomorrow? I'll have looked at this by then."

"Thanks, sir," he said. "Ah'm very grateful," and he hurried off into the darkness.

I had a lot on my mind as I drove home that evening, not least the unexpected meeting with Stan Coe. That apart, it had been a successful start for the children of Ragley and Morton. It was a new beginning and I felt optimistic. Above me the bright, eerie light of a crescent moon, like a spectre of the night, shone between the skeletal branches and cast flickering shadows across the frozen road.

It was Tuesday morning and there had been a fresh snowfall. When I arrived at school and had parked my car I stopped and smiled. There were *two* pairs of footprints in the snow heading towards the cycle shed. George Frith was there again, but this time he was not alone. Barry Stonehouse was crouched alongside and they were studying a picture in Barry's comic of He-Man and a model of a Blaster Hawk from *Masters of the Universe*.

"Hello, boys."

"Good morning, sir," said George.

"Hello, Mr Sheffield," said Barry. "Ah came in early t'keep George company."

George smiled up at me. "Yes sir . . . we're friends."

CHAPTER
TEN

Too Many Cooks

*A note was sent to parents relating to the PTA
Celebrity Cookbook Project.*
Extract from the Ragley & Morton School Logbook:
Monday, 19 January 1987

It was a frozen dawn and the pale sun in the east
touched the land with cool fingertips. The line of light
was a golden thread as it crested the ridge of the distant
hills and a monochrome snowscape stretched out to the
far horizon. Thin trails of wood smoke rose towards a
gun-metal sky while the villagers of Ragley huddled
round their log fires. It was a cold and hostile world
and the small creatures found shelter wherever they
could. The bitter rhythms of a Siberian winter had
scoured the land of life.

When John Kettley had delivered his *Countryfile*
weather forecast just over a week ago on 11 January,
he had said, "The only bright thing on this forecast is
my tie!" How true! Our favourite weatherman had
predicted correctly that we were in for freezing
temperatures and a week of blizzards. The following day
had been one of the coldest in living memory, with

sub-zero temperatures for the whole of the UK. However, on this Monday morning as I drove to school the temperature had begun to rise again and in spite of a fresh snowfall there was hope that the worst had passed.

In Bilbo Cottage Beth had left early for school and left me to give John his breakfast while waiting for Mrs Roberts to arrive. It seemed appropriate that on the radio The Communards were singing "So Cold the Night".

Three miles away in Ruby's house, Radio 1 was on full blast. Natasha had tuned in as usual to Mike Smith's *Breakfast Show* and she was swaying her hips to Alison Moyet's "Is This Love?" while frying bacon and thinking of our local bobby, PC Julian Pike, and the tickle of his moustache.

In complete contrast, in Morton Manor Vera was sipping her Earl Grey tea as she hummed along to the tranquil sounds of a Boccherini string quartet on Radio 3. We were all beginning our day differently; however, we were destined to end it in the same way.

It was a slow journey to Ragley and I needed petrol, so I pulled in at Victor Pratt's garage. His assistant, Kenny, was clearing the forecourt with a snow shovel. He propped it against the garage wall and removed the nozzle from the single pump.

"Mornin', Mr Sheffield, what'll it be?" Kenny appeared to be thriving as a car mechanic.

"Fill her up please, Kenny."

Victor lumbered out after him. "Bit sharp this mornin'," he remarked.

"Yes, it's certainly cold," I conceded as a bitter wind blew and my face began to freeze. However, this was all in a day's work for our local car mechanics.

"An' m'bronchials are playin' up," went on Victor. "M'tubes get blocked in winter. Ah need some goose grease."

Kenny grinned — he had grown used to Victor's complaints by now. I offered the usual sympathy, paid Kenny and drove off.

Vera was checking the morning post, which included a note from Mrs Earnshaw. It read, "Please excuse our Dallas from school as she has loose vowels." She smiled, made a note on her pad and looked up as Ruby popped her head round the door.

"Mornin', Mrs F," she said. "Bit parky t'day."

"It certainly is, Ruby, and how are you?"

Ruby considered this for a moment. "Fair t'middlin'," she said, "'part from our Duggie."

"Oh dear, is he unwell?"

"Not 'xactly — jus' a bit soft in the 'ead."

"And why is that?" asked Vera, wondering what was coming next.

"'E's started seein' that Tina from Thirkby again. 'Er what works in t'mattress factory."

"I see," said Vera, but in truth she didn't.

"An' you'll recall she works part-time at Tattooes-While-U-Wait in York an' 'e's 'ad TINA tattooed on 'is bum."

Vera was speechless.

"'E said it were a token of 'is undyin' love."

"Have you met this lady, Ruby? Perhaps she's what people call a *rough diamond*. It may be she has a heart of gold." Vera generally found some good in people.

"Mebbe so, but it's 'ard t'find out 'cause she never shuts up. She could talk 'til t'cows turn blue."

Vera presumed this was a long time in anyone's vocabulary, and Ruby hurried out to check the school boiler.

It was just after the bell for morning school that Vera opened the last letter in the pile on her desk. It made her shiver with excitement — it was almost too good to be true.

She read it again and again and sighed.

How wonderful, she thought.

An hour later, in Class 1, Anne was with her reception children and following up a television broadcast about animals.

"Can you name an animal with whiskers?"

Kylie Ogden's hand shot up.

"Yes, Kylie," said Anne, pleased with the little girl's enthusiasm.

"My grandma, Miss."

Anne sighed. *I'll rephrase that*, she thought.

Next door, in Pat's class, the children were busy completing a mathematics lesson.

"Let's do some mental arithmetic," said Pat. "We've got a few minutes before assembly."

"Will they be easy, middlin' or 'ard, Miss?" asked Alfie Spraggon.

"Let's start with an easy one," said Pat with an encouraging smile. "Twelve more than six."

Alfie's hand was first in the air. "Yes, Miss," he shouted out.

"What do you mean, Alfie?" asked Pat.

"Ah mean, yes, Miss — twelve *is* more than six."

It was shortly before assembly that Pat announced that it was Tracey Higginbottom's sixth birthday. Tracey was keen to share news of her present. "My mummy bought me a rabbit," she said. "It's called Fifi and my dad said it sounded French."

"Yes, I suppose it does," said Pat.

Tracey frowned. "Miss, do French rabbits speak French?"

The bell rescued Pat by providing time to consider a helpful response.

I was on duty, so I wrapped up warm in my duffel coat and scarf, collected my coffee and crunched down the frozen cobbled drive to stand by the school gate. Above me wisps of clouds drifted by like the breath of ghosts. Beyond the village green, Ragley High Street was rimed in ice and, in spite of the hint of warmer weather to come, my breath steamed in a frozen world. The villagers had a phlegmatic view of the extremes of winter weather in North Yorkshire. They called it the "killing cold". It was accepted that this was simply the way of things, and each year it took away the elderly and the weak.

As I stood at the gate I spotted an old but beautifully maintained racing-green Citroën DS. It was a distinctive car, and one of them had been credited with saving the life of French President General Charles de Gaulle when terrorist bullets had exploded the tyres but the hydropneumatic suspension had kicked in and his driver had managed an escape. However, this was clearly far from the mind of the distinguished grey-haired man at the wheel of this one as it moved carefully over the snow and ice on the High Street. I remembered I had seen this car before, but it didn't seem important at the time.

Meanwhile, undeterred by the Arctic weather, children played, made slides, threw snowballs and enjoyed their games. Stuart Ormroyd was peering through the railings towards The Royal Oak. He beckoned me to join him. "Posh car, Mr Sheffield," he said, pointing towards the green Citroën. It had parked outside our local pub. "Ah've seen it a few times, sir. Ah wonder whose it is."

Stuart was an observant little boy and loved his cars.

"I don't know, Stuart, but it's a French car, a Citroën DS, and it must be quite old because they stopped making them in 1975."

Stuart considered this. "So it's older than me, sir," and with a grin he ran off to make a snowman with George Frith and Barry Stonehouse.

In the staff-room Vera was in a state of high excitement and Marcus sat down with Anne, Sally and Pat to await her news.

Vera held up a sheet of cream headed notepaper. "A wonderful surprise, everyone: Mrs Thatcher has replied

180

— or at least her secretary has. Our Prime Minister will be too busy with matters of state."

"Is it for the recipe booklet?" asked Marcus.

"Yes, it's a response to the letter from Katie Parrish," and Vera proceeded to read it aloud:

10 Downing Street,
LONDON SW1A 2AA

Dear Katie
The Prime Minister has asked me to thank you for your recent letter and to send the enclosed recipe for Orange & Walnut Cake with her best wishes.
The Office of Margaret Thatcher

It was Sally who had encouraged a letter-writing project for the children in the top two classes as part of a *Celebrity Cookbook* project in conjunction with the PTA. It had seemed a good idea with lots of positive cross-curricular initiatives, including English, mathematics and domestic science. The children had each written to a celebrity of their choice and requested a recipe for a PTA recipe booklet.

"That's wonderful news, Vera!" exclaimed Anne.

It was clear how much this meant to our true blue secretary and even Sally kept her thoughts to herself.

"So, how many replies have we got now?" asked Pat.

"That's sixteen with Mrs Thatcher, so I'll start to prepare the booklet," said Vera.

Everyone nodded hesitantly . . . while Sally frowned.

Thirty minutes later Vera had produced the following letter to parents:

Dear Parents
CELEBRITY COOKBOOK
You will be pleased to know we have received the following replies to the children's letters and the PTA will be producing a booklet of recipes based on the responses:

Judi Dench (Katie Icklethwaite) **Barbados Cream**
Anne Diamond (Jemima Poole) **Cheese & Tomato Sandwich**
Anita Dobson (Claire Buttershaw) **Tuna Crêpe Cake**
Jimmy Greaves (George Frith) **Gladstone Hotpot**
Lenny Henry (Rufus Snodgrass) **Killer Chilli**
Nigel Mansell (Charlie Cartwright) **Normandy Chicken**
Su Pollard (Rosie Appleby) **Cheese Omelette**
President Reagan (Tom Burgess) **Pumpkin Pecan Pie**
Anneka Rice (Hayley Spraggon) **Almond & Mushroom Bake**
Cliff Richard (Ted Coggins) **Beef Curry**
Phillip Schofield (Michelle Gawthorpe) **Potato Cakes**
Delia Smith (Mandy Sedgewick) **Carrot Cake**
David Steel (Stuart Ormroyd) **Welsh Rarebit**
Margaret Thatcher (Katie Parrish) **Orange & Walnut Cake**

Daley Thompson (Barry Stonehouse) **Pear Crumble**
Wincey Willis (Siobhan Sharp) **Chinese Chicken**

Please note that Delia Smith has requested that the recipe for her Carrot Cake should be kept exactly as printed.

The recipe chosen as the favourite will be prepared for our next PTA event by our school cook, Mrs Mapplebeck.

Yours sincerely
Mrs V. Forbes-Kitchener
School Secretary

Vera smiled. It was no contest. The venerable Margaret had produced the best recipe.

It was just before the lunch break that Vera set up the Gestetner duplicating machine, filled it carefully with ink, fixed the master sheet in place without a single crease and began to turn the handle.

When I returned to my classroom Ruby was setting out the tables in the school hall for our daily Reading Workshop. I was surprised to see George Dainty coming up the drive. He called in to the school office.

"Excuse me, Mrs F," said George, "I was 'opin' ah might jus' catch Ruby afore she left."

Vera smiled. "Of course, George, it will be a lovely surprise for her."

George blinked. "Ah wanted t'tek 'er into York."

"Oh yes," said Vera nodding, "to see young Krystal, I presume."

George began to blush. "Well, not 'xactly . . . summat else."

Vera was curious but didn't pursue the point.

Ruby arrived, her cheeks flushed with the exertion of shifting the heavy tables. "Well, George, ah thought it were a pigment o' my imagination," she said looking surprised. "What y'doin' 'ere?"

"I want t'tek you int' York f'summat special, so t'speak . . . summat *private* between you an' me."

"What's that then?"

George hesitated. "Don't be offended, Ruby, but ah wanted t'buy you a new coat."

Ruby wasn't sure how to respond. She certainly needed a new coat, but this felt a little like charity. However, she didn't want to upset George's feelings. "That's very kind, George — thank you."

In our Reading Workshop six-year-old Emily Snodgrass was sitting next to her mother. We had encouraged parents to bring in items of interest that would promote language development. Mrs Snodgrass took out of her handbag an old photograph of herself when she was ten years old.

"Now, Emily, who's that, do you think?"

Emily studied it carefully and then her face lit up with excitement. "It's me, Mummy," she said. "But when I'm bigger," she added as an afterthought.

Mrs Snodgrass smiled and nodded. It made sense in a peculiar way.

184

"Mam, ah've been thinkin'," confided Emily.

"What about, luv?"

"Can we get a cat?"

Mrs Snodgrass shook her head. "We can't — your gran is allergic t'cats."

Emily considered this for a moment. "Well . . . when she dies can we get a cat?"

Mrs Snodgrass turned the next page of the Ginn Reading 360 book. "C'mon," she said, "gerron wi' y'readin'."

It was lunchtime and on the High Street in Diane's Hair Salon Claire Bradshaw was reading an article in the January edition of *Cosmopolitan*.

Diane had already flicked through the pages and had paused thoughtfully at the double-page advertisement for Benson and Hedges Special Filter — Middle Tar. It included a warning that more than thirty thousand people died each year from lung cancer and she hoped it wouldn't include her one day.

Claire's attention had been caught by the article "Smart Girls Carry Condoms". As she scanned the text she realized that the battle against AIDS had become a serious matter and she determined to discuss this with the car mechanic of her dreams, Kenny Kershaw. Now that Kenny had found regular employment at Victor's garage, she often imagined a life with her handsome lover.

"So what's it t'be, Claire?" asked Diane.

Claire opened her shopping bag and pulled out a page torn from the *TV Times*. "Like 'er please, Diane — Charlene in *Neighbours*."

Diane was puzzled. She wasn't an avid viewer of the Australian soap and was unaware of the budding romance between the feisty tomboy Charlene and Scott Robinson, played by the popular young actors Kylie Minogue and Jason Donovan. "So what y'sayin', Claire — a sort o' Blondie without t'perm?"

Claire grinned. "Ah s'ppose so."

"No problem," said Diane. She took a final puff of her cigarette, blew the smoke towards the closed window and headed for her tray of rollers.

In the Coffee Shop life had not yet returned to normal. Dorothy had been very quiet since leaving hospital and was resting upstairs. Nora had employed Natasha Smith on a part-time basis and had taken a cup of coffee and a warm meat pie up to Malcolm and Dorothy's bedroom.

"Ah bwought y'this as well," said Nora, trying hard to be positive. "It's a *TV Times* diawy wi' 'elpful 'ints from Katie Boyle an' a Wussell Gwant 'owwoscope. It pwomises good times, Dorothy."

Dorothy tried to smile, but she had forgotten how.

Deke Ramsbottom had called in to Old Tommy Piercy's butcher's shop.

"Ah'll 'ave a growler please, Tommy," said Deke.

"Jus' med 'em fresh," replied Old Tommy. He disappeared into the back room and from the warm oven selected one of his famous meat pies, known as "growlers". He double-wrapped it in a brown paper bag to keep in the warmth and handed it to Ragley's favourite cowboy.

"Thanks, Tommy," said Deke. "Jus' t'job on a cold day." He put the pie inside his shirt, buttoned up his coat and paused by the door. "Jus' thought o' summat," he added.

"What's that?"

"Ah've just seen that Stan Coe leanin' on t'fence nex' t'your cricket field, Tommy. 'E looked *shifty*, if y'know what ah mean."

Over the years, in spite of the fact that Old Tommy did not own any of the fields around Ragley, such was his devotion to his precious cricket square the locals always referred to it as Tommy's cricket pitch.

"Shifty?"

"An' 'e were talkin' t'some posh bloke," continued Deke.

"Posh bloke?"

"Yeah, 'e were tall wi' a smart coat an' a trilby 'at."

"Can't say ah know 'im," said Old Tommy thoughtfully.

"They were pointin' at t'cricket field and t'woods beyond, an' ah don't 'xpect they were admirin' t'view."

"'E'll be up t'no good ah reckon," said Old Tommy.

"Mebbe so, Tommy."

"Mark my words, Deke, summat's afoot. Ah may not allus be right . . . but ah'm nivver wrong," he added defiantly.

The children were playing on the playground and Mrs Critchley, our fierce dinner lady, was supervising. Alfie Spraggon stared at her appealingly.

"Look, Mrs Critchley," he said, pointing up at the roof, "there's testicles 'angin' down. Can we throw snowballs at 'em?"

"No y'can't," replied Mrs Critchley, "an' another thing — they're *icicles*, not what you said."

Alfie stood there picking his nose.

"An' stop that, Alfie," she said. "Ah don't ever want t'see y'do that again."

Alfie looked up with a smile that would have melted a heart of stone. "OK, Mrs Critchley — jus' close your eyes."

In the staff-room all was quiet and everyone appeared lost in their own thoughts. Anne was reading Vera's newspaper. She bypassed the gloomy news that inflation was now running at 4.2 per cent and turned to an interesting recent film. *When the Wind Blows* was based on the book by Raymond Briggs, and was a cartoon concerning the aftermath of a nuclear disaster and the heartbreaking response of an ordinary couple, Jim and Hilda Bloggs, who try to survive. The soundtrack for the film had been composed and recorded by leading musicians, including David Bowie singing the title song to great acclaim. However, Anne's mind wandered as she considered how *she* would survive . . . but, of course, she was thinking of her marriage.

On the other side of the staff-room, Sally was reading her *Guardian* newspaper.

"Well, Prince Edward didn't last long," she commented.

"What's that?" asked Vera rather sharply.

"He's left the Royal Marines after only three months."

"Oh dear," said Vera, "perhaps it didn't suit him. He has so many other talents."

"Really?" asked Sally dismissively.

Vera didn't respond, nor did she mention that she had read Joseph's Christmas present to her from cover to cover — namely, Alastair Burnet's *In Person: The Prince and Princess of Wales*. However, she had decided not to bring it into the staff-room for fear that reactions might be less than positive.

In Prudence Golightly's General Stores, Yvonne Higginbottom was looking in her purse. Mrs Higginbottom was the mother of eight-year-old Scott, six-year-old Tracey and four-year-old Chantal, who had just started full-time education in Anne's class.

"We're 'avin' a kids' party for our Chantal after school, so ah thought ah'd push t'boat out an' 'ave a few treats."

"That's a lovely idea," said Prudence.

Yvonne scanned the tightly packed shelves. "Ah'll 'ave some KitKats, please, Prudence, one o' them family packs wi' six in, an' a tube o' them Cadbury's Stackers."

"They're on offer, Yvonne," said Prudence, "as well as Chivers black cherry jelly — two for the price of one."

"Ah'll 'ave two please."

"And how is Lionel?" asked Prudence.

Yvonne shook her head and smiled. "Still doin' 'is Prudential wi' a bit o' Elvis," she said. Her husband was a Prudential Insurance man who spent his spare time doing impersonations of Elvis Presley.

"Ah'd better take some of m'posh ciggies as well," Yvonne added with a smile.

Prudence turned to the shelf behind her and selected a packet of twenty John Player Superkings, distinctive cigarettes that were ten centimetres long.

"That'll do f'now, thanks Prudence." She paid and Prudence selected a few coins from the till and passed over the change. Mrs Higginbottom walked out, opened her packet of cigarettes, lit up and inhaled deeply. It was then that she saw Stan Coe driving past in his filthy Land Rover. A thought occurred to her and she popped her head back round the door.

"Prudence," she called out, "my Lionel 'eard from 'is contacts in York that Stan Coe is after buying t'cricket field . . . finger in ev'ry pie that one."

She closed the door, the bell jingled again and the shop was silent once more. Prudence looked up at Jeremy Bear and frowned. "No good will come of that." At that moment it seemed that her beloved bear gave an imperceptible nod of agreement and she adjusted his red scarf with loving care.

The bell was about to ring for afternoon school and I was in the kitchen.

"So what do you think, Shirley?" I asked.

"Well, Mr Sheffield, there's a lot of 'em," said Shirley.

"Too many cooks, if yer ask me," retorted Mrs Critchley gruffly.

190

"Well, we 'ave t'pick jus' one, Doreen," said Shirley, trying diplomatically to find some middle ground. "That's what t'PTA wanted."

"Mebbe so," replied Doreen, "so long as it's not Mrs Milk-Snatcher."

I crept out and left them to it.

Trouble's brewing, crossed my mind.

It was just before afternoon break when Stuart Ormroyd announced, "Big Volvo 245 comin' up t'drive, Mr Sheffield." Stuart knew his cars.

The steel-grey, rubber-bumpered 245 looked like the one used by Jerry Leadbetter in the 1970s Surbiton-based sit-com *The Good Life*. It was the delivery of our new school computer. A grant from County Hall, augmented by funds from the PTA, had provided us with a state-of-the-art BBC Master computer, an upgraded version of our original BBC Model B.

In the staff-room over afternoon tea, Marcus and Pat were thrilled and animatedly discussed the benefits of the new technology.

"Lots more memory," enthused Pat, "and something called a Viewsheet, which I guess is a spreadsheet."

Marcus nodded. "Twin cartridge sockets plus sideways and private RAM."

Anne glanced up at me with a wide-eyed stare. I knew what she was thinking.

Marcus looked across at Vera, who was pouring a pan of hot milk into our coffee cups. "It's got ADFS, Vera," he said enthusiastically.

"ADFS?" queried Vera without looking up.

"Advanced Filing System," explained Marcus.

"My filing system is perfectly adequate," replied Vera crisply.

Pat gave Marcus a stern look and shook her head. Marcus accepted his coffee with particular politeness and distinctly flushed cheeks.

After the bell had announced the end of the school day I was in the office when Beth rang.

"I've got that book we were looking for," I said.

"*Postman Pat Goes Sledging?*"

"That's the one."

"By the way, I'll be late home tonight, there's a primary heads' meeting here in York."

"Fine," I said, "thanks for letting me know."

Ruby and Vera arrived in the office engaged in animated conversation.

"Well ah know summat," said Ruby.

"What's that, Ruby?" asked Vera.

"Ah 'eard Prudence talkin' in t'shop this morning about 'im who's been 'angin' around wi' Stan Coe, 'cause 'e called in t'buy a paper."

"And what did Prudence say?" I asked.

"She reckoned 'e mus' work for t'government . . . so mebbe 'e's one o' them civil serpents."

Vera smiled. "You may well be right there," and she looked knowingly in my direction.

I sat and thought about Stan Coe. His attitude appeared to have changed in the last few weeks and I couldn't understand why. I recalled that my mother had always encouraged me to see the good in people. Even

192

so, the kernel of dislike I felt for this man was overpowering. It was as if he had been wrapped in bitterness since birth and I didn't know why. For a time I carried my anger into the night like a cloak of darkness.

It was five o'clock when Vera finally put on her coat and cleared her desk. She had worked later than usual trying to prepare the *Celebrity Cookbook*. Meanwhile, I was studying the letter to parents that Vera had prepared. It was certainly an interesting set of celebrities with a few surprises, not least Margaret Thatcher and Ronald Reagan.

"I've had a word with Shirley and pointed out that she really must select Mrs Thatcher's recipe," Vera said, "as it would be unthinkable not to do so."

"Really? What did she say?"

"She said it would be better if the PTA made the selection, so, reluctantly, I've gone along with that."

Well done, Shirley, I thought. *Finally we're all singing from the same hymn sheet.*

It occurred to me that in this world where everyone had an opinion, we had *one* school cook and that was enough.

CHAPTER
ELEVEN

Oscar's Revenge

The headteacher completed responses to the document from County Hall, "A Working Paper Towards a National Curriculum". The annual service on the school boiler was completed.
Extract from the Ragley & Morton School Logbook:
Monday, 2 February 1987

It was Monday, 2 February and the morning was bright and bitterly cold while a thin light bathed the frozen land.

In our kitchen, Beth was watching John dip his toast soldiers into the runny yolk of a boiled egg, I was eating a bowl of porridge and, on the tiny television set on the worktop, BBC *Breakfast Time* was murmuring away. Frank Bough, Sally Magnusson and Jeremy Paxman were busy with the national news and Bob Wilson made a brief appearance to present his sports item. At 7.25 a.m. on the weather forecast, Francis Wilson began to tell the nation it was freezing up north, but I could have told him that. Fortunately it didn't prevent Mrs Roberts arriving on time to look after John. Five minutes later I set off for school, completely unaware that a certain feline friend was about to make an impact on the life of Ragley village . . .

On the journey into Ragley a fitful sun was trying to break through the iron-grey clouds that were being swept away by a brisk and bitter wind. The land seemed bare of life and beyond the hedgerows the furrows of the fields were frozen hard. Only the raucous cries of the rooks in the high elms disturbed the silence. Suddenly the distant hills were rimed with golden fire and I chased the dawn light as it raced across the land.

I pulled on to the forecourt of Victor Pratt's garage, where his apprentice, Kenny Kershaw, oblivious to the cold, hurried out to serve me.

"Mornin', Mr Sheffield," he greeted me with a smile and proceeded to fill up my Morris Minor Traveller with petrol.

"Morning, Kenny." I spotted Victor tinkering under the bonnet of an old Ford Granada. He looked up with a pained expression, pointed to his left leg and shook his head. Personal martyrdom was a way of life for Victor.

"How's Victor?" I asked Kenny.

"Sez 'is legs 'ave flared up again, Mr Sheffield," he said with a grin.

I was about to respond when there was a roar from behind me.

Across the road a huge commotion had erupted outside the front door of Stan Coe's farmhouse. Stan had been in the act of walking out to his mud-smeared Land Rover when a mangy cat ran across his path and tripped him up. With a bellow like an enraged buffalo,

Stan staggered to his feet and aimed a prodigious kick in the direction of the frightened cat.

As it ran off, Stan could be heard blaspheming. "Deirdre," he shouted, "ah'll drown the little bastard if it gets under my feet again."

Kenny shook his head. "'E doesn't get better with age, does 'e, Mr Sheffield?"

I gave a rueful smile, shook my head and gave Kenny a £10 note.

The weather had improved by the time I arrived on Ragley High Street under a powder-blue winter sky. A sprinkling of fresh snow crunched under my wheels as I stopped outside the General Stores.

When I walked in, Alison Gawthorpe and Tracey Higginbottom were at the counter. The two little girls were agonizing over the choice between love hearts, aniseed balls and marzipan tea cakes, while Prudence Golightly was displaying the patience of a saint. They finally decided to share a bag of love hearts.

"How's Trio, Miss Golightly?" asked Alison politely.

The three-legged cat was always an interesting sight for the children in the shop as it hopped in and out of the sacks of potatoes.

"He's fine, thank you," said Prudence as she handed over the sweets. "He's just had his breakfast."

"Can cats grow another leg?" asked Alison.

Prudence thought about this. "I don't think that's possible yet, but one day in the future a clever scientist will work out how to do it." She counted out their change carefully and placed it on the counter.

"I'd like t'be a scientist," said Tracey.

"Well, that's wonderful," said Prudence. She glanced up at Jeremy Bear, paused and then nodded. "And Jeremy says you can achieve anything if you work hard at school."

The girls stared up at Ragley's favourite furry friend. "OK, Jeremy," said Tracey. The two girls walked out and the bell above the door jingled merrily.

Prudence gave me a mischievous grin, passed over my morning paper and I walked out to my car.

Across the High Street, outside the village hall "Deadly" Duggie Smith, the undertaker's assistant, was dressed smartly in his black suit and overcoat. He was polishing the chromium headlamps of his hearse, a beautifully restored 1957 Austin FX3 and the pride of the fleet. His boss, the funeral director Septimus Bernard Flagstaff, watched in admiration.

The car looked stark in our monochrome world of snow and ice.

"Hello, Duggie," I said. "You look busy."

"Allus good business in cold winters, Mr Sheffield," replied Duggie almost apologetically.

It occurred to me that, regardless of the bitter weather, at least someone was happy.

As I drove past the Post Office Kelvin Froggat, the local chimney sweep, was parked outside and unloading his brushes prior to unblocking Amelia Postlethwaite's chimney. It was the talk of the village, particularly among the customers in Diane's Hairdresser's, that Amelia and her husband Ted preferred the hearthrug in front of a roaring log fire for their regular and very noisy lovemaking. Kelvin nodded in my direction with a startling white-toothed smile and I noticed his face was already blackened with soot. Either this wasn't his first appointment or he had gone to bed like that.

At the school gate I slowed to take in the sight. Our Victorian building looked dramatic with its roof covered in snow, icicles hanging from the gutters and frosty curved stitching patterns decorating each window pane. I parked and walked towards the entrance porch, where an agitated Ruby was waving her yard broom.

"Go on, shoo away," she shouted. Rodney Morgetroyd had delivered two crates of milk for the infants and a layer of ice covered the bottles. A pair of blue tits were pecking furiously at the foil tops to reach the head of cream. "There's crumbs on t'bird table f'you," Ruby scolded, and they flew away with a flutter of wings.

Ruby resumed clearing snow from the entrance porch steps. "Mornin', Mr Sheffield."

"Good morning, Ruby, and how are you?"

"Ah'll be fine once that boiler gets fettled."

"Yes, we need it working in this weather."

"Well ah've got it goin' full blast an' it's gettin' serviced t'day. It'll be Jim, t'boiler man from 'Arrogate, so ah'll see to 'im."

"Thanks, Ruby."

She pointed the handle of her broom towards our bird table. "Jus' look at that." A robin had perched there searching for some of the tasty titbits that Ruby provided each morning. However, a large cat was crouched nearby, presumably looking for a tasty breakfast. When it saw us it ran out of the gate and we watched as it disappeared up the road to the council estate. It looked vaguely familiar.

"That's Oscar, Deirdre Coe's cat," said Ruby. "Ah sometimes give it a saucer o' milk 'cause she don't feed it proper."

"Oh dear," I said and hurried in. There was much to do and inquisitive cats were not uppermost on my mind.

Sally and Vera were in the entrance hall and Vera was holding a birthday card in a smart lilac envelope.

"This is for Grace," she said with a smile.

Sally's daughter, Grace Eleanor Pringle, was about to celebrate her sixth birthday the following day.

"You remembered!" said Sally. "That's really thoughtful — thank you so much." Grace was now in an infant class at Easington County Primary School and Sally dropped her off each morning on her way to Ragley. She took the card and gave Vera a hug. In spite of their political differences, they remained firm friends and loyal companions.

"Good morning, Mr Sheffield," said Vera and pointed to a parcel on the pine table. "The new atlases have arrived."

"At last," I said. "They're long overdue."

"In more ways than one," agreed Sally with a smile. "Perhaps the children will now realize the British Empire isn't quite what it was." Sally was right: our ancient atlases with many countries coloured in pink made it appear as though we ruled the world. She glanced at her wristwatch. "An assembly to prepare, Jack," and she hurried off clutching her *Okki-Tokki-Unga* songbook and her guitar.

At 10.15a.m. Joseph called in to lead morning assembly and take a short lesson with the children in Pat's class. Sally opened her songbook to number 25, "Do Your Ears Hang Low?", and strummed the opening chord.

Her orchestra comprised an assortment of children from all classes playing a variety of instruments, including castanets, triangles, tambourines, recorders, Indian bells and cymbals. Katie Icklethwaite had been trusted with the large wooden xylophone, while Billy Ricketts had once again managed to secure the drum and was beating it with rather too much enthusiasm.

After this, Joseph told a story about Jesus and his life before he went to heaven. It clearly had an impact on Alfie Spraggon, who was staring at Joseph trying to make sense of the concept. It was only after Joseph's lesson with Class 2 that the little boy pursued it further.

When the bell went for morning break, Joseph was sitting at Pat's desk and reading some of the prayers that the children had written.

Billy Ricketts had written, "Dear God, Thank you for making dinosaurs extinct because it would be scary if you hadn't."

Tracey Higginbottom presumably had future relation-ships on her mind when she wrote, "Dear God, Is it you who decides who we are going to marry 'cause I definitely don't want Billy Ricketts?"

Emily Snodgrass was more concerned with God's potential errors. She had written, "Dear God, Mr Evans says you made *all* the animals but were giraffes an accident?"

200

Joseph was struggling with the logic of young children once again when he noticed six-year-old Alfie Spraggon was still in the classroom. "That were a good story 'bout Jesus, Mr Evans," he said with sincerity. Alfie liked a good story.

"Thank you, Alfie," replied Joseph. "I'm glad you enjoyed it."

Alfie shuffled from one foot to the other.

"Was there a question?" asked Joseph.

Alfie frowned and looked out of the window. "Is Jesus up there?" he asked, pointing to the sky.

Joseph considered this for a moment. "Well, Alfie," he said quietly and with a voice that was intended to convey considerable gravitas, "Jesus is *everywhere*."

"Ev'rywhere?" repeated Alfie, who at his tender age was not familiar with gravitas and wondered why this man with his shirt collar turned the wrong way round was talking as if he had a sore throat.

"Yes," said Joseph with a beatific smile. "In fact, He is with us in this room."

Alfie looked around the classroom in surprise. Then his little face lit up in perceived understanding. "So . . . are *you* Jesus?"

It was Joseph's turn to look surprised. "No, I'm not Jesus."

Alfie studied every corner of the classroom. "Then . . . am *I* Jesus?"

The sound of children playing came to Joseph's rescue and childhood logic was put to one side.

Alfie looked out of the window and smiled at Joseph as he hurried out to the playground. Then he caught sight of Scott Higginbottom making a snowman and thoughts of the whereabouts of Jesus were put to one side.

Shortly after the bell for morning break I walked into the office just as the telephone rang. Vera beckoned me to her desk. "It's Beth," she said and hurried off to the staff-room to prepare morning coffee.

Beth seemed to be in a hurry. "I've got a staff meeting after school."

"Oh well," I said. "See you later this evening."

"I've asked Mrs Roberts to stay a little later and she was fine with that."

"I shouldn't be too late, although there's that County Hall questionnaire to complete." It had arrived in the morning post requesting an immediate response. The title, "A Working Paper Towards a National Curriculum," reflected a sign of the times.

"Oh, I've done mine. It's quite straightforward."

I didn't mention that in a larger school Beth didn't have a full-time teaching commitment.

"Oh yes, Jack, just one more thing. Can you collect something for tea on your way home — something simple?"

"Fine," I said and she rang off while I removed the smart four-page questionnaire from its envelope, opened it to page one and sighed deeply. I decided I needed some fresh air.

On the playground Rosie Appleby and Jemima Poole were huddled next to the boiler-house doors. Rosie had been taught a new rhyme by her mother. "It's called a

202

tongue-twister," she explained. "Peter Piper picked a peck of pickled peppers; a peck of pickled peppers Peter Piper picked. If Peter Piper picked a peck of pickled peppers, where's the peck of pickled peppers Peter Piper picked?"

Jemima was so impressed she forgot the bitter cold. "Tell me again," she said eagerly.

Rosie sighed. Tongue-twisters were hard work. She produced a length of string from her pocket. "Why don't we play cat's cradle?"

It was time for school dinner and Shirley Mapplebeck and Doreen Critchley were serving a warming meal of mince and carrots followed by sponge pudding and purple custard.

In the queue Karl Tomkins was pushing and shoving his way to the front.

Mrs Critchley narrowed her eyes in his direction. "Behave, Karl Tomkins."

Karl looked indignant and, as always, he took the words of adults literally. "I am being HAVED!" Then he gave the dinner ladies a dazzling smile.

Mrs Critchley was thrown for a moment, then carried on serving her pudding. "'E'll go far that one," she muttered.

Meanwhile, in the staff-room, Vera opened her *Daily Telegraph*. "Oh dear," she said. "Still no sign of Terry Waite."

The forty-seven-year-old Church of England envoy, Terry Waite, had been kidnapped by an Islamic militia group. He had disappeared on 20 January, eight days after arriving in Beirut in an attempt to negotiate the release of four British hostages, including the journalist John McCarthy.

"It's worrying," said Anne quietly.

"Such a good man," murmured Vera. "I'll ask Joseph to pray for him."

On the other side of the staff-room, huddled near the gas fire, Sally had spent 18p on a *Daily Mirror* that morning. She wasn't particularly interested in the article about Gary Lineker, who had been hailed as the "King of Spanish football" following his Barcelona hat-trick in the 3–2 defeat of Real Madrid. She sighed, however, when she read that a ten-year-old boy had died of AIDS following a contaminated blood transfusion. She replaced the newspaper on the coffee table and thought of her daughter, Grace. Then she walked pensively back to her classroom to prepare for afternoon school while quietly praying there was a heaven.

At the end of lunch break Ruby arrived to clear away the dining tables, but called in to the office in a state of high anxiety. She was bursting with news. Vera was busy at her desk counting the dinner money prior to taking it to the bank.

"Mrs F," said Ruby breathlessly, "you'll never guess."

Vera sat back. "Goodness me, Ruby, come in and sit down — you've been running."

"You'll never guess, Mrs F!"

"What on earth is it?"

"It's that Stan Coe — 'e's in 'ospital."

"Hospital?" said Vera, slightly concerned with her innermost feelings at that moment.

"Ah 'eard it from Peggy in t'chemist's. Word 'as it 'im an' Deirdre 'ad jus' been in 'cause Stan had been bitten on 'is 'and — 'e were after some cream."

"Oh dear."

"But 'ccordin' t'Peggy it were right bad an' swellin' up like there was no t'morrow."

"That sounds serious."

"It mus' be, Mrs F, 'cause she said 'e'd been tekken."

"*Taken?*"

"Yes, to the 'ospital."

"So he was bitten?" asked Vera. "On his *hand*?"

"Yes, by Deirdre's cat, Oscar. That Stan is allus givin' it a kick up its backside when it gets under 'is feet. Then when 'e bent down t'chuck it out it sunk its teeth into 'im an' ran off."

"That must have been painful," said Vera with a little forced sympathy.

"Let's 'ope so," added Ruby without any shred of remorse. "Peggy said 'is 'and swelled twice the size an' 'e were yellin' like a stuffed pig."

"I'm not surprised," said Vera, wincing at the thought. She looked at the clock. "I'll make you some tea while you clear the tables."

"Thanks, Mrs F," said the red-faced Ruby, "you're a saint."

Outside Pratt's garage, a smart racing-green Citroën DS pulled in and Kenny hurried out to serve the driver.

A tall, grey-haired gentleman in a beautifully cut dark grey coat, silk scarf and immaculate collar and tie stepped out and stared across the road at Coe Farm.

"Do you know where Mr Coe might be? I was due to meet him this afternoon."

"Sorry, sir, no idea," said Kenny, "but 'is Land Rover's gone so 'e mus' be out."

"Very well," said the gentleman. "Please fill her up."

He walked round to the passenger seat. Then he picked up a leather briefcase and took out a spiral-bound booklet. He studied it for a few moments, sighed and shook his head.

Kenny watched him drive away. *Posh bloke, posh car*, he thought.

Meanwhile, ten miles away, Stan Coe was sitting in a waiting room at the hospital complaining bitterly to Deirdre.

At afternoon break Sally was on duty and Anne and I were in the staff-room drinking tea as we studied the Yorkshire Purchasing Organization catalogue and the price of squared paper. The chatter from the other side of the coffee table was animated. Marcus and Pat were really excited: our new computer had proved even better than they had hoped.

"The built-in software packages are really special," said Marcus.

"Have you seen them, Anne?" asked Pat.

"There's a spreadsheet," explained Marcus.

Anne smiled but was no wiser.

"And just look at this," enthused Marcus. He pointed to the booklet, which might as well have been written in hieroglyphics as far as I was concerned. "That ADFS feature I told you about is outstanding — you can do so much with it."

"And it's got lots more memory," added Pat for good measure.

Anne and I left them to it and walked back to our classrooms.

"Do you ever feel like a dinosaur, Jack?" she asked.

"I know what you mean," I said. "I think another computer course beckons."

"Or you could simply spend time with Rufus Snodgrass," she said forlornly. "At ten years old he's not far behind Marcus."

"It's a new world," I sighed.

"I'm not sure I want to be part of it," said Anne as she stepped into her classroom, picked up *The Tale of Mrs Tiggy-Winkle* and thanked the Lord for Beatrix Potter.

Up the Morton Road Petula Dudley-Palmer was in her state-of-the-art conservatory and had put aside her needlework. The Ragley & Morton Women's Institute had asked all members to contribute to knitting the largest blanket in the world. It would then be divided into blanket-sized strips and distributed among homeless people.

Petula was keen to do her bit, but now it was time to watch one of her favourite programmes, *The Onedin Line*. Then the telephone rang.

It was John Parsons, a handsome and recently divorced solicitor, with an invitation to join him for afternoon tea in Bettys Tea Rooms in York. They had met at a charity event in St William's College and had struck up a friendship. Petula had been attracted to this tall, engaging and well-educated man. She looked at the clock. The timing was perfect, as she could go on from there to collect her daughters from the Time School. Before donning her favourite dress and fur coat she switched off the television. The sailing saga could wait for another day.

The infants in Anne's and Pat's classes finished school at 3.15p.m., whereas the older children finished at 3.45p.m. This was a cause of concern for Dylan Fazackerly, who had recently moved up to Pat's class. He had to wait in the library area with his mother for half an hour until it was time for his big sister, Madonna, to get out of school. Dylan was a big fan of *Postman Pat* on BBC1 and it was due to start at 3.50p.m., so he was anxious to run home with his friend Cheyenne Blenkinsop to watch the latest episode of their favourite postman and Jess, his lively cat.

When his mother arrived she looked at him in dismay. "Why is it y'get so dirty?"

"'Cause ah'm closer to t'ground than you are, Mam," he replied, quick as a flash.

Mrs Fazackerly pondered this for a moment. *Getting more like his daft father every day*, she thought.

Half an hour later, Mrs Longbottom also arrived, clutching her long-overdue dinner money. She called in to the office to see Vera with Sigourney at her side. "If y'made me a packed lunch, Mam, you wouldn't 'ave t'pay dinner money."

Mrs Longbottom looked at Vera in triumph. "She's not backwards in comin' forwards, is our Sigourney," she said as she turned on her heel and strode out. "In fac', she's that sharp you'd think she'd been in t'knife drawer."

Vera wondered where these sayings came from as she took out her late-dinner-money register.

It was 4.30p.m. and I was at my desk in the school office. I had discovered that Beth was correct: the National Curriculum questionnaire looked formidable but had taken only a few minutes to complete. I sensed it was a token gesture on the part of our local authority, as the big decisions had already been made, and I left it on Vera's desk for posting.

I was about to leave when the telephone rang. It was good news from our builder, Mr Spittall.

"It's all sorted, Mr Sheffield. Planning permission is fine and the quote is as we agreed. We can start at t'end of first week in April when ah've finished my present job."

"That's good news."

"You'll 'ave y'new kitchen an' y'third bedroom wi' facilities by t'summer. It'll look lovely."

"I'll look forward to it, Mr Spittall. Many thanks for the call."

I donned my coat and scarf and ventured out to the High Street. Old Tommy Piercy's butcher's shop seemed a good option for an evening meal.

"A pound of sausages please, Mr Piercy."

"Comin' up, Mr Sheffield," he said. "Yorkshire's finest," he added without a hint of modesty.

"I heard there was some excitement this morning," I said, "concerning Mr Coe."

"Y'right there. Eugene told me all about it when 'e called by. Deirdre was all of a lather an' done up like a dog's dinner like she were seein' someone important. She went an' left 'er 'andbag so ah thought ah'd drop it off on m'rounds."

"What did she say?"

"She weren't there — probably still visitin' 'er brother. Funny thing was, there was a posh feller standin' outside t'farm gate. Looked all agitated at being kept waitin'. So ah told 'im what 'ad 'appened an' 'e drove off, p'lite like." Old Tommy thought for a moment. "'E 'ad a car ah've not seen in a while. Green it were an' foreign-lookin'."

He parcelled up the sausages after adding an extra one for young John.

"Ah 'eard there were some daft story. 'bout Stan wanting t'buy some land in t'village includin' t'cricket field. Ah nearly fell over wi' laughin'. Cricket field, ah ask you — over my dead body, ah said."

"Thank you, Mr Piercy. I'll say goodnight."

"Well, regards t'Mrs Sheffield, an' don't forget t'enjoy t'good times, Mr Sheffield, 'cause they never come back." He chuckled to himself and returned to his chopping bench and a rack of ribs.

Just round the corner beyond the end of the High Street, in Coe Farm, Stan was sitting next to the hearth

210

with a face like thunder. "All 'cause o' your cat," he muttered, looking down at his bandaged hand.

"Y'need t'get some rest, now," advised Deirdre. "Doctor said swelling'll go down in a few days."

"If ah see it again ah'll kill it."

"Oscar didn't mean it, Stan. 'E were jus' agitated."

"Ah'll give 'im summat t'be *agitated* abart. 'E's cost me a lot o' money. M'meeting t'day were important an' ah might 'ave missed m'chance. Ah've spent ages gettin' this deal set up."

"What deal?"

"Never you mind."

For Stan Coe, this day had been a disaster. Schemes, like a eulogy of bitter experience, withered in the wind and crumbled like brittle leaves . . . and all because of a cat. Deirdre had no idea what her brother was talking about and hurried off to the kitchen to make a pot of tea. It was then that Stan took a bulky envelope from the pocket of his oilskin coat and locked it away in his desk.

As I drove past Coe Farm on my way home, above me the North Star shone out brightly and the seven stars of the Plough guided my way. Around me spectral shadows reared and pranced in the swaying branches, a ghostly vision of moonlit confusion.

Suddenly, in the sharp light of my headlamps, a familiar cat leapt across the road and I braked slightly. It disappeared into the hedgerow and I drove on, completely unaware that Oscar's revenge could not have arrived at a better moment.

CHAPTER
TWELVE

Gone Fishing

We received a follow-up document from North Yorkshire County Council requesting headteachers to respond to the possible consequences of the proposed National Curriculum.
Extract from the Ragley & Morton School Logbook:
Friday, 13 March 1987

It was Friday, 13 March and winter no longer held Ragley village in its iron grip. While in the far distance the Hambleton hills appeared bleak and grey against a wind-driven sky, beneath the hard crust of earth new life was stirring. The dark days were becoming a distant memory and spring was just around the corner.

So it was with hope in my heart and a feeling of expectation that I drove along Ragley High Street. That is until I caught sight of Big Dave and Little Malcolm. They were emerging from the Coffee Shop and walking towards their refuse wagon. Big Dave had his arm draped over his cousin's shoulders while Little Malcolm stared disconsolately at the ground. It was a sad scene.

However, it was then I noticed they were both carrying fishing rods.

In the room above the Coffee Shop Nellie and Dorothy were in conversation.

"Listen t'me, Dorothy," said Nellie firmly, "you've got t'shake y'self out o' this. Life goes on an' y'need t'start thinkin' about your Malcolm. 'E's walkin' around like a lost soul."

"Ah don't know what t'say to 'im," said Dorothy forlornly.

Nellie stretched forward and took Dorothy's hand. "But your Malcolm thinks t'world o' you."

"Ah know that deep down," said Dorothy. She fingered her chunky signs-of-the-zodiac bracelet. "But ah jus' feel ah've let ev'rybody down."

"Don't be soft," said Nellie quietly. "It 'appens t'lots o' women, all over t'world . . . an' y'can try again."

"Mebbe so, but ah feel, well . . . *awkward* . . . wi' Malcolm." Dorothy looked up with tears in her eyes. "Y'know what ah'm sayin'. Ah can't relax wi' 'im like ah used to."

Nellie stood up. "Trust me — it'll 'appen when t'time is right."

"D'you think so?"

"Ah do."

Then Nellie took Dorothy's coat from the peg behind the door. "Come on, let's 'ave a treat."

"A treat?"

"Yes, let's go t'Diane's an' book in for gettin' our 'air done. Ah'm certainly due." Nellie looked at her reflection in the mirror. "Flippin' 'eck, ah look like t'wreck o' the 'Esperus."

"'Esper who?" asked a puzzled Dorothy, who had never been acquainted with the American poet Longfellow. Neither did she equate Nellie's familiar saying with the fact that she looked as though she had been sitting on the back of a motorbike in a high wind.

"Never mind, luv," said Nellie. "Jus' wash y'face an' let's go out."

Meanwhile, their husbands had the morning off work, a rarity in their busy lives, and Big Dave wanted to make sure that he and Little Malcolm could have some private time together. So they drove up the Morton Road towards the local canal, where Dave selected a familiar spot and they unloaded, placed their cane baskets on the grassy bank at the side of the canal and sat down. Dave looked anxiously at his best friend. "So . . . 'ow y'feeling, Malc'?"

Little Malcolm sighed and stared forlornly into the slow-moving waters. "Ah'm fed up wi' life," he muttered.

"Mebbe so," replied Big Dave, "but time's a 'ealer . . . so 'ow *y'really* feelin'?"

"Well, *middlin'*, ah s'ppose," said Malcolm. "Not as bad as it was."

For Big Dave this sounded encouraging. "So, y'comin' on then, bit at a time, so t'speak. There's light at t'end of t'tunnel."

There was a long pause.

"Mebbe," said Little Malcolm quietly.

Big Dave looked thoughtfully at his lifelong friend. His diminutive cousin was a proud man, tough as teak, hard as nails. In the tap room of The Royal Oak it was said that Malcolm was so tough, even his spit had muscles. He would want to hide his weakness, but Big Dave knew how to bide his time.

Both men had followed in the footsteps of their respective fathers and carried on the tradition of coarse fishing. This stretch of canal was their favourite spot. A year ago Big Dave had moved upmarket in the fishing world and had purchased a smart eighties Leeda fibreglass rod. In contrast, Little Malcolm had continued with his old-fashioned split-cane rod, which had been his dad's.

They followed a familiar routine, settling down on their old cane hamper boxes on a patch of ground by a copse of trees that would protect them from the stiff breeze. However, these rugged Yorkshiremen were used to an outdoor life and their thick work jackets provided sufficient warmth as they sat on the cold bank of the canal. Big Dave glanced at his cousin and hoped that the solitude of this private space would dull the pain that was etched on Little Malcolm's face. In silence they began to prepare for a morning's fishing.

In the temporary classroom, life was equally trying for our local vicar. Joseph was doing his best to get the children to write their own prayers.

"God is always listening."

"'E wouldn't get a chance in our 'ouse," said Tyler Longbottom. "It's too noisy 'cause m'sister never shuts up."

215

The children were invited to take turns to read out their prayers.

Ben Nobbs, aged seven, stood up first and in a clear voice read, "Dear God, please take care of my mam and my dad and my hamster and my gran. And please take care of yourself because if anything happens to you we're all in trouble."

Joseph nodded in appreciation.

Then it was Tyler Longbottom's turn. "Dear God," he recited, "you don't have to worry about me because I always use the zebra crossing."

The contributions concluded with eight-year-old Rosie Spittlehouse. "Please God, who looks after the world when you are on holiday?" It seemed a logical question, but not necessarily so to the careworn Joseph.

However, there were other concerns in the wider world and we shared these in morning assembly. It was a subdued ending when Joseph invited us all to pray. Our final prayer was for the poor souls who had been on board the Townsend Thoresen roll-on, roll-off ferry, the *Herald of Free Enterprise*. Last Friday it had capsized moments after leaving the Belgian port of Zeebrugge, killing 193 passengers and crew. The bow-door had been left open and its departure from the harbour had catastrophic results. The sea immediately flooded the decks and within minutes she was lying on her side in shallow water. When the children chorused a final "Amen" I noticed that Vera had crept in from the office and was dabbing away a tear with a tiny lace handkerchief.

216

I also noticed that Rosie Spittlehouse kept her eyes closed for a few moments longer than the children around her. I recalled Rosie telling me she missed her late grandmother and always added on a special prayer for her.

Big Dave and Little Malcolm had what they called their *routine*. Fishing followed a pattern they had perfected over the years. They began by mixing ground bait — namely, crumbs of stale bread recently discarded at Prudence Golightly's General Stores — along with a supply of maggots from Timothy Pratt's Hardware Emporium. Then they added water and rolled the sticky mixture into golf-ball-size lumps. With a sure aim, they would throw this appetizing bait upstream to attract the fish.

After attaching their reels with great care, they threaded a mono-filament line through the eyes on their rods. It was a well-practised procedure and Big Dave was pleased that Little Malcolm seemed preoccupied with something other than his turbulent love life.

Finally, they attached a float with lead shot and tied a hook to the line with a blood knot. Then, satisfied all was well, they began to fish. An added bonus for our impecunious bin men was that fishing on the canal was completely free. Also, it was very private. The tow path was completely quiet and, passed only by the occasional dog walker, they settled down in peace to enjoy one of their favourite sports.

Big Dave fixed their keep net to the bank with a stick and propped their landing net against a nearby bush. They would use this to collect fish and transfer them to the keep net. Then, after the obligatory photography session to record their catch, they would return the fish to the canal.

"Jus' minnows and gudgeon so far," remarked Big Dave after the first half hour.

"Remember that roach y'caught, Dave?" asked Little Malcolm with the first hint of enthusiasm. "It weighed one and a half pounds."

"Postie Ted's dad caught one that were nearly four pounds," recalled Big Dave.

The reputation of George Postlethwaite, the one-armed fisherman, was legendary.

Little Malcolm nodded. "Must 'ave been a record."

"This could be your day, Malc'," said Big Dave. "Ah've gorra feeling. In fac', it's time t'start lookin' towards t'future."

"'Ow d'you mean, Dave?"

Dave looked across at his cousin. "Well, Malc', life doesn't 'ave rear-view mirrors."

Little Malcolm stared into the water and gave an imperceptible nod.

Up the Morton Road, Petula Dudley-Palmer was reflecting on her date with John Parsons, her charming new companion. He had asked if they could meet again for lunch at the Dean Court Hotel and she was considering a response. Meanwhile, that morning she had switched on BBC1 shortly after 9a.m. and had enjoyed watching her other favourite man, Robert Kilroy-Silk. He was handsome, confident and, unlike her husband, he didn't look the type to be unfaithful.

It was eleven o'clock and in Sally's class the children were following up a geography lesson with mixed results.

Jeremy Urquhart had written, "In geography we learned that countries surrounded by sea are called islands and the ones without are called incontinents."

Patience Crapper had recorded that "In Scandinavia, the Danish people come from Denmark, Norwegians come from Norway and Lapdancers come from Lapland."

Charlie Cartwright had shared the information that "The closest town to France is Dover. My Aunty Jean went there on a fairy."

While Sally pondered these responses she considered that, although the content left a little to be desired, at least the sentence construction was improving.

Down the High Street, outside the General Stores, Betty Buttle tugged Margery Ackroyd's sleeve and nodded towards Petula Dudley-Palmer, who was driving steadily down the road. "Jus' look at Lady Fancy-knickers," said Betty, "all 'igh an' mighty."

"Hoity-toity," muttered Margery.

"Not normal like you an' me," added Betty for good measure.

"'Ave y'noticed she looks 'appier these days?" asked Margery.

Betty considered this for a moment. "Well she certainly deserves a bit o' 'appiness after the way 'er 'usband's been gallivantin' about."

They stared after the car as it disappeared from view on the York Road.

"An' she's slimmed off a lot recently," observed Margery.

"Mebbe she's givin' 'im a bit of 'is own medicine," speculated Betty.

They both smiled at a secret shared and walked into the village shop.

Walter Popple had got some new socks for his sixth birthday. They were bright yellow and he was very proud of his new image. In the dinner queue he was showing them to our school cook.

"Mrs Mapplebeck, ah've gorra s'prise," he announced.

Shirley smiled down at the little ginger-haired boy with the freckled face.

He stood on one leg and lifted the other. "These are m'birthday socks an' Ted Coggins said they were magic," said the eager little boy.

"Magic?"

"'E said if ah say 'Shazam' one thousand times then y'can fly."

"Fly? Why is that?"

"'Cause it's in Ted's comic book, so it mus' be right."

"Does y'mother know they're magic socks, Walter?" asked Shirley. She was concerned he might try something dangerous.

"Don't know, Mrs Mapplebeck," said Walter.

220

"Best to tell 'er when y'get 'ome."

"Why?" asked Walter.

"'Cause she'll be thrilled."

Walter smiled, received his large helping of rhubarb crumble and was pleased his socks were brighter than the custard.

Next in the queue, Karl Tomkins was pulling faces at Madonna Fazackerly.

"Ah don't want t'see you do that again, Karl Tomkins," warned Mrs Critchley firmly. Her biceps flexed as she lifted the huge jug of custard with effortless ease.

Six-year-old Karl thought about this for a moment and then his little face cheered up. "Well, Miss, can ah do it again if ah pull nicer faces?"

Mrs Critchley didn't have time to reply. There was another immediate problem. Rufus Snodgrass and Barry Stonehouse had been swapping their *Dukes of Hazzard* bubble-gum stickers and had forgotten to pick up their trays.

Sally was in the staff-room, reading her *Daily Mirror* while munching on an oatmeal biscuit. She was still sticking to the "Oxford Diet" from her copy of *The Healthy Heart Diet Book*. However, she was getting tired of muesli, oatmeal and vegetable soup. The freshly baked fruit scones prepared by Shirley in the kitchen looked particularly appetizing and she was the only one not enjoying the treat.

Sally was reading an article about the infamous Cynthia Payne. Last month the fifty-four-year-old had been acquitted on nine charges of controlling prostitutes at her home in south-west London. Finally, after wondering what strange lives other people experienced, Sally put thoughts of organized prostitution to one side, gave in to temptation and picked up a scone.

On the other side of the staff-room Marcus was studying an article concerning Mikhail Gorbachev. The Soviet leader's proposals for arms cuts had been welcomed with "cautious optimism" by Prime Minister Margaret Thatcher and the Foreign Secretary, Sir Geoffrey Howe, had also endorsed the initiative, although Marcus sensed it was through gritted teeth and he shook his head over the British government's disappointing response.

He decided not to share this snippet of news with Vera whose politics differed widely from his own. The penny had dropped last month when he saw Vera cutting out a photograph of her political heroine to add to her collection of the achievements of the venerable Margaret. Recently, the Prime Minister had visited the Centaur Clothes factory in Leeds and had attempted to machine a pocket lining. When Vera had exclaimed that Margaret's achievements knew no bounds, Marcus had volunteered to do an extra duty on the frozen waste of the school playground — it seemed the best place for a closet socialist.

After Ruby had put away the dining tables she walked back down the drive, where George Dainty was waiting for her.

"'Ello, George, you're a friendly face on a cold day."

"There were summat on m'mind."

"What's that?"

"Well, ah were thinkin' o' goin' somewhere special for our 'oneymoon."

"That's nice," said Ruby. "Y'mean like Scarborough?"

"Ah were thinkin' a bit further afield."

Ruby looked puzzled. "What, y'mean Whitby?"

"Further than that," said George with a smile.

"But there's nowt further than that," said Ruby. "After that it's jus' sea."

"Ah were thinkin' o' tekkin' you out o' Yorkshire," said George quietly.

"Out o' Yorkshire!" exclaimed Ruby. "But why?"

"Well, there's loads o' wonderful places out there in t'big wide world."

"But not like Yorkshire," reasoned Ruby. "M'mother used t'say we've got ev'rything y'could ask for i' Yorkshire."

They were walking across the village green and George put his arm around her shoulders. He stopped under the branches of the weeping willow that swayed gently in the breeze. "Ah wanted t'show you where ah've been all these years, Ruby. Ah'd like you t'see m'fish-an'-chip shop."

"But that's in Spain!"

"That's right, in Alicante. That's where m'shop T'Codfather were."

"But won't it be 'xpensive, George?"

"Mebbe a bit, Ruby, an' ah don't approve o' wastin' m'brass. It were too 'ard t'come by . . . but you are t'light o' my life an' whatever y'fancy y'can 'ave."

223

Ruby looked down at her work-red hands and sighed. No one had ever spoken to her like this before. "'Ow would we get there?"

"On a plane," said George.

"A *plane*?"

"It'll be excitin'," said George, "an' ah'll be sat nex' t'you."

Ruby took a deep breath. "Oh 'eck," she muttered.

There was a problem she would have to keep to herself.

Little Malcolm was thrilled. It was the finest catch he had ever made and he looked in admiration at a magnificent bronze-coloured bream weighing almost three pounds. A shoal had been attracted by his carefully placed ground bait. Little Malcolm had used his tried and tested trick of pinching a flake of bread between finger and thumb and adding it to his hook. Subsequently, Big Dave had taken a photograph of Little Malcolm, who had been declared champion fisherman for the day.

They sat back for a final mug of tea before packing up to return to work. Big Dave picked his moment. "'Ow long 'ave we been friends?"

Little Malcolm stared once again into the shimmering surface of the canal. "Long as ah can remember — since we were kids."

"An' we've never 'ad a cross word."

Little Malcolm nodded. "S'ppose so, Dave, never been any cause."

"Well, we might be 'avin' one now," said Big Dave firmly.

Little Malcolm looked up at his giant cousin in surprise. "'Ow come, Dave?"

The time had arrived. He needed to break the chains of his pain. They were more than cousins — they were joined together like brothers and Little Malcolm was a mirror of his soul. "It's your Dorothy," said Big Dave. "She needs you now more than ever."

Little Malcolm's body was rigid and, as he stared at the flowing water, in an instant the colour drained from his ruddy cheeks and he became as pale as death, his eyes sunken shadows. Finally he spoke. "But ah don't know what t'do, Dave — ah don't know what t'say."

"Mebbe y'don't 'ave t'say owt . . . mebbe y'jus' 'ave to 'old 'er."

It was then that Big Dave put his arm around Little Malcolm's shoulders, while in the distance only the keening cries of rooks in their high elms disturbed their cocoon of silence.

In Diane's Hair Salon Nellie and Dorothy were taking turns under the hair dryer while they waited for Diane to return from the General Stores after running out of cigarettes.

Nellie was flicking through a magazine and reading Claire Rayner's agony aunt page. It described a recipe for a healthy life. "It sez 'ere y'mus' allus be true t'your partner," said Nellie. "Ah'd never be unfaithful t'my Dave."

225

There was a long pause. Dorothy was reading her Starscope.

"An' me neither wi' my Malcolm," she echoed.

Dorothy was beginning to feel a little better by the time they returned to her room above the Coffee Shop.

Nellie switched on the television and they watched *The Liver Birds*, followed by *Knots Landing*. Chips was very upset, as his love life was becoming complicated. "Ah know 'ow 'e feels," sympathized Dorothy.

Nellie had an idea. "Why don't we 'ave a fancy tea t'night when Dave an' Malcolm come back? Y'know, check with Nora an' mek a night of it."

"OK, Nellie, good idea," said Dorothy, brightening up. "Nora's jus' got some posh buns wi' that desecrated coconut."

Nellie smiled. "We'll 'ave them, an' ah've gorra recipe."

Downstairs Anita Cuthbertson and Claire Bradshaw were listening to Boy George singing "Everything I Own" as they browsed through an old copy of *Smash Hits* magazine. Last month at the BPI Awards (which two years later would become the Brits in Grosvenor House, Dire Straits had won the best album award for *Brothers In Arms*, Kate Bush had been voted best female singer and Peter Gabriel was the winner of the male category. The best soundtrack was the theme from *Top Gun*.

However, both girls looked in alarm at the news that AIDS was in the headlines once again. Last month

Edwina Currie had announced that "Good Christians won't get AIDS", and the two young women were puzzled at the connection.

At the end of school Karl Tomkins was walking down the drive towards the gate with Madonna Fazackerly. Mrs Tomkins was waiting for him by the gate with her fifteen-month-old daughter, Kylie, asleep in her pushchair while her dog, Flossie, cocked its leg against one of the horse chestnut trees.

"Ah like your dog, Karl," said Madonna.

"It's a French poodle," said Karl. "M'mam says it's a *posh* dog."

"We've gorra 'amster," volunteered Madonna.

"A 'amster?"

"Yes," said Madonna firmly. "It's a *posh* mouse."

Madonna was taking after her mother in always making sure she came out on top in any conversation.

I decided to tackle the document from County Hall sooner rather than later. Kenneth Baker's proposed National Curriculum was certainly going to change our lives. If the Conservatives won the next election there was no doubt his ideas would be implemented and a curriculum devised by the government would be introduced. Reforms would be far-reaching, new attainment targets would become the norm and there was even a section concerning how teachers' pay might be affected.

I responded as best as I could, emphasizing that I hoped we could be permitted to keep the strengths of our current curriculum. Our children were encouraged to love learning and we were blessed with a fund of opportunities for first-hand experience in our little corner of the North Yorkshire countryside.

I quoted the old Chinese proverb, "I hear and I forget. I see and I remember. I do and I understand." It was perhaps a frivolous footnote to the document but, nevertheless, it was heartfelt and I hoped someone out there might be listening.

It was just after six o'clock when Little Malcolm walked to Ronnie's bench and sat down. The sun had just set over the vast plain of York and the sky was turning from pink to purple as darkness gradually fell.

He was lost in private thoughts when suddenly Dorothy appeared, wrapped up warm in her best winter anorak with the furry collar. Malcolm smiled: this was a good sign. Dorothy was wearing her favourite Wonder Woman boots and she usually wore those when she was in a good mood.

"'Ow's it gone?" she asked quietly.

"Good," replied Little Malcolm.

"Did y'catch any fish?"

Little Malcolm nodded. "Two big uns."

"Where are they?"

"We chucked 'em back."

"That's kind," said Dorothy.

Little Malcolm decided not to explain the customs of coarse fishing and merely nodded.

Dorothy moved a little closer and rested her head on his shoulder. "So what do you think, Malc'?" she asked in a low voice.

"'Ow d'you mean?"

"Are we gonna be all right?"

Malcolm sighed. "Course we are."

"Are y'sure?"

Malcolm held her tightly. "We'll be fine — 'cause ah love you . . . allus will."

It was getting dark when I left for home and saw Little Malcolm and Dorothy getting up from Ronnie's bench and making their way back to the Coffee Shop. They were holding hands.

Under a pale crescent moon and the cold stars, I drove home in silence and only the mournful cry of a barn owl disturbed my reverie.

In the tap room of The Royal Oak Duggie Smith was sitting with Shane and Clint Ramsbottom. Clint was pleased with his new look, wearing his baggy "parachute pants" and a collection of bright pink bangles on his wrist. It also included his new state-of-the-art Air Jordan sports shoes and just a touch of electric-blue mascara. Thanks to his home-perm kit and crimpers, his hair had moved on from a David Bowie look towards something even more artistic.

In contrast, Shane was wearing his acid-washed jeans, Doc Marten boots and his favourite Guns n' Roses T-shirt. In his *Smash Hits* magazine it had described the band as the most dangerous in the world and they were famous for "hedonistic rebelliousness". Shane wondered what that might be, but whatever it was it sounded good.

Duggie was trying to drown his sorrows. "She just up an' left," he said mournfully.

His woman-friend, Tina, had decided to seek pastures new.

"So where's she gone?" asked Shane.

"She's flown t'nest," lamented Duggie. "Gone to live wi' an ice-cream man in Walsall."

"Bloody 'ell!" exclaimed Clint. "Why would she want t'go t'Poland?"

"Not Warsaw, y'soft ha'porth," said Duggie. "It's Walsall in t'Midlands, near Birmingham."

"That meks more sense," said Shane, nodding knowingly, although his geography was no better than his brother's. "An' they prob'bly don't sell ice cream in Poland."

Clint decided it didn't seem a good idea to pursue the sale of ice cream in the capital of Poland with his psychopath brother. "D'you want another pint?" he offered.

That evening above the Coffee Shop Nora and Nellie were making a special night of it for Little Malcolm and Dorothy. They had worked hard to prepare a special buffet from a recipe in an *Ideal Home* magazine they had borrowed from Diane in the Hair Salon. It featured a Tropical Turkey Salad with mandarin segments, tinned peaches, peanuts, mayonnaise, glacé cherries plus a tin of pineapple chunks. They mixed it in a bowl and served it on top of a plate of green lettuce.

Although Big Dave looked upon it in puzzled wonderment, as it was usually egg and chips on

Fridays, they all agreed it was a treat. Best of all was the sweet course: a sliced Swiss roll drenched in sherry and served with fresh pears, tinned custard, kiwi fruit and topped with grated chocolate.

"What we celebratin'?" asked Big Dave.

Nellie smiled at Dorothy, raised her glass of Blue Nun and said simply, "Friends and family."

And a new beginning, thought Nora.

Shortly after eight o'clock they all settled down, cosy and warm, with a hot drink and a large tin of Fox's Speciality Chocolate & Creams Assortment while Nora switched on the latest episode of *Dynasty*. Together they followed the plot of Blake Carrington seeking financial backing for a natural-gas project while Joan Collins as Alexis Carrington strutted around with shoulders that resembled an American quarterback's.

It was then that Dorothy leaned over and kissed Little Malcolm gently on his stubbly face.

Nellie winked at Nora while Big Dave smiled and supped his tea. *Things are back to normal*, he thought.

And so it was that on that cold March evening, beneath the endless sky and under a blizzard of stars, both Dorothy and Little Malcolm understood the meaning of unconditional love.

CHAPTER
THIRTEEN

Knowing Me, Knowing You

End of term reading tests were completed. School closed today for the Easter holiday with 134 children on roll. The PTA supported this evening's social event in the village hall.
Extract from the Ragley & Morton School Logbook:
Friday, 10 April 1987

It was early morning on Friday, 10 April and Beth and I were on our driveway preparing to leave for the last day of the spring term. Around us the hedgerows were bursting into life and, in the distant fields, tiny lambs tottered on uncertain legs as they took their first steps. There was new life in the winter trees, while yellow petals of forsythia sparkled in the pale sunshine. The long dark days of log fires and bitter winds were over and spring had arrived in all its glory.

Beth and I stood by our gate and looked back at our home.

"Exciting times," she said.

I smiled. "It's going to be huge."

During the last week building work had begun on Bilbo Cottage. Mr Spittall and two of his labourers had arrived early and were digging out the foundations for our extension. A skip was on the road outside and they were filling it rapidly. Beth had put a spare kettle, a packet of teabags and a box of digestive biscuits on the workbench in my garden shed so they had some welcome refreshment.

"There'll be lots of room for my parents now," she said.

"And my mother and Aunt May . . . and other visitors," I added.

She squeezed my arm and kissed me on the cheek before climbing into her car. She wound down her driver's window as she prepared to set off. "Also — maybe a little friend for John one day," she called out with a mischievous smile.

In a burst of acceleration she was gone and I stood there for a moment taking in the import of her comment. My wife never failed to intrigue me. I had realized long ago that, while I would never understand women, I was certainly getting to *know* Beth a little more as the years went by.

It was still on my mind as I drove away, followed almost immediately by Mrs Roberts and John William. The builders gave us a friendly wave. We had enrolled John in a new, larger nursery in Easington and Beth had relaxed after we had met the staff. They were caring and supportive, while our energetic son clearly enjoyed the games, songs and activities. It had proved to be a good arrangement and Mrs Roberts was always on hand in case of an emergency. However, saying goodbye to our son each morning always tugged at the heartstrings and we both hoped the time we spent with him at weekends and school holidays in some way made up for our absence during this critical time in his development. Meanwhile, John seemed to take it all in his stride and was emerging as a happy, contented, gregarious and voluble little boy. As I drove towards Ragley I began to wonder if he might have a little brother or sister one day.

The landscape rushed by and I stared out of the window. A slow dawn had arrived and behind the tattered clouds the distant hills were rimed with a line of molten fire. It was on the outskirts of Ragley that the sky cleared. Then the rays of light of a new day raced across the land, casting sharp shadows over the plain of York and bathing this tiny corner of "God's Own Country" in spring sunshine. Suddenly, as I turned into the High Street, a pheasant with flapping wings and a familiar harsh, shrieking cry shattered my train of thought, and I turned my attention to the busy day that lay ahead. There were reading tests to complete, report books to go out to parents and arrangements for the Easter holiday and beyond.

In the school office Vera was dusting the frame of a beautiful watercolour painting that hung on the wall behind my desk. It had been painted five years ago by a local artist, Mary Attersthwaite, and it captured an April morning just like today with the horse chestnut trees outside school bursting into life and birds flying above our distinctive bell tower.

"Good morning, Mr Sheffield," said Vera. "A lovely morning."

"And a busy day ahead," I replied.

"Very true, and Joyce Davenport has already been in to confirm the collection of our crockery for this evening's event."

The PTA had joined with the Village Hall Social Committee to arrange a "70s Gala Night" and it had captured the imagination of the village, with one or two exceptions.

"It promises to be a lively evening."

"Not really my sort of music, Mr Sheffield, but it's important to demonstrate support," said Vera pointedly as she walked out to deliver a set of report books to Class 3.

Joseph had arrived and was striding towards the entrance hall with a new feeling of anticipation. The harsh days of winter were over. In the vicarage garden the arrowheads of daffodils were appearing in the bare hedgerows, while primroses splashed their colour on the grassy banks. Early-morning sunshine washed over his stooping figure and he smiled at Ruby, who was putting a few crumbs on the bird table.

"G'mornin', Mr Evans," she said.

"And good morning to you, Ruby, on this fine day. I've just passed Mr Dainty in the High Street and he looks as though he is walking on air. I imagine this is a wonderful time for you."

Ruby's engagement had been the talk of the village since Christmas and everyone was waiting for news of the proposed wedding, but it had not been forthcoming.

"That's good to 'ear," said Ruby cautiously.

"Easter is a time of new life," enthused Joseph, "and this is *your* time. You're like a beautiful butterfly emerging from a chrysalis."

"A what, vicar?" asked a puzzled Ruby.

"Never mind," said Joseph. "Just take it that an exciting future awaits."

Feeling he had imparted sufficient *joie de vivre*, he hurried to Sally's class to discuss music for the Easter services at St Mary's.

It was a few minutes later that Ruby tapped on the office door.

"Hello, Ruby," said Vera and immediately saw the concern on her friend's face. "Come in and sit down."

Ruby sighed deeply, shut the door and sat down in the visitor's chair.

"So, what's troubling you?"

Ruby was wringing her chamois leather as if her life depended on it. "This an' that," she said hesitantly.

"You can tell me," said Vera quietly.

Ruby nodded. "You're allus a good listener, Mrs F, an' in fac' y'brother were jus' tryin' t'be kind t'me an' sayin' nice things."

"That's lovely. What did he have to say?"

"It were about me bein' a butterfly 'mergin' from a clitoris . . . or summat."

"Oh, I see," said Vera . . . and wished she didn't.

"Y'see, ah've kept it to m'self, an' ah don't know what t'do."

Vera leaned forward. "Just say it, Ruby."

Ruby took a deep breath and brushed her chestnut curls from her eyes. "It's the 'oneymoon, Mrs F."

"Honeymoon?"

"Yes, 'e says 'e wants me t'explore 'is foreign parts."

"Foreign parts?"

"Yes, Mrs F," said Ruby. "'E wants me t'see 'is fish shop."

"In Spain?"

"Yes, in that Alicante place where 'e used t'live."

"Well, that sounds very exciting, Ruby."

"Mebbe so, but ah'm *frightened*."

"Oh dear, Ruby — why?"

"*Flyin'*, Mrs F — goin' up in a plane. Ah've never done that. In fac', ah've never been out o' Yorkshire."

Vera sighed and thought carefully about her response. "Ruby, you need to tell him. George needs to know how you feel. He's a considerate man and would never want to do anything that would cause you any upset."

"Thank you, Mrs F." Ruby returned her chamois leather to the pocket of her apron. "Ah'll 'ave t'pick m'moment."

"Perhaps at the village hall tonight."

Ruby got up to leave but paused by the office door. "Y'know . . . ah still think about my Ronnie when we were young. We used to lie back, look up at t'sky an' count t'stars," and she walked out and closed the door.

I used to count the stars as well, thought Vera. She recalled the words of her father long ago: "We all have our time in the light before our departure towards an unknown eternity."

Vera resolved she must help Ruby — and the time was now. She would have a word in George Dainty's ear.

★   ★   ★

After break the children in my class completed their project folders in preparation for taking them home to show their parents.

Last week Sally and I had taken Classes 4 and 5 to Eden Camp, a museum near the market town of Malton. It was part of our joint Second World War European history project and had proved an informative experience for the children. The camp had been open for only a few weeks and we were one of the first school parties to visit.

It had begun with an eventful journey. The April sunshine had reflected brightly on the windows of William Featherstone's cream-and-green Reliance coach and the children were excited as they clambered aboard. Although many people in Ragley thought it now belonged in a motor museum, William was proud of his ancient bus. With old-fashioned charm he welcomed each passenger and doffed his peaked cap. In his neatly ironed brown bus driver's jacket, white shirt and ex-regimental tie, he certainly looked the part.

It was no empty gesture that the words "You Can Rely on Reliance" had been painted in bright red letters under the rear window. In the midst of waving mothers, and to the accompaniment of Scargill the Yorkshire terrier's frantic barking, we had set off on the Easington Road and proceeded at a sedate pace through the byways of North Yorkshire towards Malton.

"Will there be any Germans there, sir?" asked an eager Rufus Snodgrass, clearly anticipating the adventure ahead.

"There may be, Rufus," I said, "but they will probably be *visitors* just like us."

Rufus considered this for a moment and nodded, but appeared unconvinced.

It proved to be a memorable visit. The guide explained that in 1942 the plot of land had been requisitioned by the War Office to build a camp for German and Italian prisoners of war captured from the battlefields of Africa and Europe. However, recently the collection of huts had been expertly equipped to tell the story of the Second World War through the use of sights, sounds and smells.

We had followed this up back in school with a special visitor. Seventy-five-year-old Albert Jenkins had called in to share his wartime experiences. Dressed in a familiar three-piece suit, complete with watch chain, Albert had told an enthralled audience how he had attended the village school shortly after the First World War. He spoke of a bygone age over sixty years ago when he had been taken out of school to become a fire tender worker for the railway in York.

"What's that, sir?" asked Tom Burgess.

"It was a sort of chimney sweep for the railways and I was not much older than you," explained Albert with a smile.

Charlie Cartwright raised his hand. "Ah'd like t'be a chimney sweep, sir."

Albert gave a wry smile. "It wasn't a pleasant job," he said. "I had to climb inside the firebox and clean it out with my bare hands and an old brush, while all the time I was surrounded by dangerous asbestos. My ambition was to become a train driver and twenty-six years later I fulfilled my ambition."

Albert had brought with him lots of old photographs of the giant steam engines and his time in the Army. He also recounted his memories of listening to the radio and recalled the nightly adventures of Dick Barton, Special Agent, on the BBC's Light Programme. Remarkably, he was one of fifteen million listeners and the children were puzzled why so many people would want to listen to the radio.

There were many questions, and it was only after he had left that Vera told us Albert was a very sick man. For many months he had walked with a serious illness as his constant companion.

That had been a week ago and now it was time for our final assembly of the spring term. The children sat attentively while Joseph told the familiar Easter story, then went on to share another Bible story from St John's Gospel concerning a man named Nicodemus who was keen to ask questions.

"Don't be afraid to ask a question," said Joseph, "because then you will reach an understanding." I saw Vera looking at her brother thoughtfully and wondered what was on her mind.

There was a surprise at the end when, instead of the Lord's Prayer, Joseph invited Marcus to come out to the front to recite a prayer in Latin from his old college. Marcus explained that Latin was an old Roman language relating to its people and culture. He had written the translation on an acetate and he placed it on

240

our overhead projector and encouraged the children to follow it carefully. It read:

Let all thy works give thanks to thee, O Lord, and let thy saints bless thee. We give thanks to thee, almighty God, for all thy goodness, who livest and reignest as God for ever and ever. Amen.

Then he spoke clearly and recited the prayer, which he knew from memory:

"Confiteantur tibi, Domine, omnia opera tua,
et sancti tui benedicant te.
Agimus tibi gratias, omnipotens Deus,
pro universis beneficiis tuis,
Qui vivis et regnas Deus per omnia saecula
saeculorum. Amen."

"Well, that's a first," said Anne with a smile as we returned to our classrooms.

At morning break Sally was on duty and, although she enjoyed the sunshine and fresh air while supervising the children, her mind was on something else. She had applied to be one of the five hundred volunteers required for a sponsored slim on the *That's Life!* television programme. The intention was to test different diets over a six-week period and Sally wondered if this would be the answer to her expanding waistline.

During the lunch break Marcus expressed his disappointment that Oxford had beaten Cambridge in last month's University Boat Race, particularly as Cambridge had been the favourites.

Marcus described at great length his passion for the annual race on the River Thames from Putney to Mortlake, a course of over four miles. He had expected a Cambridge victory, particularly after a so-called "mutiny" among the Oxford crew. However, Oxford won by four lengths in spite of the American members of their crew being replaced following a dispute with their coach, Dan Topolski.

Vera considered the Boat Race to be a triumph for clean-living young sportsmen and Marcus wisely kept to himself that the race was sponsored by Beefeater Gin.

"What are you doing over the holiday?" asked Sally.

Marcus smiled. "I'm spending Easter in Cambridge with my parents, so if any of you want to meet up that would be good. I could offer a tour of Emmanuel College if you wish."

"I may take you up on that," I said. "We'll be visiting Beth's parents in Hampshire, so we could call in on the way."

"That's fine, Jack," he said, "and I'm also meeting up with Fiona."

Suddenly the ladies in the staff-room all sat up quickly. "Fiona?" asked Sally and Pat in unison.

Marcus blushed slightly. "Yes, Fiona Beckwith — we were at uni together and she's . . . well, a friend."

The ladies shared unspoken thoughts, smiled and returned to their cups of tea.

Just before the bell for afternoon school a group of ladies from the Village Hall Social Committee called in to borrow our crockery and Baby Burco boiler for that evening's Gala Night. Shirley and Doreen appeared from the kitchen to give them a hand, while Ruby seemed to be directing operations.

"Word 'as it," said Doreen, "that your Duggie is goin' as John Travolta wi' 'is new girlfriend, that Sonia from t'shoe shop."

"New girlfriend!" exclaimed Ruby. "Bloomin' 'eck. 'Ere we go again."

After lunch I completed the last of my reading tests. The final reader was George Frith, who surprised me by reading "oblivion", "scintillate", "satirical", "sabre" and "beguile" on the Schonell Graded Word Recognition Test to give him a reading age two years above his chronological age.

He smiled when I praised him.

"Ah love reading, sir," he said. "It takes you into another world." He had just begun to read *The Queen's Brooch*, an excellent historical novel by Henry Treece, and had become engrossed in the battles of Queen Boudicca. I reflected that he had come a long way since that snowy morning back in January. Also, George and Barry Stonehouse had become inseparable friends and it was good to see both boys growing in confidence.

It was George who made an announcement shortly after two o'clock. "Sir, me an Barry were lookin' in t'village pond this morning and it's teeming wi' life."

"Can we go an' see it, Mr Sheffield?" shouted out Stuart Ormroyd.

I glanced at my watch. On occasions, it seemed to be a good idea to leave the planned timetable, particularly on the last afternoon of term.

"Come on then," I agreed. "Get your coats on."

The sun shone from a powder-blue sky as we walked out to the village green and the scent of wallflowers was refreshing after the overnight rain. The new leaves on the weeping willow weighed down the graceful branches and, on the far side of the pond in front of The Royal Oak, Albert Jenkins was sitting on a bench and feeding the ducks.

We gathered around the edge of the pond and soon there were excited discoveries as the children spotted lots of tiny creatures, including water boatmen balancing precariously on the surface tension of the still water.

"It's like *their* world in *our* world," said Michelle Gawthorpe.

When it was time for afternoon break we returned to school and Albert walked beside me. He had always maintained his great interest in our school and his wisdom and support were sorely missed on the governing body.

"Takes me back," he said as he watched the children full of animated chatter after their experience by the pond.

"Schooldays," I mused, "the happiest days of your life."

244

Albert smiled. "That's what R. C. Sheriff said a long time ago." I remembered that Albert was one of the best-read scholars in Ragley.

"I'm not familiar with the name."

"He was a captain in the First World War and he wrote successful plays and award-winning screenplays — a remarkable man. I recall that was one of his quotes."

"He was right," I said, "but just occasionally it's a rocky road."

Albert wasn't regarded as the shrewdest man in the village without reason. "You mean Stan Coe," he said quietly.

I nodded.

"Yes, Jack, keep your eye out for him. There's rumours in the village among those in the know. I'll report back when I have more information. In the meantime, watch your back."

"Thanks, Albert."

"It is excellent to have a giant's strength; but it is tyrannous to use it like a giant," he quoted. Albert loved his Shakespeare.

"*Measure for Measure*," I murmured with some hesitation.

Albert nodded. "If it's the last thing I do I'll make sure that dreadful man doesn't spoil this village for ever."

The children were excited when the bell rang for the end of school. I walked out with them and opened the giant oak door.

"Guess what, sir," said an enthusiastic George Frith. "We saw a robin's nest, sir. All mossy it was an' there were eggs. Four white uns, sir, wi' pink spots."

"But we never touched 'em, sir," added Barry Stonehouse.

I found myself reminiscing as I watched them scamper down the worn stone steps towards the freedom of a school holiday. The river of life had pattered down these steps for more than a century. So many children . . . so many faces. It was a time for expectation and a different sort of eggs — chocolate ones.

At seven o'clock Natasha Smith arrived to look after John while Beth stood in the hallway admiring her new coat. It was a fully lined grey trenchcoat, double-breasted and with button-down epaulettes. It stretched down to her calves and looked terrific.

I put my arms around her waist and stared at her reflection in the mirror. "The picture of the modern woman," I said and she smiled up at me.

The village hall was packed by the time we arrived. Don Bradshaw had set up a bar and Clint Ramsbottom, dressed as Michael Jackson, was disc jockey for the evening. Clint's "Disco Experience" comprised three coloured light bulbs and a scratchy record deck, but as he was working for nothing we couldn't complain.

He had a good record collection and suddenly we were transported back to the previous decade. Clint opened up with Pink Floyd's "Another Brick in the Wall", followed by Queen's "Bohemian Rhapsody",

Blondie's "Heart of Glass" and "Sultans of Swing" by Dire Straits.

The ladies of the Social Committee, with reinforcements from the Women's Institute, had prepared a refreshments table. They were discussing the treats displayed inside Jane Asher's *Quick Party Cakes*, a recent purchase from her book club by Petula Dudley-Palmer, which everyone agreed was 75p well spent.

The dancing was energetic to say the least. Duggie Smith and his new partner, Sonia from the shoe shop in Easington, were doing their impression of Olivia Newton-John and John Travolta in *Grease*, while Old Tommy Piercy watched in amazement from the trestle-table bar at the back of the hall. Ruby was pleased that Sonia was comfortably twenty years younger than Duggie's previous partner and hoped he was returning to the straight and narrow.

Mrs Ricketts, predictably, had come as Suzi Quatro and was dancing with her daughter, Suzi-Quatro, who had come as herself. The liveliest group was undoubtedly Big Dave, Nellie, Little Malcolm and Dorothy. They had hired Abba outfits and Dorothy in particular was proud of her Agnetha Fältskog hair-do.

Betty Buttle was sitting with her husband, Harry. "They look 'appy again," she said. "Dorothy's been through a tough time."

Harry, who had come as Alice Cooper, shook his head. "Ah 'adn't noticed."

"That's t'trouble wi' you, y'great lump, y'never do." Harry's wig had made him too hot and Betty used it to wipe beer spillage from their table top. "Men," she muttered. "No idea."

Beth and I hadn't considered fancy dress, but many people had found outfits for the occasion. Deke Ramsbottom picked up the microphone to announce that Sheila from The Royal Oak had donated prizes for the best costumes. Kenny Kershaw and Claire Bradshaw were thrilled to come first in their Luke Skywalker and Princess Leia outfits and received a bottle of Tia Maria coffee liqueur.

Several runners-up were announced, including Shane Ramsbottom, who had dug out his dad's mothballed Teddy-boy outfit and arrived as a member of Showaddywaddy, and Old Tommy Piercy, who had put on his best suit, stuck his familiar pipe in his mouth and arrived as Harold Wilson. In contrast, Vera was not pleased to receive applause as the final runner-up for her Margaret Thatcher outfit, especially as she was wearing her normal clothes.

The evening was a success, and Big Dave had to return to The Royal Oak for a second barrel of Chestnut Mild. Meanwhile, in the far corner of the hall, George and Ruby were deep in conversation.

"Summat's up," said George, looking concerned. "Mrs F 'as said we need t'talk."

Ruby shook her head. "M'mother allus said, 'There'll be tears afore bedtime.' So ah don't want no argy-bargy, George."

George took her hand in his. "There'll never be owt like that, Ruby. So, tell me, why are y'frettin'?"

"Ah'm not sure ah can say."

"Y'can tell me."

"You'll think ah'm daft."

"Ah would never think that."

Ruby took a deep breath. "Well . . . it's flyin' — ah'm scared o' flyin'."

George looked relieved. It was exactly as Mrs Forbes-Kitchener had said. "Is that all? Well, we can soon sort that."

"Ah'm sorry, George, ah were jus' a bit nervous."

"No, it were my fault," said George. "Ah were rushin' things. So — where would y'like t'go?"

Clint put "Message In a Bottle" by The Police on the turntable and Ruby looked up into the disco light. "Once, when ah were a young girl, we went on a lovely 'oliday."

"And where were that — where did y'go?"

"Whitby, George — it were Whitby."

The evening was drawing to a close and Abba's 1976 hit "Knowing Me, Knowing You" was on the turntable. Clint turned up the volume.

"This record is about the break-up of a relationship, Jack," said Beth.

"I hope that's not the case with Ruby," I said. "She was upset today."

"Whatever the problem is, at least they're discussing it," she replied pointedly. "Perhaps that's what we need to do."

"What do you mean?"

"*Know each other* a little more."

"I don't understand."

Beth smiled. "That's part of your charm, Jack. You never did."

I held her close and felt the whisper of skin beneath her silk blouse. The scent of her perfume, Rive Gauche by Yves Saint Laurent, filled my senses.

She gently stroked my lapels and looked up at me expectantly.

"What is it?" I asked.

"Don't you know?"

Then she stretched up and kissed me on the lips, gossamer-soft yet firm with the need of lovers.

CHAPTER
FOURTEEN

Cambridge Blues

The headteacher checked doors and windows for security and collected mail. Mrs Grainger and Mrs Pringle will take charge of the school choir during the Easter Sunday service at St Mary's Church, as the headteacher is visiting Hampshire.
Extract from the Ragley & Morton School Logbook:
Wednesday, 15 April 1987.

Hand in hand we stood to admire this city of ancient beauty. Our journey to Cambridge had been a release for us both.

It was just the two of us, as Beth's parents had spent a short holiday at Bilbo Cottage prior to returning to their home in Hampshire with our son, John. He was to spend a few days with his grandparents and seemed excited by the prospect when he waved goodbye. On Wednesday morning, 15 April, I had collected mail from the school and checked it for security prior to packing for our journey south.

Bright and early on Maundy Thursday we had departed for a one-night break in one of England's finest cities, with its stunning architecture of chapels,

251

courtyards and gardens. After checking into a small hotel on Trumpington Street, it was early afternoon when we set off in the sunshine for the market place in the heart of the city. We had arranged to meet Marcus Potts in his favourite coffee shop. What we didn't expect was the beautiful young woman sitting by his side.

Marcus stood up and waved, and we made our way through the crowds of ambling tourists to his table. He looked relaxed in an old blue cord suit. A slim young woman, shorter than Marcus, was standing beside him. She had long fair hair and was casually dressed in blue jeans and a T-shirt that professed "Peace & Love".

"This is Fiona," said Marcus with a shy smile.

It was clear from his demeanour that he was "smitten", as Ruby would say, while Fiona appeared oblivious to his attention. Although quite tiny, we soon realized she had a huge personality. She waved now to the waitress, who nodded in recognition and four coffees arrived almost as we took our seats.

"I've heard so much about you," she said, "and thanks for believing in Potty. It was the opportunity he had been looking for."

"Potty?" I enquired. Fiona grinned, Marcus blushed profusely and Beth gave me a hard stare.

"My nickname at uni, I'm afraid," murmured Marcus.

Introductions over, we relaxed, ate our sandwiches, sipped our coffee and learned much about this self-assured young woman. Like Marcus, she had completed her studies at Emmanuel College and had moved on to a business degree at Harvard in America. She had flown home for the Easter holiday to spend time with her father, a professor at King's College. Ten years ago her mother had died of cancer and she had become the dominant female in the household. For a time Fiona waxed lyrical about her city of revolutionary thinkers such as Isaac Newton and Charles Darwin. Then, over a second coffee, she regaled us with stories of Frank Whittle's first jet engine and Ernest Rutherford splitting the atom. All the while Marcus hung on her every word and Beth gave me a knowing, wide-eyed stare. I had seen a new side to our recently appointed teacher. He was clearly in love and his heartache was palpable.

"It's a lovely day," said the vivacious Fiona. "Shall we explore?"

Marcus insisted on paying for our refreshments and Fiona slipped on a skimpy leather jacket. We strolled towards St Andrew's Street and into Emmanuel College. Although we were only a few paces from the vibrant city centre, we entered a world of peace among beautiful trees, extensive lawns and medieval buildings.

Immediately, Fiona took the lead. "We have a slightly incongruous chapel," she said with a grin. "It points north-south, which reflects the nonconformity of the early seventeenth century."

It was simply magnificent, the stuff of dreams, and I envied the students who had the opportunity to be part of this historic seat of learning. Founded in 1584 on the site of a Dominican priory by Sir Walter Mildmay, who was Chancellor of the Exchequer to Elizabeth I, it was now a mixed college and had been for the past seven years.

Fiona proved to be the perfect guide, with Marcus chipping in on occasions. We stopped by the pond in the Paddock on the site of what was once the friars' fishpond, and she told us how in the seventeenth century many Emmanuel scholars had been Puritans and sought refuge from persecution in America.

"One of them was John Harvard," she explained. "After gaining his degree here, he married and moved to New England in 1637."

"It was there he provided the funds for America's first university," added Marcus.

Fiona nodded. "Yes, sadly he died young but he bequeathed his library and one half of his estate to the new college."

"Hence the links between the two universities," finished off Marcus.

"I had heard of John Harvard," said Beth, "but I confess I didn't know much about him."

"What's it like at Harvard?" I asked.

"Simply wonderful," enthused Fiona. "Lots of new friends, a challenging course and a passport into the world of business."

"And what is it you hope to do?" asked Beth.

"Something in the financial sector, perhaps in London or New York," said Fiona breathlessly. Life was an adventure for this dynamic young woman and the doting Marcus appeared to be no more that flotsam in her wake. It was clear that both their hearts were restless — but for different reasons.

254

"Shall we go down to the river?" suggested Marcus.

"Good idea," agreed Fiona and took his hand. I had never seen Marcus look so happy. Beth and I followed the young couple as they wandered along Sidney Street towards Bridge Street and we stopped outside The Pickerel Inn.

"Interesting place," said Marcus. "It used to be an opium den and a gin palace."

"And even a brothel," added Fiona with a mischievous smile.

Marcus blinked and Fiona took his hand more firmly and strode off towards Magdalene Bridge. Down below us on the quayside tourists were queuing for a gentle punting experience on the Cam.

We leaned on the parapet of the bridge and Beth nodded towards Marcus. "Young love," she whispered.

The views across the river were spectacular on this perfect afternoon. In the distance cherry trees were filled with tight buds waiting for the trigger of life to burst open. Warm days had returned as the earth shifted subtly on its axis.

"Let's hire a punt," said Fiona. "It will be fun."

This time I insisted on paying and we clambered on to our wooden seats and settled back to enjoy the experience. Along the Backs, the land between the six riverside colleges and Queen's Road, carpets of daffodils and bluebells lifted the spirits as we joined the other punts moving lazily up the river. I admired the skill of our punter as he lifted the pole out of the water with metronomic regularity before letting it slip again until it touched the river bottom. With perfect balance he pushed

255

steadily, moving his hands along the pole and propelling it forward. Finally he twisted the pole, allowing it to float to the surface where he used it as a rudder to correct our course.

Fiona pointed out St John's and the Wren Library at Trinity College, but then appeared to forget about us at the back of the punt and soon the young couple were in animated conversation.

"We could live here," I said suddenly.

Beth was surprised. "This isn't like you."

"Think about it, Beth. John could grow up in this wonderful city. He starts school next year."

"But you've just started a new headship and there will always be new opportunities."

I was even surprising myself. "Sorry . . . just thinking out loud."

"And we've just begun to extend Bilbo Cottage."

There was silence as we drifted by the great lawn in front of King's College. The view was quite magical, but Beth had other things on her mind. "Apart from my headship, there's Ragley, of course. You've always said how much you love it there."

"I do — it's my life. I love teaching, always have, always will. It's what I do best."

Beth sighed and took my hand. "I know, Jack — I know . . . and I understand."

"Don't worry," I said, "it's just that this is the most beautiful place."

Perhaps it was a flight of fancy on my part. Maybe I had relaxed for the first time in weeks. Then again,

256

somewhere in the back of my mind, the high moors of North Yorkshire were calling me home.

Back on dry land Marcus said, "Shall we go to Auntie's Tea Shop? Jack and Beth might like some refreshment."

"Let's," agreed Fiona with a smile.

We found our way back to King's Parade and paused when we saw a huge poster advertising a production by the Cambridge Actors' Society of *The Happiest Days of Your Life* by John Dighton. It was described as "a much-loved farce", opening on 28 April.

"Shall we go?" asked Fiona suddenly.

Marcus sighed. "I'll be back at school by then."

Fiona considered this for a moment. "And come to think of it, I fly back to America on the twenty-ninth."

Marcus stopped suddenly and spoke to Fiona in a low voice, but Beth and I couldn't help but overhear him. "Do you have to? I wish you could stay."

Fiona looked at him curiously, as if becoming aware for the first time of what lay behind the sadness in the eyes of her friend.

"Oh, Potty," she said quietly, "I have to go. You know that, and there will be other days."

"I hope so," said Marcus, "because there was something I needed to ask you."

"Perhaps you should keep it for later," she said with a gentle smile.

Soon we were in Auntie's Tea Shop in St Mary's Passage, where we enjoyed an excellent cream tea. We chatted happily and Fiona shared a story that, in his student days, Marcus had discovered his own form of refrigeration by hanging plastic bags of food outside his window.

"And he was captain of the University Tiddlywinks Club," she added. "Marcus is a man of many talents."

"Well, we're pleased he came to North Yorkshire and our village school," I said.

"But he won't be there for ever," said Fiona confidently. "Marcus is destined for greater things."

I noticed Beth nodding in agreement, while Marcus looked uncomfortable and I guessed the reason why.

An hour later we said goodbye and watched them walk away hand in hand. Beth murmured almost to herself, "I wonder what will become of them?"

After a meal in the hotel we settled down for an early night. It was good to relax together without the prospect of our son wandering into our bedroom during the early hours. It was also noticeable that we didn't pursue our earlier conversation. I guessed Beth would pick her moment.

The next day after breakfast Beth did some last-minute shopping while I sat in the hotel lounge to scan the complimentary copy of the *Cambridge Evening News*. There was a four-page pull-out special about the Queen's visit to Ely and complaints that holiday traffic on the A1 had come to a grinding halt. Locally, there appeared to be a row over who should be the next Mayor of Cambridge and an announcement that all major shops would be closed on Bank Holiday Monday, including Boots, Woolworths, Marks &

Spencer, Sainsbury's and WH Smith, and it was causing an uproar.

Meanwhile a Cambridge team had won the National Lego Building Competition. Their "Easter Enterprise" zone was based on the trade war between Japan and England. I hadn't realized that Lego was taken quite so seriously. Also, for a moment, I considered changing my car after seeing the striking advertisement for the new, British-built, Peugeot 309 GEX. It included a radio cassette, sunroof, mud flaps, special striping and attractive wheel trims. However, apart from the fact that the price of £5,295 was way beyond my means, I couldn't bear to lose my classic Morris Minor.

At lunchtime we loaded up again and set off for Austen Cottage. Soon the familiar flint-faced walls of Hampshire reflected the April sunshine and we slowed on entering the tiny village of Little Chawton.

We drove past The Cricketer public house, which overlooked the village green, and paused by an ancient cast-iron water pump. Then we negotiated a few market stalls and crawled past the local church with its square Norman tower. Finally we arrived at a row of half-timbered houses and turned into the gateway of Austen Cottage.

As we crunched to a halt on the gravelled driveway, Beth's father came out to greet us. He hugged Beth and the warm bond between them was immediately obvious. John Henderson looked relaxed in his baggy denim shirt and cord trousers with mud on the knees. He turned to me. "Hello, Jack."

"Hello again, John, good to see you."

Diane was making final preparations to her famous watercress soup. She turned, took off her apron and pushed back a strand of blonde hair, tucking it behind one ear — reminiscent of a habit of Beth's.

"Welcome home," she said and glanced at me, "both of you."

It was a relaxed evening in their low-beamed lounge, with a log fire and quiet conversation. Beth and Diane were discussing Laura's experiences in Australia while John, as a member of the local railway preservation society, explained that their tenth anniversary had arrived and a first ride on a steam train awaited his grandson.

On Saturday morning I was sitting with Beth in the kitchen, sipping a cup of tea and listening to the news. Our son was running around the terracotta-tiled floor playing hide-and-seek with his grandfather, while Diane was at the sink washing up the breakfast bowls. A vase of daffodils stood in the bay window and on the old Welsh dresser, beneath a complete set of Jane Austen novels, was a collection of framed photographs of Beth and Laura. Happy, innocent faces in a long-ago time of childhood.

On the radio Kenneth Baker had announced, "We can no longer leave individual teachers, schools or local education authorities to devise the curriculum children should follow."

"Oh dear," I said.

"Interesting," murmured Beth.

Famous for wearing Brylcreem, our Secretary of State for Education cut a slightly comic figure, but he was certainly making a name for himself. I heard Beth sigh. His speech was delivered in true Thatcherite terms and I wondered if the venerable Margaret had written his script.

"Big changes ahead," said Beth.

It was hard to decide who was the most excited when we arrived at Alton railway station. It was like stepping back in time. The station master wore a smart black three-piece suit, white shirt and red tie, plus a cap, and greeted us with a smile.

On the iron fencing that bordered the platform there were enamel advertisement signs for Colman's Mustard, Rinso, Capstan Navy Cut cigarettes and Camp Coffee. I bought a ticket for myself for a £3.80 return to the pretty Georgian market town of Alresford and a child's ticket for £1.90, which seemed a bargain for such a special experience.

"Come and look at the engine," said John, lifting his grandson on to his shoulders. We walked past a coach with a red line on top and John explained it was a buffet coach and included the guard's van. When we reached the engine he introduced us to the driver, fireman and a trainee fireman, and young John was allowed to stand on the footplate.

"Can I drive the engine please, Grandad?" he asked.

I thought my father-in-law was about to burst into tears. "One day, John," he said. "Maybe one day."

We stepped up into a 1950s coach with a corridor down the side and sliding doors that opened into individual compartments that seated six passengers. It took me back to journeys to the seaside when I was a small boy. The guard asked the onlookers to stand back to ensure a line of sight for the driver. Then he waved his flag and with a shrill whistle we were off, and smoke and steam wafted past our window. The ticket inspector punched our tickets and had a friendly word with young John. He knew my father-in-law, smiled in acknowledgement and explained there were four stations on the line — Alton, Medstead and Four Marks, Ropley, and Alresford.

When we stopped at Ropley station there was a large engine shed with three railway lines running through it. John explained that he was working with a team of volunteers on the steam locomotive T9 30120 and his job was to repair the ash pan in the boiler. He said it was a 0-8-0, which referred to the pairs of wheels, and, as I listened to him, it was clear that the volunteers were creating a marvellous return to the age of steam following the Beeching cuts of the sixties. It was a wonderful day, with much to reflect upon when we returned to the cottage.

On Sunday we all went to the lovely church in nearby Medstead for their Easter service, followed by lunch in Winchester. It was a happy end to our visit and on the morning of Easter Monday we packed the car and set off to return to Yorkshire.

The miles swept by as we travelled north and John nodded off in the back seat. The radio was murmuring away. A sports reporter announced that a promising teenage cricketer, Michael Atherton, had rescued Cambridge University from humiliation with a battling 73 not out when he defied County Champions Essex at Fenners.

"John loved the steam train," I said.

"It's been a good holiday for all of us," said Beth, "and it's opened my eyes."

"So, what's on your mind?"

There was silence for a while. I sensed Beth was choosing her words carefully.

"John will be four in the summer. He will be starting school before we know it."

I wondered where this was going. "He's certainly well prepared," I said. "Nursery has done him a world of good."

"Jack, I was thinking over what you said about Cambridge."

I had guessed this was coming. "It simply struck me it could be the perfect place to settle as a family."

Beth took a deep breath. "You have a new headship, I've just been appointed to a new post, your Masters degree is progressing well and, in case you've forgotten, there are builders extending the cottage."

"I'm aware of all this. You know that. It's just that I thought . . . is this it?"

We settled back as the miles sped by and listened to the news on the radio. There was talk of industrial action by teachers' unions in protest against teachers having to cover for absent colleagues. The work-to-contract guidelines had caused unrest and teachers were urged to count their hours and stop work when they had completed their annual quota of 1,265 hours.

Meanwhile, at the teachers' conference in Eastbourne, delegates voted overwhelmingly to support the scheme to give more spending power to schools.

"But who pays for sick teachers?" asked Beth and turned down the volume control. It was becoming too depressing.

"So many changes," I muttered.

It was later that Beth spoke up again. "Tell me — why the change of heart?"

"Having to reapply for my job hit me harder than I realized."

"Are you unhappy?"

"Not exactly. I love my new job, but . . ."

"Do you feel you could be doing more?"

We were getting to the heart of it. "I'm one of the older students on my uni course and there's a new generation of teachers who will be overtaking me. It occurred to me I was being left behind."

"You mean left behind in a job you love."

I smiled. "I suppose so."

There was a heavy shower as we drove through South Yorkshire and we were silent as the rain pattered against the windscreen.

Eventually, Beth said, "Let's leave it for now and think again before the end of the holiday."

Finally, as we approached the plain of York and drove through familiar villages, Beth said, "I think Marcus is in love."

"Perhaps he is."

264

"It's obvious, Jack. He dotes on that young woman, but he's being left in her slipstream. He needs to be more active and make the running. The poor man has the Cambridge Blues."

"It sounds familiar," I said and we drove on in silence.

CHAPTER
FIFTEEN

Hogging the Headlines

*School will close on Friday for the May Day holiday
and will reopen on Tuesday, 5 May. Mrs Grainger
and Mrs Pringle held a rehearsal for the display of
maypole dancing.*
Extract from the Ragley & Morton School Logbook:
Wednesday, 29 April 1987

The first soft kiss of sunlight caressed the distant hills
and lit up the horizon. Like a thin band of gold the hills
shimmered beneath a ring of fire. It was Wednesday, 29
April and the countryside around me lifted the spirits
as I pulled up on the forecourt of Pratt's garage.

Almond trees were in blossom, the heavy scent of
wallflowers was in the air and, across the road, darting
swallows had returned to their nesting sites in the eaves
of Stan Coe's outbuildings. The annual May Day
holiday beckoned and all seemed well — that is, until
Victor ambled out to greet me.

"A lovely morning, Victor," I said.

"Mebbe so, but not f'one o' those poor buggers," he
replied as he unscrewed my petrol cap. He nodded
towards Stan Coe's farm.

"Pardon?"

"Ah mean one o' them pigs, Mr Sheffield."

The penny dropped. Old Tommy Piercy's hog roast was a highlight of the May Day activities on the village green. "Oh, I see," I said lamely, wishing I didn't enjoy crackling quite so much.

As I drove off I saw Mrs Higginbottom and Mrs Gawthorpe chatting by the fence that bordered Stan Coe's farm. They waved as I passed, while their daughters, Tracey and Alison, stood on one of the bars of the wooden fence watching the pigs. I smiled. It was always fascinating to watch young children observe the wonders of nature within the bounty of our North Yorkshire countryside.

However, the girls seemed to be attracted to an unlikely companion. A particularly large pig was snuffling around a clump of thistles on the other side of the fence. I slowed up and smiled. It appeared they had made a friend. As I drove off towards the High Street I had little idea of the chain of events that was to follow and was destined to be the talk of the village for many months to come.

Alison, meanwhile, leaned over the fence to look more closely at the smiling pig. Then she took a biscuit from her pocket and, on cue, the eager animal waddled over to her.

It was a ritual that had taken place for over a month, ever since Alison had received a camera for her seventh birthday. After that she had become an eager photographer and her first roll of film had been processed in Boots the Chemist in York. The twenty-four exposures included a photo of her big sister, Michelle, playing on the swings, one of her mother feeding their cat, ten more of their cat in various poses, while the remaining twelve comprised studies of her favourite pig eating, sleeping and, on occasions, rolling in the mud.

"Ah call 'im Peaches," she said, "'cause 'is cheeks are soft an' rosy."

"Peaches," echoed Tracey, nodding in agreement. "That's a lovely name."

At that moment Healthcliffe Earnshaw arrived on his bicycle with an empty satchel swinging from his shoulder. Fifteen-year-old Heathcliffe had just delivered his last newspaper of the morning and was on his way back to Prudence Golightly's General Stores.

He parked his bicycle against the fence, took a half-eaten apple from his pocket and held it up by the stalk. "Here y'are, piggy," he said and stretched out his hand. Peaches rumbled forward, collected the grubby core with a slap of its wet tongue and swallowed it in an instant.

"That were brave, 'Eathcliffe," said an admiring Tracey.

Heathcliffe accepted the hero-worship with a modest smile.

"'E's a fast eater," said Alison in admiration.

"We've got some apples at 'ome," said Tracey.

"An' we've got a bag of pears," said Alison. "I bet Peaches likes pears as well."

"Peaches?" queried Heathcliffe.

"Yes, Alison calls 'im Peaches," explained Tracey.

"'E's our favourite," added Alison.

"'E's *my* favourite an' all," agreed Heathcliffe. "'E's best of t'lot. Ah allus give 'im a treat when ah'm passin'."

The three of them stared at Peaches.

Tracey sighed. "'E's got a lovely smile."

"An' that's what meks 'im diff'rent to t'others," said Alison.

"Well, ah can pick 'im out dead easy," said Heathcliffe with confidence.

"'Ow come?" said Alison.

"'Cause of 'is droopy ear."

It was true. One ear pointed towards the heavens while the other hung down towards the ground — incongruous but endearing.

Meanwhile, Peaches seemed to revel in the attention and gave them what they took to be another vacant smile. However, the huge pig had been hoping for another tasty titbit from the strange humans. Eventually, with a grunt and a snort, he waddled off to join his brothers and sisters at the trough to enjoy his third helping of breakfast.

Sadly, Peaches was completely unaware that he weighed exactly ninety pounds. In his contented world of eating, sleeping and snuffling, this would have meant little to this friendly pig. But according to Old Tommy Piercy, Ragley's champion butcher, it was the perfect weight for a spit roast.

Sally and Vera were in the entrance hall when I walked into school. Sally was holding an armful of colourful streamers provided by Vera in readiness for the maypole-dancing practice on the village green.

"I thought we would nip out after morning break, Jack," she said. "I've arranged with Anne for the rest of my class to be supervised. She'll be doing some music in the hall. Also, Val Flint said she would call round to give me a hand."

"That's fine," I said, "and thanks for all your efforts. It will be the highlight of the day."

"Along with the Women's Institute tent with our special cream teas," said Vera without a hint of modesty.

"And Old Tommy's hog roast," added Sally with a grin. "That always goes down well."

On the High Street, a group of pupils from Easington Comprehensive School had gathered at the bus stop. Heathcliffe and Terry Earnshaw were standing outside the General Stores, staring at the large jars of sweets in the window.

Heathcliffe was completely unaware of an ardent admirer. Maureen Hartley had just become a teenager and was wearing her big sister's cast-off school blazer. She was staring at her spiky-haired hero in rapt adoration. Little Mo, as she was known to her friends, had no idea what hormones were, but they had begun to make their presence felt in this happy, carefree girl. She was the youngest of five daughters and her father worked tirelessly to support them following the death of his wife after a long illness.

Outside the butcher's shop next door, Stan Coe was in conversation with one of his duck-shooting friends, Boris Drudgeon, the landlord of The Pig & Ferret.

"Ah'm sellin' one o' m'pigs t'night for t'May Day 'og roast," said Stan.

Heathcliffe forgot the mouthwatering display of his favourite sweets and listened in.

"You allus pick a good un," said Boris with a bucktoothed smile, unaware that he was known as Bugs Bunny to many of his regulars.

Stan took a final puff of his cigarette and flicked the stub on to the pavement. "'Erbert's comin' round in 'is van t'night t'collect it," he said. "Ah've got one that's t'perfec' weight."

"'Ow d'you know which one?" asked Boris.

Stan gave an evil grin. "You can't miss 'im — big bugger's gorra droopy ear."

Boris wandered off up the High Street while Stan returned to his filthy, mud-streaked Land Rover, leaving Heathcliffe looking thoughtful.

"What's t'matter, 'Eath?" asked Terry.

Heathcliffe gave his kid brother a determined look. "We've gorra job t'do straight after school."

"What is it?"

"We're gonna save a pig," said Heathcliffe.

"A pig?"

"That's right, Terry — a pig called Peaches."

It had been a busy morning in school and in our Reading Workshop Mrs Gawthorpe was listening to her daughter Alison reading her Ginn Reading 360 story book and jotting down the words with which she was struggling.

"Ah've got loads o' photos of a pig, Mummy," said Alison.

"Ah've seen 'em," said Mrs Gawthorpe. "An' that camera o' yours'll be t'death of me!"

Meanwhile, in his butcher's shop, Old Tommy Piercy was waxing lyrical to Deke Ramsbottom. The singing cowboy had called in for a pork pie.

"Ah'm lookin' forward to the 'og roast," said Deke. "Best treat o' May Day f'me."

Old Tommy glanced up at his calendar on the tiled wall. "It'll need to be slaughtered soon."

"Ah s'ppose it will."

"Y'see, Deke," explained Old Tommy, "young pigs are hung longer than old pigs."

"'Ow come?"

"It's to allow time for t'muscles to relax after t'rigor mortis has set in!"

"Bloody 'ell," said Deke. "Sounds 'orrible."

Old Tommy merely smiled. "That's slaughterin' for you. It's normally one week from slaughter to roasting, but ah've gorrit down to a fine art."

"Ah guess you 'ave, Tommy," said Deke. "Practice meks perfec'."

It was shortly after four o'clock when the school bus returned to the High Street. As soon as it pulled up, Heathcliffe and Terry hurried towards Stan Coe's farm. Heathcliffe stopped to break off two sticks from the copse of trees next to the fence.

272

"Here y'are, Terry," he said. "We need these t'encourage Peaches to shift 'imself."

After checking no one was around, our two intrepid heroes jumped over the fence and persuaded Peaches to amble at his own speed towards the gate that led to freedom.

"Where we tekkin' 'im, 'Eath?" asked the faithful Terry, who had always been Robin to his big brother's Batman.

"Ah reckon that ol' barn in Twenty Acre Field," said Heathcliffe. "No one ever goes there an' Peaches'll be out o' sight."

It was shortly before six o'clock that Herbert Cronk drove his rusty white van into Stan Coe's farmyard. On the side of the van were the words:

PERFECT PIGS
Cronk's Crackling:
Quality Hog Roast Supplier

Herbert's van was well known in Ragley village and I had seen it many times. The sign always appeared to me to be a perfect porcine oxymoron: there was certainly nothing perfect about a healthy and happy pig who was about to be spit-roasted.

Deirdre Coe came to the door. "'E's jus' comin', 'Erbert," she said. "Jus' gettin' 'is wellies on."

Stan emerged, puffing a cigarette and with a smile on his face. There was no doubt that, with his heavy jowls,

273

he bore a strong resemblance to his precious pigs. "Ah've gorra a real beauty this time, 'Erbert," he said.

Together they walked towards the pig pens.

"Where's that bloody pig gone?" shouted Stan.

On Thursday morning Heathcliffe and Terry arrived at the old barn in Twenty Acre Field. They had brought some scraps of food plus a couple of apples. However, the door was ajar, presumably opened by a powerful snout in a bid for freedom. Peaches had escaped!

"Bloomin' 'eck, Terry," exclaimed Heathcliffe, aghast, "'e's done a runner — 'e's gone!"

"What we gonna do, 'Eath?"

Heathcliffe heard the church clock strike half past eight. It was time to get to the bus stop. "We'll come back after school an' find 'im then."

It was just before morning assembly when Stuart Ormroyd called out, "Mr Coe comin' up t'drive, Mr Sheffield, wi' that copper."

"That's Police Constable Pike, Stuart," I said. "He won't appreciate you calling him a copper."

"OK, sir, but they don't look too pleased."

Vera's manner was almost glacial as she kept both men in the entrance hall to await my arrival.

"Ah want t'see that 'eadmaster o' yours," demanded Stan bluntly.

"Only when it's convenient, Mrs Forbes-Kitchener," interjected Julian Pike quickly. He looked sternly at Stan. "I suggest you sit down, Mr Coe, and remember we're guests in the school." He glanced apologetically

274

at Vera. "Sorry, you'll appreciate I'm just doing my job at present."

"Of course, Julian," said Vera with calm assurance. "And how is your mother — well, I hope?"

"Yes, thank you," replied the nervous bobby. He was out of his depth with our dominant school secretary and he knew it.

Meanwhile, the children were gathering in the school hall. When they were all seated, Anne played the opening bars of "Morning Has Broken" and Sally stood up to lead the assembly.

I arrived in the entrance hall to find Vera standing there in a determined fashion, her lips pursed. There was obviously a problem.

"What can I do for you, gentlemen?" I asked.

"It'll be some of 'is kids be'ind all this. They're allus 'angin' abart near my land," said Stan angrily.

This was the *old* Stan Coe — the one we knew so well.

"I suggest you remain silent for now, Mr Coe," warned PC Pike sternly. He looked up at me. "I've been asked to investigate the disappearance of one of Mr Coe's pigs."

"A pig?"

"Yes, Mr Sheffield. It's a serious matter. The pig in question was due to be sold yesterday evening, so a significant amount of money is involved."

"I see," I said. "It's assembly time now, so would you like me to ask the children if they have seen anything?"

"An' who stole it," muttered Stan.

I ignored him completely and shook hands with our local constable. "I'll do what I can and let you know."

"Thanks, Mr Sheffield, and in the meantime I'll organize a search." Julian looked at Vera. "Sorry to have bothered you, Mrs Forbes-Kitchener."

Vera smiled at the young policeman, turned on her heel and disappeared into the sanctuary of the office.

They left with Stan grumbling loudly, "Ah'll 'ave t'give 'Erbert a diff'rent pig."

Back in the school hall, my announcement concerning the missing pig caused a buzz of conversation among the children. Tracey Higginbottom and Alison Gawthorpe stayed behind to have a word with me.

"Ah think the missing pig is Peaches, Mr Sheffield," said Alison. "'E weren't there this morning when we passed."

"Ah brought him some fruit to eat," added a concerned Tracey.

"Peaches?"

"No, apples, Mr Sheffield."

"I mean you said the pig's name was Peaches?"

"Yes, sir, that's what we call 'im 'cause of 'is pink cheeks."

"An' 'e's got a droopy ear," added Tracey. "Y'can't miss 'im."

Word got round the village very quickly and Joseph called in to speak to his sister.

"There's a lot of fuss about this missing pig," he said, "and I heard PC Pike is on the case."

"He is a charming and determined young man, Joseph, so I'm sure he will sort it out so long as Mr Coe doesn't interfere. He was very rude when he visited school."

"Perhaps he didn't mean it — he was probably upset," ventured Joseph, who always tried to find a little bit of goodness in everyone.

Vera looked at her brother and shook her head. "You are one of the most caring and honourable men I have ever known." Joseph would have smiled, but he knew when there was a "but" coming. "But on occasions," continued Vera, "you can be so naive."

Later, during morning break, Vera took a telephone call.

"It's for you, Mr Sheffield," she said and added with a cautious smile, "a gentleman of the press."

"Hello again, Mr Sheffield, Merry here, features editor from the *Herald*." It hadn't taken our local newspaper, the *Easington Herald & Pioneer*, long to spot an emerging story in the locality. "I wondered if I might call in? Word has it there's a pig missing and a couple of young girls in your school may know something about it."

"I have no objection to you calling in, but if you wish to speak to any of the children their parents would have to give permission and also be present."

"In that case I'll call on them at their homes," he said. Mr Merry was used to cutting corners.

It was late afternoon when the Earnshaw brothers returned to the scene of the crime.

"'E's definitely gone," said Heathcliffe. He scanned the distant field, but there was no sign of the pig.

"What we gonna do, 'Eath?"

"Nowt," said Heathcliffe. "Peaches is a free pig now."

"Mebbe 'e'll think 'e's on 'oliday."

Heathcliffe considered this for a moment. He wasn't sure PC Pike would agree. "Y'right, Terry, everybody deserves a 'oliday . . . even pigs."

It was late when I drove home that evening. Above me the stars shone down like celestial guardians, a million watchtowers in a vast purple sky. Although my headlights picked out a few small creatures, there was no sign of the errant pig and I wondered where he might be and what would become of him. By the time I got out of my car at home, all that was left was silence, except for the distant sounds of the night — a hooting owl, bats beating their leathery wings and the strange cry of a solitary fox.

In the meantime, Peaches was free.

By Friday lunchtime it was the talk of the village — and, as no one liked Stan Coe, there was huge local support for the fugitive pig.

The previous evening Mr Merry, the features editor, had interviewed Tracey and Alison and had enough photographs of Peaches in various poses to capture the imagination of his readers with a double-page spread.

He also spoke to Petula Dudley-Palmer, who had seen a large pig enter her garden, rumble across the Japanese bridge and stop by her lily pond for a quick drink. Ted Postlethwaite was next on his list: our local postman had spotted a pig peeping over the hedge at him when he was delivering mail up Chauntsinger Lane. Everyone had an opinion and Mr Merry was happy to print them all.

On Friday evening the newspaper featured a large front-page photograph of Peaches looking up from a trough of food with a quizzical expression. Under the banner headline "A Pig Called Peaches", Mr Merry had written, "Support is increasing for Ragley's fugitive pig. Peaches has been spotted on several occasions but he continues his flight for freedom." There was also a plan of Ragley village and the sightings were indicated with more crosses than a treasure map.

However, it was Saturday's newspaper that finally brought closure and an unexpected finale to the dramatic tale. An even bigger photograph of Ragley's most famous pig giving a lop-sided grin was splashed across the front page. Peaches had at last been cornered near the cricket field by a team of volunteers from the local animal sanctuary. Mr Merry's report read as follows:

A certain benevolent lady, Lady Emmeline de Courcy, Chair of the North Yorkshire Animal Sanctuary, has taken it upon herself to provide Peaches with the freedom he so desires. The brave pig that has captured the hearts of the people of North Yorkshire is to be saved. The eminent animal rights campaigner has given Mr Coe of

Coe Farm *nominal compensation* and Peaches will enjoy a lifetime of food, fun and frolics.

Mr Merry was always pleased with his alliteration.

Prudence Golightly was also pleased. She had never sold so many copies of our local paper.

Outside the shop, Heathcliffe had followed the story.

"Did we do owt wrong, 'Eath?" asked Terry.

Heathcliffe studied his brother's innocent expression and gave a considered response. "Well, it were *illegal* . . . but we didn't do owt wrong."

It was May Day and I held John's hand as Beth and I walked across the village green. It was a fine sunny day and we had heard our first cuckoo.

As usual it seemed as though the whole village had turned out to watch the maypole dancing and sample the delights of the cream teas in the Women's Institute tent. John enjoyed Captain Fantastic's Punch & Judy Show, Big Dave won the Wellington-boot-throwing competition and Shane and Clint Ramsbottom were the first to complete the pram race around the village, finishing at The Royal Oak.

George and Ruby were sitting on Ronnie's bench, where George had shared a new plan for their honeymoon.

"George Dainty, m'mother used t'say nothin' ventured nothing gained. So ah'll do it. Ah've never been out o' Yorkshire but there's a first time for ev'rythin'. Ah can't wait t'tell Mrs F we'll be goin' t'London on t'train."

"Go tell 'er now if y'like," urged George.

"Ah will," said Ruby, "an' ah'll tell'er we've picked a wedding day on Saturday the twenty-fifth of July, first day of t'summer 'oliday." And she kissed George on his cheek and hurried off towards the Women's Institute marquee.

Later that afternoon, as I sat on the grass with John eating ice-cream cornets, I looked around me at the scene. Everyone seemed relaxed and happy except for one person.

Old Tommy Piercy's hog roast was having a quiet day.

CHAPTER
SIXTEEN

The Yuppie

The school supported the Village Hall Committee's fund-raising event this evening to promote the work of local artists. Mrs Pringle organized a selection of children's artwork to be displayed.
Extract from the Ragley & Morton School Logbook:
Friday, 22 May 1987

In the kitchen of Morton Manor only the cawing of the rooks in the high elms disturbed Vera's peaceful start to her day. It was Friday, 22 May and our school secretary was at peace in her world. She sipped Earl Grey tea from a china cup and stared out of the window.

In the far distance, beyond the hawthorn hedgerows, cattle were grazing contentedly in the open pasture land. The warmer days had broadened the leaves of an avenue of sycamore trees and they sheltered beneath the welcome shade. Rupert had left earlier for his morning "constitutional" with a brisk walk to meet his daughter, Virginia Anastasia, at the nearby stables and Vera reflected on the changes in her life. Finally, she washed and dried her cup and saucer, switched off Radio 3's *Morning Concert*, said goodbye to her cats, collected her handbag and car keys from the hall table, donned a silk scarf and walked out of the front door.

On the spacious driveway the gravel crunched beneath her feet as she walked past the wild raspberry canes that covered the Victorian brick walls. Soft pink petals from the cherry trees drifted in the gentle breeze, while above her head a flock of black-headed gulls swept across the sky in graceful formation. Vera gave a contented smile as she climbed into her car and set off for school.

In her working life, however, Vera was aware that you never knew what might be in store. No two days were the same. Occasionally, one stood out from the others — and such a day awaited our intrepid secretary today.

At Bilbo Cottage rapid progress was being made, as the walls of the extension had been completed and work on the roof had begun. The builders had started early and gave me a wave as I set off for school.

As I passed Pratt's garage I noticed the now familiar green Citroën once again parked outside. Standing next to it was a tall, distinguished gentleman staring across the fields towards Stan Coe's farm.

Vera was very busy when I walked into the office. "It's a special night in the village hall this evening, Mr Sheffield. I do hope you might be able to come. We need to support our local artists and all the proceeds are going to the Village Hall Preservation Fund. So it's a worthy cause."

"Yes, I'll be there."

"Also," added Vera, "Sally is taking the opportunity to show off some of the children's artwork."

It had been well advertised in the *Herald* that twenty-five local artists had each donated a painting, with all the proceeds going towards the redecoration of the village hall.

It was just before morning break when Stuart Ormroyd made his first announcement of the day.

"Flash car comin' up t'drive, Mr Sheffield."

A cranberry-red metallic Jaguar XJ6 had screeched to a halt in front of the NO PARKING sign outside the boiler house and a tall man wearing an airforce-blue suit stepped out confidently. He looked as if he were auditioning for *Miami Vice*. He was joined in the car park by a dark-haired girl, who had emerged nervously from the passenger seat. She was smartly dressed and clutching a new leather satchel.

The man checked his reflection in his car window, picked up a Filofax and a mobile phone that resembled a large brick, depressed its aerial, beckoned to his daughter and strode confidently towards the entrance porch.

At that moment Tom Burgess rang the bell for morning break and the children poured out of school to enjoy the sunshine.

When I walked into the office there was an overpowering scent of strong aftershave and Vera was adding a name to her admissions register.

"Mr Sheffield, this is Mr Collingwood and his daughter, Candice. They have moved into the area from

284

Leeds. You may remember we had a telephone call from Mrs Collingwood last week and we have received all the relevant paperwork from the previous school. So all is in order." She glanced down at her neat copperplate writing. "Candice is ten years old and will go into Class Five."

I noted a hint of disapproval in Vera's tone but merely went into professional mode. "Welcome to Ragley School, Mr Collingwood," and I shook his hand. It was soft and limp. "And hello, Candice. I'm Mr Sheffield and I will be your new teacher."

The young girl fiddled with the buttons of her new cardigan and gave me a cautious smile.

Mr Collingwood ran his fingers through his slicked-back hair and smiled. "We're renting on the outskirts of the village, so Candice won't be here long," he said. "Just until the end of term. We've got her name down for the Time School for Girls in York."

He placed his mobile phone on Vera's desk. In doing so he disturbed the photograph of her three cats. Vera was not impressed and moved the photograph to the other side. I looked curiously at the mobile phone and considered it would have made a good door stop. I could never imagine owning one myself. It looked to be such a cumbersome accessory.

"We're awaiting the completion of one of the exec' properties on the York Road. Apparently there's a hold-up with the indoor swimming pool." He gave a disparaging smile. "You know what builders are like." Unperturbed, he took an expensive-looking wallet from his pocket. "My card," he said and proffered it between

the first two fingers of his right hand, "in case you need
to get in touch."

I looked down. It read:

JONNY COLLINGWOOD
VISIONS DELIVERY MANAGER
UNILEVER

It was followed by a Leeds telephone number.

"Visions delivery?" I said.

"Yes, I'm the visions delivery manager at Unilever."

"Really?" I was no wiser.

"You know — tomorrow's ideas today."

"I see," I replied . . . but I didn't, and he knew it.

"The present project is Signal toothpaste. You'll
recall it was introduced way back in the early sixties,
then we extended it to the fluoride label. Last year we
introduced the anti-tartar formula, so it's cutting-edge
stuff."

"I've never really thought about it," I admitted.

"You ought to," he said. "This is the new world of
business." He glanced down at Vera's electric
typewriter. "Computer technology is the key. I work on
an IBM green screen PC with twin floppies using Coral
66 or maybe Delta — you know, a Cobol generator. So
I write everything myself, no packages of course."

I could see Vera was bored by this incomprehensible
computer-speak. "Mr Collingwood's rented property is
in our catchment area," she said.

"Yes," he responded brightly, "just a temporary
measure. It's convenient for my early-morning train

286

into Leeds or London." He gave a cursory nod towards Vera. "So, according to your PA, we appear to be in the most convenient school."

I saw Vera stiffen in her seat at being called my "PA". "Yes, that's correct," I said.

He looked down at Vera. "The end of term is when?"

Vera opened her drawer and took out the latest school newsletter. "All the relevant dates and events are listed here."

He folded it roughly and put it in his inside jacket pocket. Then, much to Vera's dismay, he tossed his Filofax Personal Organiser on to her desk. I recalled an article in the paper saying that the Filofax was an "indispensable organiser and a must-have status symbol for the '80s executive". He fingered through the loose-leaf pages. "So the last day of term is . . . when?"

Vera pointed towards the academic-year calendar on the wall. "July the twenty-fourth," she replied coldly.

When he reached July he added a note to the busy scrawl. "And what time do you finish?"

"The children are dismissed at three forty-five," replied Vera.

"Really?" He added the time. "And with homework, I hope."

I saw his daughter frown.

"We can discuss that once Candice is settled in," I said.

He picked up his Filofax and mobile phone. "My wife, JJ, said she would call in at the end of school, so you'll meet her then."

"JJ?" said Vera.

"Jackie Jane," he said. "I call her JJ. In future, she will bring in Candice at eight forty-five a.m.," he gave a self-satisfied smile, "as I'll have been working for over an hour by then."

I ignored the implied criticism. "Would you like to come with Candice to my classroom?" I asked.

He held up his wrist and turned the face of his watch towards me. It was a stainless-steel Omega Constellation. "Sorry, things to do . . . another time." He bent down, kissed Candice on the forehead, flicked his foppish hair out of his eyes and headed for the door.

In the entrance hall Anne and Pat were helping Sally to prepare a folder of children's artwork. They looked with interest as our visitors emerged and Anne reacted quickly. "Ah, you must be Candice," she said with a friendly smile. "We've been expecting you. I'm Mrs Grainger, the deputy headteacher." She glanced up at Mr Collingwood. "Would you like to look around the school?"

"You go," said Mr Collingwood and gave his daughter a gentle push. Anne caught my eye and I nodded.

"Come on, Candice," said Anne, "we'll visit your classroom first."

"You appear to be a busy man," I said.

That self-satisfied smile appeared once again. "I work hard and play hard."

He hurried out to the car park, unlocked his car and settled into the biscuit-leather seat. Then he started the engine, flicked a switch on the walnut dashboard to open the electric sunroof and, with the full-throated hum of six-cylinder power, he drove out of the school gate and turned left towards York.

When I looked round the office door Vera said, "What an unusual and slightly irritating man — in fact, a dreadful show-off."

"Well, he's certainly different."

"*Visions*,' indeed," muttered Vera and I closed the door quietly.

Pat and Sally were sharing a joke. "What is it?" I asked.

"He's a Yuppie," said Pat.

"A Yuppie?"

Sally laughed and winked at Pat. "You're out of touch, Jack. It's an acronym."

"A *young urban professional*," explained Pat.

"There was an article in my *Cosmopolitan*," said Sally. "Young urban professionals are supposed to be ambitious, ruthless and they love buying so-called *great stuff*."

"Great stuff?"

"Yes," said Sally. "Cars, clothes, gadgets, houses."

"The image is a sharp suit and a flashy car," went on Pat, "and that guy certainly fits the bill."

"Having said that," mused Sally, "when I've got Colin to go home to, a world of glamour, wine bars and nightclubs does have its appeal."

"Yes," said Pat thoughtfully, "but it's generally regarded as the shallow side of the materialistic eighties and, sadly, there's a ruthlessness and selfishness that goes hand in hand with it."

Sally looked towards the closed office door and lowered her voice. "Don't tell Vera," she added conspiratorially, "but they're also known as *Thatcher's children*."

After break Mrs Spittlehouse had arrived to take Rosie to the dentist. Her daughter was staring at her mother's bright red blouse with padded shoulders, orange cord trousers and Chris Evert trainers. Mrs Spittlehouse had dressed hastily that morning.

"Mummy, why do my clothes have to match and yours don't?"

During the lunch break in the staff-room the talk was of the Yuppie.

I was puzzled. "I didn't understand half of what he was talking about. Marcus, what's a green screen?"

Marcus grinned. "Well, computers include a cathode ray so, as the screen is green with white writing, it's known as a green screen."

"So now you know, Jack," whispered Anne with a smile.

Meanwhile, in The Royal Oak, Old Tommy Piercy was sitting on his favourite stool at the bar.

"Ah don't know what t'world's comin' to," he said. "Ah couldn't believe m'eyes this morning. Y'could 'ave knocked me down wi' a feather."

"What was it, Tommy?" asked Don, putting down a pint of frothing beer in front of our curmudgeonly butcher.

290

"It were Ernie Morgetroyd on 'is milk float, large as life — a milkman selling WATER!"

"*Water?*" repeated Don from behind the bar. "Y'mus' be jokin'."

"No, as true as ah'm standing 'ere," insisted Old Tommy defiantly.

No one dared mention he was actually *sitting*.

"So 'ow come Ernie is selling water?" asked Don.

"Ah asked 'im that very question an' 'e said t'world were changin' an' they were importin' it from across t'Channel. So it's not even proper Yorkshire water. It's foreign muck."

"Teks all sorts," said Don.

Old Tommy supped deeply on his pint. "Daft, I call it — bloody daft!"

By afternoon break Candice had settled in well and I soon realized she was a bright girl. She approached my desk with her new friend, Michelle Gawthorpe.

"Show it to Mr Sheffield," urged Michelle.

Candice rummaged in her satchel. "It's called Rubik's Magic, Mr Sheffield."

I later discovered from Marcus that sales of this latest puzzle had passed over £1.5 million and it was expected to out-sell its famous forerunner, the Rubik's Cube. The task appeared to involve rearranging a series of rings printed on hinged pieces of flat plastic so that the rings become interlocked. It had captured the imagination of children throughout the country and the Rubik's Magic National Championship was due to take place next week on ITV's *Get Fresh*.

Candice solved the puzzle in only ten seconds, but the incessant clicking was getting on my nerves so I suggested she took it outside.

A crowd of girls gathered round her on the playground.

"Are they expensive?" asked Michelle.

"Yes, but my father's rich," replied Candice.

Michelle considered this. "My dad says 'e used to be rich . . . but then 'e married m'mother."

In the staff-room the talk had turned to Yuppies and "Thatcherism".

"Maggie's promotion of privatization concerns me," said Sally, "and have you noticed how important designer labels are?"

"They've become status symbols," said Marcus.

"There's certainly a lot of fashion designer goods in the new shopping centres," said Pat.

Sally sensed she had acquired an ally. "The idea that 'greed is good' is gaining credence. I just don't like it."

Vera stood by the sink and kept quiet. She loved Margaret's power suits; for her they were the symbol of the Prime Minister's success in the eighties. Mrs Thatcher had also called for a General Election on 11 June and Vera gave a secret smile.

Back in my class I had planned a project aimed at broadening the children's geographical understanding. I had used Tolkien's *The Hobbit* to describe a journey through a wild countryside of mountains, valleys and rivers. I had developed the task to encourage their

292

knowledge of contour lines on Ordnance Survey maps. A group of children including Rosie Appleby, Jemima Poole, Candice Collingwood, Michelle Gawthorpe, George Frith and Barry Stonehouse had completed a relief model of the Lonely Mountain. They had made a three-dimensional contour map using a layer of polystyrene for each 100-metre contour. The result was quite dramatic and I wished I had thought of this before. You never stopped learning as a teacher and this was another of those light-bulb moments.

Just before the end of school, a sleek Audi 100 purred into the car park and a tall, slim woman with long dark hair stepped out and walked into the entrance hall.

Candice Collingwood looked up. "That's my mother, Mr Sheffield."

"Go and meet her, Candice, and say I'll be there in a moment."

It was noticeable that Mrs Collingwood did not share her husband's world of excess, but was calm, sensible and charming.

She greeted me with a smile. "Thank you so much, Mr Sheffield. Candice has already made friends and is clearly happy in your school." Her daughter was sitting at the far end of the library engrossed in a copy of *The Hobbit*. "I'm really grateful — life has been rather hectic lately."

"I understood that from your husband."

There was a pause and she lowered her voice. "Yes, you will have gathered that Jonny is obsessed with financial success." I kept a respectful silence. "Don't worry, Mr Sheffield, it's patently obvious." She sighed. "I just want Candice to be *normal*, but it's difficult sometimes." She let it linger until she saw Sally arranging the children's artwork into a huge folder. "Oh I love art — I try to paint myself."

"It's for a display in the village hall," said Sally. "Do come along — it starts at seven thirty."

Mrs Collingwood looked at her daughter and smiled. "Yes, we must, and it will give us a chance to meet other people."

When they left Sally and I carried the folder of work to her car. "Lovely lady," said Sally. "Pity she's married to a Yuppie."

By seven thirty the village hall was busy. The paintings of local artists filled the walls while villagers assessed their work. Sally's display of the children's pictures was next to the refreshment area and had created lots of interest.

I joined the crowd and viewed the wide range of paintings. On the bottom right-hand corner of each one was a small peel-off sticky label indicating the price. These ranged from Lollipop Lil's *York Minster in the Mist* at £2.50 and Joyce Davenport's *Ragley High Street at Dawn* at £5, up to the *pièce de résistance*, Mary Attersthwaite's magnificent *Mrs Thatcher with Blue Bow* at the top price of £50.

I was keen to show support, so I selected Joyce Davenport's watercolour for a modest £5, which was as much as I could afford. Elsie Crapper was in charge of collecting the money and she peeled off the price label, wrapped the painting in brown paper and tied it with baling twine.

Our road-crossing patrol officer, Lillian Figgins, was staring at her painting. She had copied a photograph of York Minster but, after she had pegged it on her washing line to dry, the paint had run horribly and it was smeared badly.

Dallas Sue-Ellen Earnshaw and Suzi-Quatro Ricketts came to stand beside her. "What's the matter, Mrs Figgins?" asked Dallas.

Lollipop Lil' gave the girls a wry smile. "Nothing really, Dallas, it's just that ah like paintin' but mine's 'opeless compared to all t'rest — that's why it's t'cheapest."

"Well, ah think it's lovely," said Suzi-Quatro.

"That's kind of you t'say," replied Lillian and wandered off to the far end of the hall to share a cup of tea with the other artists.

"Ah like Mrs Figgins," said Dallas.

"Me too," agreed Suzi-Quatro. "She gave me a 'umbug once."

Dallas shook her head. "Ah wish we could cheer 'er up."

Suzi-Quatro looked thoughtful. "Ah know 'ow," and with a quick glance to make sure no one was looking she peeled off the price label.

"What y'doin'?" asked Dallas.

"Mekkin' Mrs Figgins' paintin' more expensive," said Suzi-Quatro with a grin.

I saw Mr and Mrs Collingwood arrive with their daughter Candice. Mrs Collingwood gave me a wave while Candice offered a shy smile. They went to study the display of children's work and talk to Sally and a few of the other mothers. Mr Collingwood had changed from his airforce-blue "power suit" and arrived wearing a preppy-style seersucker blazer with a distinctive and quite deliberate wrinkled appearance, along with a white Oxford shirt and baggy cream trousers.

He came to stand beside me and looked down at the brown-paper package under my arm. "A bargain I hope," he said.

"Yes, thanks," I said.

We stood there staring at the paintings. Partly to make conversation, I asked, "Just a thought — how do they get the stripes in Signal toothpaste?"

He gave that familiar self-satisfied smirk. "Well, it's not exactly rocket science . . . they put the red in first and the cap has grooves in it. So the white flows through the cap and drags the stripe on to it."

With that air of irritating confidence he walked away to look at the paintings and I went to the refreshment stall to talk to Vera and Rupert.

Jonny Collingwood wasn't the visions delivery manager for nothing. He made a rapid assessment of the paintings, picked up the one by Lollipop Lil', looked at the price and took it to Elsie Crapper at the table. Elsie blinked as she peeled off the label. "That will be fifty pounds, please."

He took out his wallet, removed five £10 notes and Elsie put them in her metal money box. She was puzzled that someone would pay so much for a painting that looked as though it had been put through a quick rinse in a washing machine. She wrapped it up and Mr Collingwood went to find his wife.

"I see you've bought a painting, Mr Collingwood," remarked Vera.

"Yes, Mrs Forbes-Kitchener," he replied with a smug smile. "You've either got an eye for a bargain or not. The world isn't standing still and you have to be ahead of the game."

"Really? What have you purchased?"

"A superb abstract — *York Minster in the Mist.* Clearly a talented artist."

Vera's eyes widened. She was familiar with the artistic disaster that was the lowest-priced item on display. "An interesting choice, Mr Collingwood."

"It comes naturally." He tucked the painting under his arm, beckoned to his wife and daughter and turned back to Vera. "You simply need *vision*, Mrs Forbes-Kitchener."

"And you have clearly got it, Mr Collingwood," said Vera without a hint of sarcasm.

That evening in Morton Manor Vera had a surprise. Before they had left the village hall, Rupert had spotted the painting *Mrs Thatcher with Blue Bow* for a bargain price and knew Vera would appreciate it. He secreted it into the boot of her car before they left and went out to retrieve it after their evening meal.

"I bought this for you, my dear."

Vera was thrilled when she unwrapped her unexpected gift. "It's wonderful, Rupert. What a kind thought." She was also aware that at £50 it was the highlight of the show. "And so *generous*."

Rupert was slightly puzzled that Vera was so impressed with a painting that had cost him a mere £2.50.

Vera looked up at her husband in sheer admiration.

Now there is a man with vision, she thought.

CHAPTER
SEVENTEEN

Maggie For Ever

School will close tomorrow for one day and will reopen on Friday, 12 June. The hall is being used as a polling station for the General Election on Thursday, 11 June.
Extract from the Ragley & Morton School Logbook:
Wednesday, 10 June 1987

It was a perfect morning on Wednesday, 10 June. In the back garden of Bilbo Cottage bright-winged butterflies were hovering above the buddleia bushes, while the drone of bees could be heard in their never-ending search for pollen. Cuckoo spit nestled in the lavender leaves, sparkling like bright foam. The scent of roses hung in the air like a lover's embrace and the sun was warm on my back as I drove into school.

"Everything is in place for tomorrow, Mr Sheffield," said Vera.

Our school had been selected as a polling station and would be closed for the General Election. "The voting booths have been delivered and Ruby said she will erect them at the end of school."

A big day was in store for Vera. She was the officer in charge of our polling station and her beloved Mrs Thatcher was seeking a third term in office.

It was a busy day in school and everyone enjoyed morning assembly. The little ones in Anne's class showed off their paintings and read their wonderful poems.

At the end, Anne sat at the piano, opened her *Count Me In* songbook and led the children in a lively rendition of an old favourite:

> Six sticky buns in a baker's shop,
> Big and brown with a currant on top.
> A boy came along with a penny one day,
> He paid one penny and took a bun away.

After lunch the children in my class were busy exploring an aspect of physical science through the study of cranes. My intention was to encourage them to develop a greater understanding of structure, stress and mass. They had looked at a selection of photographs of cranes used in building work in the centre of York and, as a follow-up, we were making balsa-wood models. After much trial and error, we discovered the relationship between the weight of a load and the length of a jib.

When the bell rang for afternoon break no one moved.

"Can we stay in t'finish it, sir?" asked Barry Stonehouse, "'cause our model's brilliant."

"An' it works," added an eager George Frith.

A cup of tea would have been welcome, but as the children were so keen to continue we carried on. I recalled that Sally had mentioned this work was now known as "design technology", which sounded rather grand. However, whatever we chose to call it, the opportunity to develop scientific and mathematical knowledge was clear to see.

It was at times like this I realized I had the best job in the world. If I had sought the headship of a larger school, experiences such as this would likely be limited and I reflected on the excitement of children's learning.

At the end of school Ruby transformed a flat-pack construction kit into a set of three voting booths. Finally, she walked down the drive with Vera and fixed a large sign to the school gate. It read "POLLING STATION" with an arrow pointing towards the school. Then Vera hurried home. A busy evening was in store.

By 7.30 the village hall was full and the ladies of the Ragley & Morton Women's Institute had gathered in large numbers. Vera had invited a local beekeeper, Lofthouse Grimble, to give a talk. However, it wasn't so much that the ladies were interested in beekeeping, rather that it provided a good opportunity to discuss the contrasting fortunes of Neil Kinnock and Margaret Thatcher prior to the General Election.

"Margaret will prevail," declared Vera with confidence. "We can't let that vociferous little Welshman into Number Ten."

"I think his wife, Glenys, was a teacher," said Bronwyn Bickerstaff evenly.

Vera considered this for a moment. "Well in that case she can't be that bad," she conceded. "However," she added, "it still remains a pity she married a ginger-haired activist."

It wasn't clear whether it was Neil Kinnock's ginger hair or his politics that proved the final straw. Whatever it was, Vera was determined not to show a shred of compassion for the leader of the Labour Party.

Lofthouse Grimble resided with his wife, Pearl, in the tiny hamlet of Cold Hampton close to the local airfield. His neighbour was Lillian Figgins, our road-crossing patrol officer. They both lived in pretty thatched cottages and kept themselves to themselves.

One of the reasons for this was that Lollipop Lil' had little time for men. Many years ago she had succumbed to the charms of a diminutive bookmaker from Batley. His Brylcreem quiff and the back seat of his Hillman Imp were indelibly etched on her memory but, after he had run off with a leggy usherette, she had decided that, as far as men were concerned, enough was enough. Nevertheless, as a show of support, Lillian had found a seat in the front row next to Vera.

Vera thought very highly of Lillian, who was in charge of the church-cleaning rota. It was a thankless task, but Lillian was a dedicated soul and each week the dark mahogany pews shone with the lustre of her furniture polish.

It was Vera's job as events secretary to introduce the speaker and she tried hard to ignore the fact that with his ginger hair he looked like Neil Kinnock's twin brother.

"So, ladies, please welcome our speaker for this evening, Mr Lofthouse Grimble, the president of the North Yorkshire Beekeepers Society, who will provide an illustrated talk entitled 'A Taste of Honey'."

Pearl switched on the carousel slide projector, adjusted the focus and the audience settled back to an insight into the life of bees. The majority of the ladies considered the industrious little insects were fine in their place — namely *outside* and not in their kitchens. Vera was content in the knowledge that they pollinated her fruit trees. However, woe betide any stray bee that came in through the window of Morton Manor. It received short shrift along with an eye-watering spray of Timothy Pratt's finest insecticide. For the meantime, though, Vera put this thought to the back of her mind as she stared at the first slide showing a picture of Mr Grimble's back garden. It was full to bursting with beehives.

"I wonder where she hangs her washing?" murmured Joyce Davenport.

"Quite so," replied Vera.

Lofthouse was clearly an authority on his subject. "Bees created the perfect hexagonal honeycomb before geometry was understood," he informed them as Pearl switched to an image of a honeycomb.

"They cooperate and make good decisions."

He gave Pearl a hard stare. "They *cooperate* . . ." he repeated in a loud voice.

"Oh sorry, dear," said Pearl, who was sick to the back teeth of her husband's monotone voice and the boring talk she had heard a hundred times. She pressed the switch for the next slide.

"Their search for a suitable food supply is particularly interesting," continued Lofthouse with authority. "The bee scouts venture out into the unknown and the queen and the rest of the colony wait for their return." He puffed out his chest. "They are the hunters, just like the cavemen of old."

"Well 'e wouldn't 'ave lasted long," muttered Margery Ackroyd.

"Y'reight there, Marge," said Betty Buttle. "'E couldn't knock skin off a rice puddin'.'"

Undeterred by the whispering from the back row, Lofthouse pressed on. His big moment had arrived. He gave Pearl a searching look and she flicked through a sequence of slides that resembled a bee trying its hand, or to be more precise legs and antennae, at a Michael Jackson breakdance.

"Here you see the scout bees returning to the hive and performing a very special ritual dance. The better the food source, the more extravagant the dance."

"Bit strange, if y'ask me," muttered Betty. "Ah can't see my 'Arry doin' a Shakin' Stevens when 'e comes back from Asda."

Vera turned sharply and frowned at the ladies on the back row. After all, even though this Neil Kinnock look-alike was one of the most boring men she had ever met, he was still a *guest* of the Women's Institute and there were *standards*.

At this point ... thought Pearl as she moved smoothly into the final sequence of slides.

304

"At this point," said Lofthouse, "other bees check this food supply and return with a similar dance."

"They do a lot o' bloody dancin' do these bees," whispered Betty.

"Ah'm gonna buy some spray from Timothy," said Margery with a finality that brooked no argument. Little did she realize that the majority of the audience were having the same thought and Pratt's Hardware Emporium was about to experience bumper sales of insect repellent.

It was Thursday morning, Election Day, and an early-morning mist covered the lawns of Morton Manor like a cloak of secrets. At 6.30 Vera arrived at school to ensure all was ready for the first voters. A large black metal box had been delivered and Vera prepared her electoral list and checked the special hole-punch to validate each voting slip.

At 6.45 a.m. her assistant, Delia Morgetroyd, Ernie the milkman's wife, came trundling up the school drive and Vera sighed deeply. Fifteen hours of listening to stories of Delia's dysfunctional family was bad enough, but as her hobby was collecting spoons, conversation was destined to be limited for our school secretary.

At ten o'clock, when Beth and I arrived with John, Vera looked pleased to see us. She underlined our names on the electoral list and punched our voting slips. After we had voted we folded the slips and posted them through the slit in the metal box. I decided to make Vera and Delia a cup of coffee and Vera seemed to enjoy the change of roles.

305

Then we walked across the High Street to Pratt's Hardware Emporium to buy some light bulbs for the new bedroom in our extension. We found Timothy in a state of high excitement. His friend, Walter Crapper, was due to visit him on Sunday afternoon.

"We've combined our Meccano sets, Mr Sheffield, and we're going t'build a Class B1 LNER locomotive."

"Sounds fun, Timothy," I said.

"Can't wait," said the eager Timothy and he hurried off to rearrange his display of dome-headed screws.

We decided to call in to Nora's Coffee Shop for a hot drink and as we walked in Whitney Houston's number-one record "I Wanna Dance with Somebody" was on the juke-box.

Anita Cuthbertson and Claire Bradshaw were at a table just inside the door.

"'Ello, sir," said Anita. "Young John's growin' up fast."

Beth went to order while I chatted with my ex-pupils.

"We're goin' t'Glastonbury," said Claire.

They had saved up and bought their tickets for the CND Glastonbury Festival for the weekend after next and had planned their trip to Pilton in Somerset. Kenny Kershaw had arranged to borrow a car from Victor Pratt and the three of them were intending to share a tent.

"There's Elvis Costello, sir," said Anita, full of excitement.

"An' Van Morrison," added Claire.

"It should be great," said Anita, "an' my cousin is goin' an' 'e says 'e'll introduce me to 'is friend in the Mighty Lemon Drops, 'cause they're playin' as well."

"The Mighty Lemon Drops?"

"Yes, they used t'be called the Sherbet Monsters but they changed their name," explained Anita.

"I can see why," I said.

However, it occurred to me that although it wasn't quite in the realm of the Dave Clark Five or the Rolling Stones, it did have a catchy appeal.

We decided to make the most of our day off and drove into York, parked in Lord Mayor's Walk and strolled up Gillygate into the city centre. Soon we were in the Computer Store where a prematurely balding young man suffering from severe acne approached us. The purple badge fixed to his orange polo shirt read: Trevor Drabble — Computer Sales Executive.

"I've made a decision," said Beth. "We need a new computer and this looks perfect."

It was an Amstrad PCW 8512, described as "Arguably the best word processor in the world". I had no intention of arguing. There was no budging Beth once she had made up her mind.

Trevor was very persuasive. "It includes a free starter pack an' two thousand sheets o' paper."

"Sounds good," I said without conviction.

Beth was studying the literature very carefully.

"Also it's gorra s'phisticated accounts database," added Trevor.

"That should be helpful," said Beth. "And how much is it?"

"Five hundred and forty-nine pounds ninety-five pence, includin' VAT."

Beth paused, thinking hard.

Trevor went for the kill. "Wi'" five diskettes and top o' t'range word processing software, it's a 'ceptional offer."

"What do you think, Jack — shall we take it?" asked Beth.

I smiled and nodded.

It was Friday morning and the election was over. I was listening to the early-morning news on my car radio as I drove into school. Margaret Thatcher had celebrated her third general election victory after defeating Labour by 376 seats to 229.

There were losers, of course, including the defeated Labour Leader, Neil Kinnock, and the Conservative Enoch Powell, who had lost his seat in parliament after thirty-seven years.

In the office Vera was looking in admiration at a photograph of Margaret Thatcher on the front page of her newspaper. The Prime Minister was wearing a royal blue woollen suit and Vera pointed to a gold and semi-precious stone bracelet.

"It was a present from Dennis," she said. "Such a devoted husband."

"Impressive," I said neutrally. Even so, Mrs Thatcher had become the first Prime Minister for more than 160 years to win three successive terms of office.

Later that morning I called in to Class 2, where Pat Brookside was busy with a science lesson. She was sitting alongside Julie Tricklebank and the Jackson twins. The three girls, all now seven years old, were testing various objects to see if they would conduct electricity. Pat had provided a simple circuit board, two electrical cells and a bulb from her torch.

"So what have you found out?" asked Pat.

Hermione looked thoughtful. "Well, when we put the wires on this side of the tin lid it lights up."

"But when we put them on the other side," added Honeysuckle, "it doesn't light up."

"Why do you think that is?" asked Pat.

"It's coloured blue," said Julie, "and the top is just metal."

"So it must be . . ." began Hermione.

". . . the paint," concluded Honeysuckle. It came naturally to them to complete each other's sentences.

"That's right," said Pat, "the paint insulates the metal."

"Insulates?" queried Julie.

Pat smiled and sat down next to them to explain the process of insulation and I walked out, pleased to have seen the challenges that she was providing for the children in her care.

During morning break Sally wished she hadn't spent 20p on a *Daily Mirror* on her way into school. The headline "THATCHER BACK AT NO. 10" filled her with despair. She flicked through the pages and came across another irritating piece of news.

"Vera, what do you think of Prince Edward's television spectacular?"

Vera looked up from brewing a pot of tea. "What's that?"

"The event at Alton Towers — *It's a Royal Knockout*."

It was the brainchild of would-be media giant Prince Edward.

Pat looked up from marking her spelling test. "I heard they've roped in Jenny Agutter, Aled Jones, Cliff Richard and Paul Daniels, along with Gary Lineker." For a moment she went all misty-eyed at the thought of Gary Lineker, then she returned to the children's books.

"It's embarrassing," said Vera. "Certainly the Queen and Prince Charles will not approve."

"I agree," said Anne.

"It will do little for the House of Windsor," added Vera as she poured out the tea.

"Cringeworthy," muttered Sally.

Vera wondered if there was such a word, but decided not to comment. She was happy that for once she and Sally agreed on something relating to the royal family. Meanwhile, Sally discarded her *Daily Mirror* and returned to her *Cosmopolitan* magazine. An article entitled "Clitoral Stimulation" had caught her attention; however, she had decided to tuck it away in her ethnic shoulder bag for perusal at a later hour — preferably while Colin was watching *World Snooker* presented by the handsome but slightly quirky David Icke.

It was during the lunch break that Pat Brookside announced to everyone's surprise that she had voted

310

for the SDP and was disappointed that Liberal leader David Steel had described the result as merely "a setback". Both Vera and Sally considered it to be a wasted vote, but said nothing.

"I think the government will be privatizing water and electricity," said Marcus.

"Perhaps it will be for the better," said Vera quietly.

Sally looked up. "I'll tell you something that won't be better."

"And what's that?" asked Anne.

Sally picked up a custard cream from the biscuit tin on the coffee table and headed for the door. "Maggie is going to replace local rates with a community charge — she's calling it a 'poll tax'." With that she closed the door firmly and I reflected that politics in the staff-room always seemed to promote lively debate and sadly, on occasions, the gradual erosion of friendship.

Our school health visitor, Staff Nurse Sue Phillips, was no happier with the political climate. Sue had called in to check for head lice as there had been another outbreak in the village.

"It's still a struggle, Jack," she said. "I'm in it for life because I believe in the NHS, but recruiting and keeping good nurses is difficult."

"I saw the pay award in the paper," I said. "Won't that help?"

"Yes, it's a nine and a half per cent pay increase and a newly qualified nurse will now earn seven thousand pounds per annum but, sadly, staff nurses are still underpaid."

She picked up her metal nit comb and strode off with purpose.

I was in the school hall shortly after Tom Burgess had rung the bell for afternoon break.

"Mr Coe's in t'entrance 'all, Mr Sheffield," Tom informed me.

"Oh yes?"

"'E said 'e wanted t'see you."

"What did you say, Tom?"

"Nothing, sir, 'e jus' told me to get lost."

"Thanks Tom," I said, slightly puzzled.

When I walked into the entrance hall it was obvious there was trouble brewing. Stan Coe was leaning against the display board holding up an official-looking letter. There were no smiles any more, only a scowl.

"Yes, Mr Coe?"

"No bloody sense, them idiots at County 'All," he snarled.

"Perhaps you can refrain from bad language. You're in school now."

As usual his wellington boots were covered in mud.

"Well they're useless."

"What can I do to help, Mr Coe?"

"We need t'talk," he said abruptly.

"I'm available after school," I replied. "You'll appreciate I have a class to teach."

"Mr Timmings was allus available at Morton," snapped Stan.

"Perhaps he didn't teach full-time as I do."

"Per'aps 'e were a better 'eadmaster."

312

I ignored the insult. "Would you care to come back at four thirty, Mr Coe?"

"No, ah think ah'll ring that Miss Cleverley up at County 'All an' tell 'er y'too busy t'talk to one of y'school governors 'bout an important matter."

"And what might that be?"

"This refusal f'me to put up a new fence on my land."

I recalled my recent telephone conversation with Joseph about the request to replace the school fence that adjoined Stan Coe's land. I had followed it up with County Hall.

"Yes, sorry, Mr Coe, but it was out of the question. I told the Education Office it was something we would not consider."

It had been clear from the drawing we received that we would lose a significant piece of land. The siting of the new fence would also provide Stan with space for a new access to his land that bordered the local football pitch and cricket field.

"You're a school governor, Mr Coe. Surely you should have raised this at a governors' meeting . . . And why did you make the request in the first place?"

He waved the letter in my face. "That's f'me t'know an' you t'find out, Mr 'Igh an' Mighty 'Eadmaster."

"I see."

"No y'don't, but let's jus' say you'll find out when ah'm good an' ready."

He barged his way out of the entrance hall to his Land Rover and drove away.

I sighed. The *status quo* had returned.

At the end of school Ruby and Vera were busy discussing Ruby's forthcoming wedding.

"I'm thrilled, Ruby," said Vera, "and I would love to be your matron of honour."

"Me an' George 'ave seen Mr Evans and we're all set. 'E's asked Deke t'be 'is best man 'cause they were friends when they were boys an' my Andy will be walkin' me down t'aisle."

"It will be a wonderful day, Ruby, and I'm so pleased for you."

Ruby dabbed a tear from her eye with her chamois leather. "An' ah'll allus be grateful t'you, Mrs F."

Vera said nothing — she simply got up and gave her friend a hug.

That evening Vera was not happy with her husband and he knew it.

After spotting a mouse in the kitchen she had visited Timothy Pratt's Hardware Emporium and purchased a state-of-the-art Trip-Trap Patent Mouse Encapsulator. It was a plastic tube that a mouse would enter after being attracted by food. Then the mouse would be released into "the environment". For Vera this was without doubt the humane approach towards all God's creatures.

Unfortunately, the mouse had immediately returned and was promptly killed by Rupert with a yard broom! Rupert's pleas that this was how he had been brought up to deal with unwelcome rodents fell on deaf ears and, for the time being, a stony silence pervaded the kitchen of Morton Manor.

However, when they settled down to watch the television news, Vera calmed down, particularly when Mrs Thatcher appeared in all her glory. On the steps of Conservative Headquarters, the Prime Minister said, "It is wonderful to be entrusted with the government of this great country once again."

"Isn't she simply the best?" murmured Vera.

Margaret was in full flow. "The greater the trust . . . the greater the duty upon us to be worthy of that trust."

"Well, you got your wish, my dear," said Rupert. "Your favourite lady lives to fight another day."

"It really is a great day. I wish it would never end."

Rupert smiled. "All good things come to an end," he said, and he got up to switch off the television.

But not Maggie, thought Vera. *She will go on for ever.*

CHAPTER
EIGHTEEN

He Who Waits

School closed today for the summer holiday with 139 children on roll and will reopen on Monday, 7 September. A presentation was made to Mrs Ruby Smith, school caretaker, prior to her wedding tomorrow. 15 fourth-year juniors left today to commence full-time education at their secondary schools in September.

Extract from the Ragley & Morton School Logbook:
Friday, 24 July 1987

It was Friday, 24 July, the final day of the school year and in the early-morning sunshine the air was already hot and humid. It had been a stifling night and Beth had tossed and turned. She had been off-colour lately and the summer holiday couldn't come soon enough for her.

At breakfast her cheeks had been flushed and damp.

Wavy strands of blonde hair framed her face. She smiled wearily. "Almost there."

As I drove to school I wound down my window to welcome a refreshing breeze. Honeysuckle and wild roses intertwined in the hedgerows and in the fields cattle were chewing the cud in the shade of the sycamores. The end of my tenth year as headteacher had arrived and an eventful day awaited me.

It wasn't simply a summer storm that was heading my way. The old saying that everything comes to him who waits was about to be realized.

The High Street was coming alive and I felt happy that after all these years I was finally part of the fabric of this beautiful village.

In the General Stores Prudence Golightly had dressed Jeremy Bear in a white sailor suit and a straw boater. She gave me a wave as she watered her hanging baskets. Next door, in the butcher's shop, Old Tommy Piercy was telling his grandson that one day this empire would be his and that he planned to expand his home-delivery service to the neighbouring villages. To this end, Old Tommy had purchased a white van, which was parked outside. In the thick dust on the rear doors Terry Earnshaw had written "NO PIES ARE LEFT IN THIS VAN OVERNIGHT". Meanwhile, outside the village Pharmacy, Eugene Scrimshaw, with his Captain Kirk uniform hidden discreetly under his white coat, had been reprimanded by his wife, Peggy. He was sweeping the forecourt while swearing in Klingon under his breath.

In the doorway of his Hardware Emporium, Timothy Pratt was talking to his best friend, Walter Crapper. Between them they had purchased a new Sprite Finesse touring caravan for £2,850 and had planned a holiday together in Skegness. A week away from boot-scrapers, countersunk screws and garden gnomes awaited the pernickety Timothy and he couldn't wait to type out a detailed itinerary.

In the Coffee Shop there was a celebration going on. Both Dorothy and Nellie had discovered they were pregnant and Big Dave and Little Malcolm had taken the morning off work to learn a new skill: talking to their wives about something other than football.

In the Hair Salon Diane Wigglesworth had opened early to cater for the constant flow of ladies who wanted to look their best at tomorrow's wedding. In contrast, it was a more relaxed start to the day in the Post Office. Ted Postlethwaite had finished his first delivery and Amelia was in the kitchen frying bacon. The smiling postmistress was wearing nothing but an apron and Ted was relishing the smell of the bacon and, of course, the view.

Outside The Royal Oak, Deke Ramsbottom was checking arrangements for the wedding with Don and Sheila Bradshaw. The singing cowboy was taking his role as George Dainty's best man very seriously. In fact, he had used most of a tin of Brasso on his sheriff's badge and spurs.

"So 'ave y'got entertainment as well as a bar in t'village 'all?" asked Deke.

Sheila put her hands on her hips and stuck out her chest, which, momentarily, made Deke forget his question. "We're trying something a bit different, Deke. Don's bought in a group from Cleckheaton, Harvey Coleclough and the Wallbangers. 'E's gorra wonderful voice — jus' like that Placebo Domingo."

"Were they expensive?"

"Well," said Don, "we're givin' 'em a free pea and pie supper an' a bottle o' stout."

"So a top group then, Don," said Deke with absolute sincerity.

Ruby was talking to Vera in the entrance hall when I walked in.

"G'mornin', Mr Sheffield," said Ruby. "Ah were jus' tellin' Mrs F that ah'm all set for m'big day."

"We're all looking forward to it," I said.

"Ruby got her wish, Mr Sheffield," said Vera, "and she and George will be going to a lovely hotel in Whitby tomorrow evening."

"Then on Monday we're goin' t'London f'three days t'see all t'sights." Ruby's face was flushed with excitement. "George says 'e'll tek me to Nelson's Colon, Piccalilly Circus an' that A an' E Museum."

Vera gave me a conspiratorial smile.

"I'm sure you'll enjoy London," I said and I walked into the office to check the morning mail.

Ruby picked up her galvanized bucket and mop and looked searchingly at Vera. "An' all m'children will be there."

"It will be a day to remember," Vera assured her.

Our caretaker breathed a huge sigh and looked thoughtful. "It were a big decision."

"And the right one."

"Are y'sure?" She rubbed a tear from her eye. "Mrs F — am ah doin' right?"

"Yes," said Vera softly, "you are."

★   ★   ★

It was the Leavers' Assembly and by ten o'clock the hall was full of excited children, with rows of parents and grandparents seated at the back. Anne was at the piano and Pat and Marcus were sitting next to their classes. Sally was with her choir and orchestra at the front of the hall, while I was sitting with Rupert, who was about to present each school leaver with a book.

Shirley and Doreen were standing by the kitchen door in their best summer frocks, and Vera was sitting next to a tearful Ruby by the double doors that led to the entrance hall. Our final assembly of the school year was always a special time in the school calendar. It was a time of exits and entrances and there were a few tears as the eleven-year-olds walked out one by one to collect their books. I called out their names. "Rosie Appleby, Claire Buttershaw, Candice Collingwood."

I watched each child as they shook hands with the major. Every one of them had a story to tell. I glanced down at my list: "George Frith, Michelle Gawthorpe, Sigourney Longbottom, Jemima Poole," and so it went on. Each one collected their prize full of optimism. A summer holiday stretched out in front of them, followed by a new school with forty-minute lessons, exams, new teachers and teenage acne. For them life was a never-ending stream and they knew with the certainty of youth that they would live for ever.

The ceremony was followed by a presentation to Ruby and it was fitting that her closest friend, Vera, handed over a gift of a fine vase and a bunch of roses, Ruby's favourite flower.

320

★ ★ ★

After assembly Joseph used the opportunity to call in to Class 3 and tell the story of how God created the world. "He made the bees, whales and slippery snails," he said with a benevolent smile.

It was during morning break that he read some of the follow-up poems. Jeremy Urquhart had written:

> God made the bees,
> Bees make the honey,
> Children do the work,
> While teachers get the money.

Joseph frowned and wondered if he had communicated the right message.

I was on duty and I stood by the school wall under the welcome shade of the horse chestnut trees. As I sipped my tea I watched events on the other side of the village green. The local thatcher, Neville Crump from Morton, had pulled up in his van with "Maggie's Thatchers" painted on the side. His son Noel had gone into Pat's class back in January and Pat had organized a class visit to watch the thatcher at work. His wife, Maggie Crump, was a domineering woman who kept Neville firmly in check, ran the business with shrewd accountancy and in a manner that didn't suffer fools. While she often dreamed of those carefree times in the sixties when Adam Faith was top of the charts, the price of a home was £2,500 and a pint of milk cost threepence, she had embraced the reality of eighties

Britain. Business was booming and Neville was in great demand, with a two-year waiting list.

It was Stuart Ormroyd who called out to me, "Look, sir, it's that car again."

The familiar green Citroën drove past quickly towards the end of the High Street . . . or perhaps to Coe Farm. I noticed he was followed by PC Pike and a fellow officer in his little grey van. They too appeared to be in a hurry.

In the Coffee Shop Nora was sitting behind the counter while the rest of her customers were congratulating Dorothy and Nellie. Nora was reading an article in her *TV Times* while thinking back on her acting career. The highlight had been the time she was a non-speaking extra in the television soap opera *Crossroads*. Sadly, it was being axed and would come to an end next spring after twenty-four years. The new producer had taken drastic steps, killing off many of the main characters and giving the motel a new look; however, more viewers were turning to *EastEnders*. Nora felt a little sad as another small piece of her life slipped away.

When Ruby arrived to clear away the dining tables she popped her head round the office door. "There's summat goin' on at Stan Coe's farm by all accounts."

"What is it?" asked Vera.

"Dunno, but Old Tommy said t'police were there."

Vera pursed her lips. "As you sow, so shall you reap."

"Y'right there, Mrs F. Like they say, ev'ry silver linin' 'as a cloud."

322

Both incorrect and correct, thought Vera with a wry smile and set off for the staff-room to prepare a pot of tea.

In the staff-room Pat was examining her most recent North Yorkshire County Council payslip. Her total pay for the month was a little over £900. After tax, superannuation and National Insurance, it left her with £600 and she wondered about the elusive dream of buying a home.

Also, she had received a number of thank-you cards from the children who were leaving her class and moving up to Class 3 next September. However, one in particular was a mixed blessing. It read:

> Dear Miss Brookside, you are my second best teacher ever.
> Love Suzi-Quatro

As Anne had been her only previous teacher, Pat knew where she came in the pecking order.

I was at my desk as the telephone rang. It was Beth.

"Are you alone in the office?"

"Yes, why?"

She lowered her voice. "Jack, I'm only suggesting this because of how you felt about having to apply for your own job."

"Yes, it was a difficult time."

"I'm also thinking about our conversation in Cambridge when you said you were . . . *unsettled*."

"What's on your mind?"

"Well . . . I've just heard that there's a headship coming up — a big one in York. John Foggety will be retiring from Ousebank Primary in a year's time. He's told his governors and Miss B-H knows."

This was out of the blue. "Oh, I see . . . well, thanks for letting me know."

"If you were interested, perhaps it's something to consider for the future and it wouldn't mean we would have to move, particularly after the house extension. Bilbo Cottage has been transformed — it's lovely now."

"Yes, I see what you mean."

"I'm sure Miss B-H would see you as an excellent candidate, particularly now you're doing your Masters degree. Come to think of it, so would Richard Gomersall and the other advisers."

There had been times when I wondered if I was my own man or merely one who walked in Beth's shadow — but not any more. It was good we could share and plan together.

"Something else cropped up today," I said. "We can discuss it tonight."

"Very well, let's do that," she said and there was a moment of quiet while she waited for my response. "And don't forget John's party."

In a spinning world there was only stillness in our cocoon of silence.

"See you tonight," I said quietly.

"Love you," she whispered and I knew she was alone in her office.

It was then that there was a tap on the door. "Someone's here, Beth, I'll have to go."

324

"OK, bye."

Ruby appeared in the doorway. "Ah'm jus' clearin' away now, Mr Sheffield, an' then ah'll be off."

"Thanks for all your work, Ruby, and good luck for tomorrow."

"Ah'm all excited." She looked up at the clock. "Ah've got t'call in t'see m'mother t'mek sure she's got everything she needs for the mornin'."

"How is she?"

"'Er eyesight's gone, Mr Sheffield. Ah think she's gorra detached rectum or summat."

"Oh dear," I said and I meant it.

Vera was putting on her coat. "Another year over," she said.

There was the clatter of a galvanized bucket outside as Ruby cleared away. She was singing "Edelweiss" at the top of her voice.

Vera smiled. "Just like old times."

"Well, I hope all goes well tomorrow. You have an important job."

"Yes, a special day, and I'm so pleased for Ruby." She picked up her handbag and stood there looking at her desk. "I wonder what she will decide to do next term. She won't really need to work any more."

"I think she loves the job — and the children."

"She does, but it must be a temptation not to have to clean floors and toilets and keep that old boiler going, particularly on cold mornings. She suffers a lot now with her hands."

"Well, let's see what she decides."

Vera was standing by the door as if there was something else she wanted to say.

"And what about you, Vera? We've completed a decade of service together."

Vera looked at the photographs that filled the walls and sighed. "We all have to move on at some stage, Jack. All good things come to an end and my time is coming soon."

Vera didn't often call me Jack and the significance was not lost on me.

She walked out and closed the door quietly behind her.

I sat back in my chair and, once again, I pondered my future . . . to stay or to go.

All good things come to an end.

Perhaps I had been a flame in a shuttered lamp for too long.

I was about to leave when suddenly there was a firm knock on the door.

"Come in."

It was PC Pike. "Could I have a private word, Mr Sheffield?"

With him was a tall man in a smart suit. "This is Mr Stafford Bywater of the York Planning Department. He was keen to meet you and visit the school."

He shook my hand. It was a firm handshake. "I used to attend Ragley School fifty years ago."

"Pleased to meet you, Mr Bywater. What can I do to help?"

Julian Pike was clearly in professional mode. "I thought it appropriate to speak to you, as it will be all round the village tomorrow morning and the local press are already on the case."

"Yes?"

"Also, as Mr Stan Coe is a school governor here, it seemed important to let you know."

"What about?" I asked.

"Mr Coe was arrested this afternoon and is currently down at York Police Station."

I was speechless.

"Perhaps I can explain, Mr Sheffield," said Mr Bywater. "Mr Coe gave a cash bribe of five thousand pounds to a member of my planning department. He wanted to make land purchases at agricultural prices in the knowledge that planning permission would be granted. He even had plans for twelve properties on the Ragley cricket field. It promised to make a profit of half a million pounds for your local pig farmer."

"I see," I said as the full seriousness dawned.

"Mr Coe has been unscrupulous in his dealings," added PC Pike, "and the evidence against him is overwhelming."

Mr Bywater smiled. "I've been acting as the go-between, rather like Robert Redford and Paul Newman in *The Sting*, but not quite so dramatic. I'm afraid it's been a sordid story from the start. There was a moment when we almost lost the opportunity, but I recall there was an incident with a cat that laid him low. It gave us time to regroup and put another plan into operation."

I smiled. "That was Oscar."

"Oscar?"

"His cat — it bit him."

"Well, Oscar did us a favour."

"I appreciate you letting me know," I said, "and there will be implications for the governing body after I've contacted County Hall."

PC Pike looked at his watch. "If you'll excuse me, I have to leave now." His cheeks coloured slightly and I presumed another date with Natasha Smith awaited the young policeman. He hurried off while I walked down the drive with Mr Bywater.

We paused in the playground while he stared up at the bell tower and grinned as he reminisced about his time here as a young boy. "I climbed that once. The headteacher was not pleased. I never did it again."

We reached the school gate. "I sense there was more at stake here, Mr Bywater."

He gave me a shrewd glance and nodded. "An astute observation. It's a long story, but suffice to say I'm off to visit my mother, Victoria. She is eighty-three and a resident here at the local retirement home. She was impressed by the children singing at Christmas."

"We do our best."

"It's good of you to go out into the community in this way."

We walked on to his car. "How is your mother?"

He considered his reply. "My mother is a plain-speaking woman, Mr Sheffield, and she says it's a lovely place for a group of coffin-dodgers."

I laughed. "She sounds quite a lady."

"With an interesting life." His craggy face softened a little at the memory. "She was born in Sheffield on the fourth of May nineteen hundred and four. It was the day of the unveiling of Queen Victoria's statue in the city centre. At the age of ten she moved to Doncaster because her father found work at Edlington Colliery. His shift at the coal face earned him eight shillings and threepence. So it was a hard life. Then in nineteen twenty-five she married a miner, my dad, Tom Bywater." He smiled at the memory. "I'm told he was a tough, uncompromising Yorkshireman and they had a daughter and a son."

"You have a sister?"

"Yes, Evelyn. She is healthy and well now but she had a very difficult childhood. She was a victim of polio."

"I'm so sorry, that must have been terrible."

"So little was known about it when we were children. There were large epidemics in the thirties and forties, so it was an anxious time. Public places like cinemas and swimming pools were closed to try to control it. I recall hearing it was caused by an infectious pathogen, but it wasn't until the nineteen fifties that we knew how it was transmitted."

I thought back to my childhood. "I had a polio vaccination when I was at primary school in Leeds. I remember queuing up for it full of trepidation."

"You were lucky, Mr Sheffield. That wasn't available to my sister. She had a metal brace on her leg and needed a crutch for support. That's when we first came into contact with Stan Coe. Evelyn and I attended this school while we stayed in rented accommodation before moving to a pit village in Nottingham. We were only here for a few weeks, but I never forgot this school."

"And Mr Coe?"

"He clearly does not remember me . . . but I never forgot him. Stan was a cowardly bully, sly and unkind to my sister. He mocked her disability and she was frightened to tell anyone. I was just a small boy at the time. It was much later when she confided in me."

"That must have been very distressing."

"It was part of a forgotten and distant past until I moved into North Yorkshire. Then his name was mentioned by a colleague in one of my meetings. That was a year ago and I've been on the case since. In fact, I've been leading him a merry dance."

He opened the driver's door of his green Citroën, smiled and shook my hand. "It's been good to meet you and good luck for the future. By all accounts you have a fine school here."

"Thank you for sharing your story with me."

He climbed into the car and looked up at me before driving off. "Mr Sheffield — everything comes to him who waits."

The heat was oppressive as I drove home and I saw lightning in the far distance. Heaven's marching army was coming our way and thunderheads were gathering.

Beth was in our spacious new kitchen putting the finishing touches to a birthday cake with blue and white icing. She was wearing a baggy checked shirt with rolled sleeves along with sky-blue leggings. John's party had begun in the lounge.

I put my arms around her waist and she turned and kissed me hastily. "Sorry, Jack, I'm busy."

"So am I," I replied and kissed her again, "and we're on holiday."

"Thank goodness," she murmured. "I've been very tired lately."

"I have some news."

Beth lit four candles on the cake. "Can you save it for later?"

It made sense to save such a story. After all, it wasn't every day that one of our school governors was arrested.

In a few minutes John was blowing out his candles assisted by his eager little friends, followed by a rendition of "Happy Birthday". It was a party of noise, games and lots of good things to eat until, finally, his friends were collected, we cleared up and the house was quiet once again.

I told Beth about Stan Coe's arrest and she nodded as if it was not entirely unexpected.

"He was always up to no good, Jack, so good riddance. He's been a thorn in your side for long enough."

Later we sat on the sofa drinking a welcome cup of coffee. The storm had passed but the oppressive heat remained.

Beth rested her head on my shoulder. "So, what was on your mind when I rang earlier?"

"I've had another letter from Jim Fairbank at the College in York."

Beth sat up. "Really?"

"There's another job offer for a senior lectureship."

Beth was quiet for a moment. "Miss B-H wouldn't be happy after appointing you to the new headship only a short time ago. The headship I mentioned is a year off."

"Yes, but so is this. Their head of department has said he will be leaving at the end of next year, along with another colleague. So it's a long time away."

Beth looked pensive. "It's an opportunity, Jack, and maybe the time will be right. Who would have thought — two opportunities in one day."

We were still discussing it when we climbed the stairs to bed.

It was the early hours and, while thunder roared, I lay awake on this hot, oppressive night. I was confused. There was a lot on my mind.

I had searched for peace within and found it in the woman I loved. Beneath a sky of cinnamon, the scent of jasmine was in her hair. Her green eyes were gentle with hope for the future as I touched her smooth skin. The knotted fibres of my mind had untangled and the grey mist of doubt had evaporated. It was as if the tricolour of my heart had fluttered free.

There was a time when I thought I had caged a bird with bright wings, but now I knew it was not so. The way ahead was clear. Like a single shaft of hope,

332

answers tumbled into place and pierced my troubled dreams. It was time to move on.

With a final embrace we drifted into sleep while the thunder faded into the distance, the heat subsided and a fresh wind sprang up.

A fine day was about to dawn.

CHAPTER
NINETEEN

Happiest Days

Today was the first day of the school holiday and staff and children celebrated the wedding of our school caretaker, Mrs Ruby Smith, at St Mary's Church.
Extract from the Ragley & Morton School Logbook:
Saturday, 25 July 1987

It was a perfect morning and, where the sky met the earth, sunlight lit up the horizon with a rim of golden fire. The air was warm and a breathless promise hung over the fields of golden barley. The branches of the sycamores stirred with a sibilant whisper as the world awoke to a new day. It was Saturday, 25 July, Ruby's wedding day, and a shaft of light streamed into our new kitchen.

It was eight o'clock and Beth was preparing to leave. "I've pressed your suit," she said, "and you'll remember I'm going in early to help Vera with the flowers in church."

"That's fine," I said, "and I'll follow on with John. I'll be there for ten thirty. I'm reading a lesson so I need to be prepared."

Beth looked the perfect English rose in a pale blue two-piece suit with her honey-blonde hair in a French plait under a matching broad-brimmed hat.

"I'll meet you there," she called over her shoulder as she checked her appearance for the final time in the hall mirror. "And I've a couple of other things to do in Ragley."

She picked up her gloves and handbag and hurried out.

Vera had already called in to 7 School View to check that all was well.

Diane Wigglesworth had arrived at the crack of dawn with her hairdressing equipment and a busy couple of hours awaited the Ragley hairdresser. However, she had done this many times.

"Come on, Ruby," she said. "You first, then the bridesmaids."

Joseph had gone for an early-morning walk to clear his head and he stopped outside George and Mary Hardisty's cottage. With the summer colour of bright geraniums and the autumn fire of Virginia creeper on its white-washed walls, it was a picture-postcard home. George was Ragley's champion gardener and Joseph admired the scene. Beyond the colourful summer blooms and perfect lawn, George was busy hoeing between his rows of prize vegetables.

Joseph gestured towards Ragley's finest garden. "Isn't God great?" he said.

George looked up and nodded with phlegmatic grace. "Yes, vicar, y'right there . . . but y'should 'ave seen this place when 'E 'ad it to 'Imself."

Good point, thought Joseph, but he remained silent and walked on.

It was ten o'clock when I set off with John. All roads seemed to lead to St Mary's and its ancient stone was lit up in the sunshine. It felt as though God was in His heaven and all was well on this momentous day.

We parked near the church and walked up the path to the entrance, where men in lively groups and ladies in summer dresses milled around. Our son was wearing a new suit and I had never seen him look so smart. How long he would stay like that was another matter.

Ruby's son Duggie was acting as usher and giving out service sheets. Duggie only had one suit: the black frock coat he wore when he was walking in front of a funeral cortège. Consequently, he looked as if he was an extra in a remake of *High Noon*. Wisely, he had left his tall black top hat in the wardrobe at the funeral parlour.

"Here y'are, Mr Sheffield," said Duggie, giving me a service sheet. "Sit where y'like."

His new girlfriend, sexy Sonia from the shoe shop, was hovering in the background in a skimpy dress and sparkly six-inch stilettos. When she had asked Duggie why he had "TINA" tattooed on his bum he said that Tina Turner was his favourite singer and that Sonia was his "Private Dancer", and she had been daft enough to believe him. Meanwhile, Duggie was secretly pleased

336

that her previous partner, a colour-blind wallpaper sales-man from Hartlepool, had returned to the north-east.

The church shimmered in the morning heat haze, but inside it was cool and calm. Elsie Crapper had taken her Valium and was playing soothing music. The church had never looked more beautiful. Everything, from the candles to the altar cloth, was in place. The ladies from the cross-stitch club had contributed a floral display next to the pulpit and the tireless efforts of the flower-arranging group had added fragrance and colour. John and I found a seat at the end of a pew and Beth came to join us. I looked around. Suddenly sharp refracted sunlight from the stained-glass windows lit up the ancient stone and the altar. The pews were filling up rapidly and I looked at the friends I knew so well.

Major Rupert Forbes-Kitchener, looking every inch the local squire, was sitting with his daughter, the confident and elegant Virginia Anastasia. Rupert had provided his classic Bentley for the bride, with his chauffeur, the immaculate Tomkins, at the wheel.

Anne Grainger looked stunning in a mauve two-piece suit. She smiled in my direction and appeared more relaxed than usual. Next to her John Grainger was not only in a smart suit but he was also clean-shaven. John was being particularly attentive and Anne had wondered about his sudden change of heart during the last few days. Her DIY-obsessed husband had been replaced by an active and willing partner who reminded her of their early life together. It would be later when John confessed he had realized he was losing her to a handsome antiques dealer. For now he was trying to repair their fractured life and Anne had welcomed his change of heart.

Sally Pringle, as always, lived up to her extravagant dress sense with a bright yellow-and-pink summer outfit along with a spiky and ostentatious feathered hat that brought to mind an electrocuted flamingo. Colin, in a sober grey suit, had their daughter, Grace, on his knee and the happy little girl was looking more like her mother every day.

Pat Brookside was classically dressed in a beautiful navy blue suit. Next to her was her handsome partner, David Beckinsdale, and rumour had it, according to Vera, that they were about to become engaged.

The big surprise was Marcus Potts, who arrived with his girlfriend, Fiona. They walked into church hand in hand and Marcus could not have looked more content. Fiona had flown home from America to spend the summer vacation with her father in Cambridge. However, Marcus had persuaded the free-spirited young woman to join him for a week in York. They both waved in my direction and settled down near the back of the church.

Meanwhile, Shirley and Doreen, our cook and dinner lady, had made sure they were sitting at the end of the pew so they had the best view of Ruby when she walked down the aisle.

In the silent vestry Joseph opened the old wardrobe, took out his long black cassock and slipped it over his tall, gaunt frame. From the shelf above he selected a white surplice and cope and added them to his sartorial ensemble.

Finally, he held his white stole in his hands and stared at it for a long time. Vera had edged it with the most wonderful and intricate array of gold crosses and he cherished the memory. He lifted it to his face and kissed it gently. As he arranged it around his neck he shed private tears in the quiet sanctuary of this secluded space. He missed the companionship of his sister more than she would ever know and he carried his loneliness like a millstone of memories.

Earlier, George Dainty and Deke Ramsbottom had met with Joseph. They had visited the vestry and completed the formalities of payment for the legal fees and bell-ringers. Now they were sitting on the front pew waiting in anticipation.

George had bought a new three-piece suit from Harry Solomon in York and in his buttonhole he sported a white carnation. Deke had pulled out all the stops and gone for a Doc Holliday look straight out of *Gunfight at the O.K. Corral*. He was wearing a long black duster coat, pinstriped trousers, wing-collar shirt, bootlace tie, Paisley waistcoat and black boots. While his sheriff's badge was polished to a high shine, he had decided, on reflection, to leave his spurs at home as they jingled when he walked and he didn't want to cause a distraction during the service.

At the front of the church, Ruby's family had gathered. Thirty-three-year-old Racquel was sitting next to her husband at the end of a pew to keep an eye on little Krystal. Ruby's granddaughter was to be a bridesmaid along with her youngest daughter, Hazel.

Sharon looked a picture as she held hands with Rodney Morgetroyd, who had delivered his milk earlier than usual to give him time to change into his Duran Duran suit. Meanwhile, Natasha was secretly holding hands with PC Julian Pike, who was dressed in his best uniform. They were seated next to Sergeant Dan Hunter and his wife Jo, who had been on the staff when I arrived at Ragley School. They waved in our direction from their pew and it was good to see they appeared content in their life together. I remembered the day they had first met in our village school. It really had been love at first sight.

Elsie Crapper rummaged through her pile of scores and selected a piece of music that would set the scene. It had been chosen by George. "That advert on t'telly," he said, "y'know, where they say 'appiness is a cigar called 'Amlet . . . the mild cigar."

It was the only piece of classical music that George could recall.

Elsie spread out her sheet music of J. S. Bach's *Air on the G String* and began to play. Predictably, there was a muttering among the men in the congregation keen to show their knowledge of popular cigar advertisements. She followed this with Luigi Boccherini's "Minuet in A" from *String Quintet in E Major, Opus 13, No. 5*, one of her favourites which, for Elsie, was almost as good as Valium.

Ruby arrived in style in the Major's classic Bentley, complete with Tomkins the chauffeur. There was a

340

cheer from the parents and children who had gathered by the lych-gate outside the church.

By her side was her eldest son, Andy, who was pleased that his mother had found some happiness at last. He knew times had been difficult for her over many years, but that was about to change. In recent months he and George had talked long into the night and he knew his mother was marrying a good man.

"Jus' look at t'bridesmaids, Margery — pretty as a picture," said Betty Buttle.

"Takes y'back," said Margery wistfully.

"A bit of 'appiness at last for Ruby," said Betty.

Margery nodded knowingly. "An' she deserves it."

Hazel and Krystal wore pink short-sleeved dresses with matching jackets. Each girl carried a tiny posy and had summer flowers in her hair, and Hazel was keeping a careful eye on her little niece.

Vera looked the picture of elegance in a beautiful lace-trimmed lilac dress. Outside the church door she was making final adjustments to Ruby's collar. The bride's outfit was simple in design but perfect for her special day. With Vera's help, Ruby had selected a flowing light blue silk skirt with a matching long jacket and a pale cream blouse. Diane the hairdresser had worked wonders with Ruby's chestnut curls and they framed her rosy, dimpled cheeks. Her bouquet comprised six roses, one to represent each of her children, and the fragrant flowers had been selected with exquisite care by Vera from her garden.

"There," said Vera, after she had rearranged the bow on Ruby's blouse. "Just perfect."

"Ah never thought ah were beautiful enough t'get married, Mrs F."

Vera looked at her friend. "My dear Ruby," she said softly, "this is your day and you look lovely. George is a lucky man."

Andy stepped forward. "Time t'go, Mam."

There was a hushed whisper among the congregation as Elsie played the first bars of the "Bridal March" and everyone turned their heads to see the arrival of the bride. Andy, immaculate in his army sergeant's uniform, looked with deep affection at his mother. Ruby linked arms with her first-born and together they walked down the aisle.

The service was one I shall always remember. George looked with pride at the woman he loved and, as Ruby turned to pass her bouquet to Vera, she whispered, "Thank you," and Vera squeezed her hand. It was a tiny gesture that meant so much.

It was my turn for the first reading. I walked to the front of the chancel and mounted the step behind the brass lectern. The huge Bible was resting on the wings of a wondrous eagle and a red ribbon marked the page. It was the popular reading from Corinthians, chapter 13, verses 4–8, and I spoke in a slow, clear voice that echoed above the heads of the congregation.

"*Love is patient and kind; love is not jealous or boastful; it is not arrogant or rude. Love does not insist on its own way; it is not irritable or resentful; it does not rejoice at wrong, but rejoices in the right. Love bears all things, believes all things, hopes all things, endures all things. Love never ends.*"

I looked up and saw Vera smile and nod in acknowledgement. It was a job well done.

We sang hymns, including Ruby's favourite, "Love Divine, All Loves Excelling", until finally the moment arrived and a hush descended as we heard the words we all knew so well.

Joseph did not need to look at his service book. "Wilt thou have this woman to thy wedded wife," he asked, "and, forsaking all others, keep thee only unto her, so long as ye both shall live?"

His voice was soft, but it was a message bound in iron.

So it was on that long-ago summer's day that Ruby Smith, our school caretaker, became Mrs Dainty and all who knew her rejoiced.

When George and Ruby emerged into the sunshine, Nora, Dorothy and Nellie threw handfuls of confetti and cheered. Big Dave and Little Malcolm flanked Tyrone Crabtree as they leaned against the lych-gate and watched their excited partners. Nora gave a searching look in Tyrone's direction and hoped it might be her turn next. Unknown to the Coffee Shop owner, Tyrone was thinking the same thing.

"Y'can't beat a good weddin'," said Big Dave.

"Y'reight there, Dave," agreed Little Malcolm.

In the village hall there were toasts and speeches, followed by a wonderful feast.

The live group rattled the walls, Clint Ramsbottom played his records and everyone danced. I had never seen Ruby look happier and, by popular demand, Old

Tommy Piercy played the piano and the bride stood on the stage and sang "Edelweiss".

It was a moment to savour and everyone stood up to applaud.

Later, when the festivities were dying down, Ruby and George set off for Whitby. Beth was talking with her friends while John played hide-and-seek under the tables with Krystal. I walked out and welcomed the fresh air, then on impulse decided to call in to school for a final check before the holiday.

I unlocked the old oak door and stepped into the entrance hall. A shaft of light lit up the office door and I remembered the first time I had seen it. On that day almost a decade ago, my predecessor, a smiling Mr Pruett, had opened it and invited me in. It had been the beginning of a journey I would never forget. Then I opened the double doors that led to the school hall and recalled the generations of children singing hymns and listening to stories in morning assembly. The empty school was filled with the echoes of those who had gone before — the five-year-olds who were now teenagers . . . Elisabeth Dudley-Palmer, Heathcliffe Earnshaw, Jimmy Poole, Hazel Smith and so many more.

I returned to the office and looked around at a room I knew so well. There was Vera's empty desk, the filing cabinet that was her domain and hers only, the smiling faces of the children in the photographs, memories of times past. Finally, I locked the door and said a silent goodbye to the academic year 1986/87. It had been an eventful one and I wondered what the future would bring.

When I walked down the drive I paused at the gate. My name was there on the school sign and I was proud to have played my part in the history of this little village school.

It was a warm, sultry evening and the earth was returning the heat of the sun. Beth was sitting on the village green playing with John. She waved and I went to join them.

"Jack," she called out to me, "there's something I want to tell you."

"Yes?"

"I've been waiting for the right time. It's a surprise."

I pushed a lock of honey-blonde hair from her eyes. "Really?"

"Yes — but a good one."

She beckoned me towards Ronnie's bench and tugged my arm. "Let's sit here."

We settled down side by side and I put my arm around her shoulders. "So, what is it?"

"We're lucky aren't we — having all this?"

We surveyed the scene around us.

"Yes, we are."

John was playing with handfuls of the new-mown grass under the weeping willow. Nearby, Old Tommy Piercy was smoking his pipe as he fed the ducks on the pond. Deke Ramsbottom with his three sons, Shane, Clint and Wayne, waved to us as they wandered into The Royal Oak for a drink. Down the High Street Margery Ackroyd and Betty Buttle were discussing the wedding, while outside the village hall Heathcliffe Earnshaw was chatting with Mo Hartley, who in later years was to become his wife. His brother Terry looked on from a distance with a puzzled frown. Meanwhile, Timothy Pratt was shooing away Scargill the Yorkshire terrier from the forecourt of his Hardware Emporium.

Life in Ragley village was getting back to normal and continuing its timeless cycle.

In front of us my school stood like a silent sentinel with its bell tower and steeply sloping slate roof. Summer sunshine reflected from the Victorian windows, the avenue of horse chestnut trees swayed in the gentle breeze and I recalled the first time I had experienced this tiny part of North Yorkshire many years ago. Over time I had grown to love it . . . my world, my land, my home.

Finally Beth decided to break the silence.

"I've got some news," she said softly.

I looked into her green eyes, wide and loving, open pages of affection. "What is it, Beth?" I asked.

Gently, I kissed her neck and the breath of roses filled my thoughts.

She held my hand while I said nothing, simply waiting.

"Can't you guess?" she said with that mischievous smile I knew so well.

I sat back and shook my head.

"Oh Jack, you're a lovely man but sometimes you just miss the obvious."

"Go on then," I said, "tell me."

She took a deep breath, held me close and whispered in my ear. "I'm expecting a baby."

And in a heartbeat my life was complete.